Enchantress from the Stars

WALKER & COMPANY   NEW YORK

Enchantress from the Stars

Sylvia Louise Engdahl

Foreword by Lois Lowry

Illustrations by Leo and Diane Dillon

To My Mother,

Mildred Butler Engdahl, 1897–1987

Copyright © 1970 by Sylvia Louise Engdahl
Foreword copyright © 2001 by Lois Lowry
Illustrations copyright © 2001 by Leo and Diane Dillon

First published in the United States of America in
1970 by Atheneum Publishers, New York.
This edition published in the United States of America in 2001 by
Walker Publishing Company, Inc.

Minor changes to text, type style, and punctuation have been made since
the first printing of the original edition. This edition should be
considered definitive over all previous editions.

Published simultaneously in Canada by
Fitzhenry and Whiteside, Markham, Ontario L3R 4T8

Library of Congress Cataloging-in-Publication Data

Engdahl, Sylvia Louise.

Enchantress from the stars / Sylvia Louise Engdahl; foreword by Lois Lowry;
illustrations by Leo and Diane Dillon.
p. cm.
Summary: When young Elana unexpectedly joins the team leaving the
spaceship to study the planet Andrecia, she becomes an integral part of an
adventure involving three very different civilizations, each one centered on the
third planet from the star in its own solar system.
ISBN: 0-8027-8764-9
[1. Space and time–Fiction. 2. Choice–Fiction. 3. Responsibility–Fiction. 4.
Science fiction.] I. Dillon, Leo, ill. II. Dillon, Diane, ill. III. Title.

PZ7.E6985 En 2001

[Fic]–dc21

Book design by Ellen Cipriano

Printed in the United States of America

2 4 6 8 10 9 7 5 3 1

Contents

Foreword to the 2001 Edition

✳ How lush a literary landscape is the one that enables a reader to enter several worlds and make a home in each.

Sylvia Engdahl, the author of *Enchantress from the Stars*, says, in its preface, that it is not very important whether any of the people in her story are our ancestors or our descendants. Still, because she created them, and placed them there for both our scrutiny and our delight, it should be important to us, in my opinion, that they could be part of our future—and our past. Feeling a familiarity in fiction is what makes it live. Recognizing ourselves and our possibilities is what keeps us turning pages to the end, and keeps the story lingering in our thoughts, as this one does, long after the last page is turned.

Elana, the spunky stowaway who travels both forward and back—and confronts the moral issues inherent in the journeys—is the now in each of us. With her enthusiasm, her occasional petulance, her introspection, she could be my daughter, or my neighbor, or even my long-ago self.

Life works well for Elana. She has a sturdy footing in her own world and her own family: a knowledge of her place and an understandable pride in her role.

Then, quite unexpectedly, she is tumbled backward into the world of myth, magic, and dragons—and of Georyn, with whom she falls in love. (Who among us has not, at some time, been jolted to find that the past is not entirely past?)

And for Georyn, she becomes the Enchantress.

As a writer, I am impressed by the deftness with which Sylvia Engdahl veers between several points of view and several styles of language—even, amazingly, melding Georyn's formal speech with Elana's casual vernacular into a believable back-and-forth that moves from conversation into a deep emotional connection. At the same time she maintains the fine balance in Elana's character, so that even as she pretends to sophisticated powers of enchantment to manipulate Georyn, she genuinely enchants him with her very human charm. Yet throughout, she is still Elana: guilty, dutiful, frightened, and very young. Like every teenager, she speaks in a jaunty flippancy and stirs with rebellion as well. Newly stunned by the awareness that she—despite the technology of her highly evolved society—cannot change the injustice of the world, she asks, "Father, haven't you ever questioned this policy?"

With that hesitant question, later to become a firmer, more confident plea, Elana joins the multitudes of literature's impassioned young protagonists forced to face the inadequacies and hypocrisies of their parents' generation: my own Jonas, Robert Cormier's Jerry, Katherine Paterson's Lyddie, even E. B. White's Fern. One by one they do what they can to set things right, to make things fair.

And Georyn! What a heartbreaking, wonderful hero

he is! The remarkable dexterity with which the author shifts viewpoint and voice brings us into Georyn's world, a world that embraces chivalrous honor and the structure of fairy tales as well. There is a sense of familiarity when he faces the three tasks (of course there are three! There are always three!) given him—the disk, the light, and the cup—in order to be able to confront and slay the dragon.

In the predictability of the once-upon-a-time world, however, his courage would earn him the hand of the princess. Here, in the multilayered world where past and present briefly blend, it will not be possible. Reading, we know it will not. The demands of the complex world preclude the romantic resolution we have learned to expect from fairy tales.

He knew all along. His brother warned him. "Think, Georyn: even if she should let you look through such a door, the time will surely come when it will be sealed again; and when that happens you will be not on her side of it, but on ours."

The story of lovers from different and opposing worlds has been told for centuries, yet we love it no less for its repetition or the sad inevitability of its ending. Juliet will whisper sweet nothings from her balcony, but she and Romeo will die eventually anyway. Pinkerton and Butterfly will never live happily ever after. But as readers, we yearn for the possibility of it, and our hearts break as those doors close.

> *Then, as the Lady's voice faded, he glimpsed the world as she saw it, from above....*
>
> *And after that, she was lost to him. Yet he was sure, as he would be sure for ever after, that the powers that were hers to tap would endure beyond time and space.*

*   *   *

Even in these days when politicians overlook the separation mandated constitutionally and invoke religion in their campaign rhetoric, spirituality remains a topic largely unaddressed in fiction for young adults. But in essence, *Enchantress from the Stars* is a story about sacrifice and compassion, two of the main ingredients of religious faith, and about the power of believing in that which one cannot understand. His belief in an unexplainable power saves Georyn's life. Elana's sacrifice of her own happiness restores Georyn's future. And the compassion of the Starwatcher—the overseer, the father—is the orchestrating chord.

Many books, including some of my own, contain a character like the Starwatcher: the elderly adviser, the one who understands outcomes and risks, the one who steers a young protagonist, points the way, and then lets go. Parents, of course, know the pain of that letting-go. I remember writing the passage in which The Giver, in the book of that title, tells Jonas that he will not go with him on the final, difficult journey. It was hard for me to send Jonas off without him in exactly the same way that it had been hard for me to see my own children move out into the world beyond my protection.

Elana's father undertook such a task with the wisdom, courage, and blind surging faith it requires. When she asks how he had known enough to stand aside and let things happen as they did, he tells her, "I didn't. I trusted *you*."

Maybe trust is the key element in the book. All good Young Adult literature is about leaving childhood and innocence behind. It is about the recognition and acceptance of responsibility. But every young person who goes forth—Jonas, Elana, Gilly, Maniac, and countless others—does so buoyed and strengthened by the knowledge and trust of those who have made the journey before them.

Today's children find some of those empowering mentors only in books. For them, and for all of us, it is a wonderful thing that the Starwatcher is still there.

—*Lois Lowry*

Preface

The locale of this story can be fixed neither in space nor in time. Perhaps it is the planet Earth—but then again, perhaps not, for whether this is a tale of the past or of the future is anybody's guess. Scientists now believe that the universe may contain countless worlds upon which life has evolved; who is to say how many such worlds happen to be third planets of medium-sized yellow stars? And who can predict how far the sons and daughters of Earth may someday travel?

Three peoples of different levels of advancement appear here; whether any of them are our ancestors or our descendants is not really very important. If other peoples exist, their symbols are not ours; yet a story must be told in familiar terms. Thus, the elements of this one may seem commonplace: As magical charms and fearsome dragons are the traditional ingredients of yesterday's legends, so ray guns and interplanetary invasions are those of today's. All such legends are unrealistic in a literal sense. This narrative is no more a prophecy than a history. Yet this, within the limits of its   form, is how things may have been . . . or how they will be . . . or how they now are, somewhere beyond the Earth we know.

Enchantress from the Stars

Prologue

The planet shines below us, cloud-flecked, dazzling against the dark backdrop of space. Down there it is cool and green and peaceful. In a little while we will take the ship out of orbit and leave this world behind, a mere speck in the vast currents of the universe. This world, which we call Andrecia—the third planet of a quite ordinary yellow sun . . . but that's just coincidence, of course. What difference does it make that just such a planet was my own people's ancestral home?

I am not supposed to cry. I am not supposed to let my personal feelings get involved. How could a girl ever become a field agent if it affected her this way every time? Maybe I'm upset now only because of Georyn. Or maybe I should never have joined the Anthropological Service at all, though it's a little late to decide that now. I've been warned often enough that an agent's life is not easy. I used to think people meant simply that you had to study hard and work hard, and that you were sometimes in danger; but I guess that's not the point. . . .

Last night when we got back to the ship, Father said that he hoped I saw now why people as young as I (I'm still a First Phase student) are not normally allowed to make contact with Younglings. But Father's a compassionate person, and he's well aware that I'm not sorry I got myself into this. Pretty soon he took me in his arms and smoothed my hair and said that it was his fault as much as mine for allowing it to happen. He admitted that he'd used me, and that he had had no right to because I wasn't ready. Yet we did accomplish something on Andrecia . . . without me, perhaps we couldn't have. And in the end I didn't cause any of the disasters untrained people can cause; there's been no harmful disclosure, and if Georyn and Jarel were hurt by their contact with us, it was only because they had to be. Anyway, I keep telling myself that.

But I wish I could know, really *know,* how it was down there. Was it only a hoax, a sham? Or was there real magic after all? I'm afraid I haven't much of the empathy that Father says an agent needs most of all. (*He* says I do have, perhaps too much, only I'm too young to channel it properly.) All the same, I've got to try to put together the pieces, not only to prepare my report but because it's important to me. There's a lot I don't understand yet. . . . The things Younglings take seriously—are they all real underneath, as a tree is real no matter what language you describe it in? Was Georyn not deluded, but only attuned to another kind of truth? Can believing something make it a fact? Is the Stone more than a stone, *really*?

That's one set of questions, the ones I may be able to answer. I'll try not to get bogged down with the others. The ones like why do Younglings have to be Younglings at all. Why, for instance, must Georyn be capable of wanting something that he'll never be able to reach? Why must a man like Jarel, a good man, have clearer sight for the dark side of human progress than for the bright? And why should a person be stuck in the wrong age, anyway?

Well, I'll never get anywhere worrying over *those* things.

Because the starship was diverted to Andrecia, Father and I won't be coming to the family reunion, and it's just as well for I'm no longer in any mood for a vacation. You'll see why; I am going to record the whole story and send it to you, since we are not only cousins but friends, I think, although we've never met. You asked me what the Service is like, and I can't think of any better way to tell you. This account may help you make up your mind about applying to the Academy, but I honestly don't know which way you're likely to be swayed.

Since I'll be putting in a lot of detail, I'll keep a copy of the tape and edit it later for my report. The report won't be a formal, official one. Father will write that. It'll be simply the personal account required from every agent who's involved in a mission. I've been asked to cover the Andrecians' and the Imperials' viewpoints as well as my own reactions; the Service often requests this because they want you to learn to look at things the way Younglings do. (They demand that you be totally objective about the picture anyone you contacted got of you, even if this causes you to make yourself sound better, sometimes, than you really were. So please forgive what may seem like distortions in my favor!) It's easy now for me to see through Georyn's eyes and to speak in the words appropriate to his view of the world. With Jarel it is harder, since I didn't know him well; still I can try to imagine how he must have felt. This, then, is the way I *think* it was: for Georyn's people, for Jarel's, and for us. . . .

The Mission

At the edge of the Enchanted Forest there lived a poor woodcutter who had four sons, the youngest of whom was named Georyn. They were able to earn a meager living by selling wood to the folk of the village, and although there was seldom more than dry bread or thin gruel on their table, they were not miserable.

Yet the brothers, as they grew to manhood, found little satisfaction in their lot. Often, as they toiled at the hewing of a tree on the outskirts of the wood, they stopped to watch the huntsmen of the King ride by to hunt in the Enchanted Forest, which their father had forbidden them to enter. And the eldest son would say, "Ah, if I but had the power of the King and a hundred servants to do my bidding!" And the next brother would laugh and reply, "Myself, I would settle for the King's treasure, for gold buys all that a man could wish for." And the next would tell them, "You are both fools, but if a man could win a fair bride such as the King's daughter, he would be well content."

Georyn, the youngest, would say nothing; yet in his own heart he would whisper, "Had I the wisdom of the King and his councillors, I would not be merely a wood-cutter, and indeed I would not be hungry, nor would the villagers. And I would know the secret of the Enchanted Forest and be free to hunt there, and someday I might go even beyond it!"

Now to that country there came a time of great sorrow, for on the far side of the Enchanted Forest there appeared a monstrous Dragon that breathed fire, and its roaring could be heard far and wide over the land; and many folk fled in terror, fearing that their homes would be laid waste. Many of the King's huntsmen went to fight the Dragon, yet the Dragon remained and no men returned.

At last the King sent forth a decree, and in every village it was proclaimed: whosoever should free the land of the terrible Dragon would be given whatever reward his heart should desire, even to a half of the kingdom. Yet the people were afraid. If the King's own huntsmen had failed, how could mere villagers face the monster and kill it? And few men entertained thoughts of the King's reward.

But the woodcutter's sons had dreamed long of possessing such as the King could give, and they begged their father for permission to travel to the King and ask his blessing in the quest. The woodcutter himself, however, opposed them. "Even to enter the Enchanted Forest is death for such as you!" he cried. "Yet you talk of dragons! I forbid it; you shall not go."

The three elder brothers went angrily to their beds and whispered far into the night, making plans to disobey their father and set out together at first light, for they believed their valor equal to that of nobles and huntsmen.

But Georyn talked further with the woodcutter, asking, "Why should it be death to enter the Forest, when the King and his followers have hunted there since before I was born?"

"As I have often told you," replied the woodcutter, "the Enchanted Forest is the home of evil spirits, who have laid a curse on all who go there, though they dare not touch the King's companions. This was true even before the Dragon appeared to ravage our land."

"Then if the King should send us, they would not touch us either."

"Perhaps not. But how could you hope to slay the Dragon, you who have never before held a sword? It is impossible, Georyn."

Now Georyn knew this, for though he was quite as brave as his brothers, he was not so foolish as to consider himself abler than the King's huntsmen at killing. But these men had failed, and if they had failed then perhaps the Dragon could not be killed with a sword at all. "There may be a way to overcome the monster, Father," he said. "But it will not be found by those who fear it! I can have no happiness until I have at least tried."

And so at last, seeing that he could not dissuade them, the woodcutter allowed his sons to seek the aid of the King. They set forth the next morning, following the river that circled the wood. When they had gone but a short distance, they came to a fork in the path: one way kept to the course of the stream, while the other led to the King's castle by a shorter route, through the forest.

"Let us take the quickest way," said the eldest brother.

"That would not be wise," protested Georyn. "That way leads directly into the Enchanted Forest."

His brothers laughed, saying, "What, do you believe such foolishness? Do you fear that we will be bewitched?"

"Not all tales of enchantment are foolish ones," replied Georyn. "There will be a time when we must challenge that which lies within the Forest, but to do so now, unnecessarily, would be no better than folly. We have no knowledge of what we face."

Thereupon the brothers stopped and debated; for they remembered that they had indeed heard fearsome tales of the Enchanted Forest, and they were not anxious to test the truth of them. So at length they were persuaded to take the familiar way, and for the rest of that day they continued along the riverbank. It was a bright, springtime morning; the leaves were young and green, the water sparkled in the sunlight, and as the young men walked, they whistled.

When the sun had sunk low behind the dark profiles of the fir trees, however, the Forest beyond the river loomed larger, both in the brothers' eyes and in their thoughts. The foaming roar of the water seemed less cheering, and upon the opposite shore a faint trace of mist began to form. And then it was that the brothers came upon a small stone hut, which surprised them greatly, for it had not been there in the past when they had cut wood near that place. As they were wondering at this, a tall, dark-haired maiden stepped forth from the hut; and the woodcutter's sons stood silent in amazement and awe, for she was unlike any mortal maiden they had ever seen, and they knew at once that she was an enchantress.

I was not supposed to be in the landing party at all—I was supposed to be studying. That was part of the bargain when Father decided we should go in the first place; I agreed to prepare for First Phase exams on shipboard, to make up for the time I would be missing at the Academy. For that matter, the Academy itself wouldn't have granted me leave on any other basis. Father's wish was enough to get us passage, since the starship was to make a stop at the world on which our family reunion's to be held, but even that wouldn't have carried much weight with the Dean.

A Service starship is a good place to study; you have lots of free time at your disposal, especially if you are neither part of a survey team nor a member of the crew. But who wants to study all the time? I had never been off my home world before; since I'm from a Service family, even entering the Academy hadn't meant a trip for me. And I was dying to see something! I knew that I would not be permitted to accompany any regular team for a long time. So when the Andrecian situation came up and Father was appointed Senior Agent to handle it, I begged him to take me with him.

"It's out of the question, Elana," he said gravely. "We are not going on a sightseeing trip. You know that."

"Evrek's going!"

"Evrek has completed Third Phase; he has taken the Oath. He's ready for a field assignment, and while I wouldn't have chosen a thing like this for his first one, it's his job."

It was true enough that Evrek and I were not really in the same category anymore. The Oath makes a difference, personally as well as officially; since Evrek was sworn, I'd hardly known him. Practically from the moment of his investiture, which had taken place only a few days before we left home, he had seemed changed in some subtle way that I couldn't quite define. One thing was sure: it wasn't only the new white uniform. Agents don't wear their uniforms anyway, except on dress occasions.

But as you know, Evrek and I are close friends—well,

more than friends. Someday we will marry and will be a field team in the same sense that Father and Mother were before Mother was killed, many years ago, on that ill-fated exploratory expedition. Despite the temporary gulf between us, I was not about to stand by while Evrek went down to Andrecia without me.

"Please, Father?" I persisted. "I won't be in the way, I promise!".

"I'm sorry. But it would be dangerous, not only for you but for the mission."

I didn't reply aloud; though language is a useful tool, sometimes you get further telepathically. *I'm not afraid . . . and I'll learn from it!*

You're too young, you're not yet sworn!

This was about the answer I had expected. Sometimes it seemed that the closer I got to my own investiture, the harder it was to wait. You're not invested until the end of Third Phase; I wasn't even through First Phase yet. And I'd nearly forgotten that last year the big hurdle was simply to get admitted to the Academy.

All my life I've wanted a career in the Anthropological Service; I've lived and breathed it ever since I was old enough to know what a Youngling world is. Of course it's natural, in my case, since besides my parents being Service people my grandfather and grandmother—Mother's parents, with whom I lived most of my childhood—are both retired field agents. But even for someone with my background, the Academy is not easy to get into. The stories you hear about the entrance tests being such an awful ordeal are true. They're carefully designed to be, because you're not meant to pass unless you want to pretty desperately. It's not just a matter of being smart—though you do have to be, of course—or of having high aptitude for the control of psychic powers like psychokinesis and the

Shield as well as ordinary telepathy. It's more a question of having the right personality. The Service is not about to turn anybody loose on a Youngling world who's not fitted for the responsibility. So there are all sorts of psychological tests . . . and some other things they throw in to weed out anyone who hasn't sufficient—well, fortitude. Being an agent isn't always fun, and you are supposed to take the first steps toward finding that out before you get in too deep.

So they do everything they can to discourage you—but it's a very good arrangement, because the Service is not just a job. After all, once you take the Oath you are in for life; it's irrevocable, and you renounce your allegiance to your native world. There are a number of reasons why it was set up this way, but the main one is that they just don't want you if you don't feel that strongly about it. The power to influence Youngling civilizations is not a thing to be taken lightly.

But if you are truly serious about it, if you are willing to make the sacrifices the Oath demands, all the worlds of the universe are open to you! If you are not in the Service you will never see anything but Federation planets, for the worlds of Younglings—peoples who are not yet mature enough to qualify for Federation membership—are strictly off limits to everyone but trained field agents. The reasons are very complex, but what it boils down to is that if Youngling peoples were to find out that they aren't the most advanced humans in the universe, their civilizations just wouldn't develop properly. They wouldn't ever realize their own potential. The Federation doesn't want to dominate other peoples, only to study them—so we don't reveal ourselves.

Of course, the Service is more than a chance to travel to exciting places. To begin with, it's a fellowship like none other. Service people are of all races, from all over the universe; yet we're like one family. Once sworn, you're Service first and differences in background don't matter. There's not even any rank among agents; though they're rated by ability and experience and given responsibility accordingly, these ratings aren't announced. Naturally, for any specific mission someone's appointed Senior Agent and all others are bound to obey him; but at other times and places he's the peer of the rest and probably best friends with some of them.

The really big thing about the Service, though, the thing that makes you want to give your life to it, is the opportunity to do something worthwhile . . . more than worthwhile, actually *significant*. Because, while our main objective is to study the Younglings, there are occasions on which we do take action. There are times when we may, literally, save a world—save its people, I mean, from slavery or from extinction. Not that we meddle in any planet's internal affairs; that is absolutely forbidden, for the Federation knows that however benevolent this might seem in some cases, it would be ultimately harmful. But we do try to save Youngling peoples from each other, when we can.

For some Youngling civilizations, the most advanced ones, have starships. It takes a lot less maturity to build a starship than to understand what to do with one when you get it. With their starships, they begin to expand to planets besides their own, which is both natural and right. The trouble is, they don't stick to uninhabited planets; they're just as likely to grab one that belongs to somebody else: either they invade it, or they unwittingly destroy its culture through peaceful contact. We stop that if it's feasible, but we do it in a very quiet manner. Oh, it would be easy to use force! It would be easy to lay down ultimatums and that kind of thing, because we of the Federation have all sorts of powers that nobody else has; but we'd do more harm than good that way.

So we don't send in a fully armed starship and an army of men. We send two or three field agents, unarmed, just as if it were an ordinary data-gathering expedition.

You may wonder why we don't simply avoid the trouble in the first place by shielding the Youngling planets, as we shield our own, so that they can't be found by a science less advanced than ours. Well, it's a nice idea, but it just wouldn't be practical. In the first place it would be awfully expensive. You can't shield only the inhabited planets, you've got to shield all the planets in their solar systems, because otherwise any astronomer who took the trouble to calculate planetary orbits would realize that something peculiar was going on. It's one thing to do this for the Federation solar systems, but something else again to do it for every Youngling system that's been charted. And even if we could, it wouldn't solve anything; after all, we've explored comparatively few of the millions of Youngling systems that exist.

More than this, though, if we kept on Youngling planets the men and equipment that would be needed to shield them, there'd be a very substantial risk of disclosure to the people of those planets. And that would be a risk we couldn't take, because the chances of their being harmed by it would be much greater than the chances of their being picked for invasion. The Service has learned when to leave well enough alone.

It's a frustrating problem. It's heartbreaking, even, when you really think about it. We have so much power, yet we can accomplish so little! Our primary mission is to observe and to learn. The sad fact is that Youngling peoples are often wiped out, either through colonization of their planet or through some other disaster that we haven't any idea of how to prevent . . . and we may not even know about it until it's too late. Once in a while, though, it happens that we are in the right place at the right time to come to the rescue. In the case of Andrecia—and I knew that Andrecia must be such a case, for mysterious unscheduled stops aren't made otherwise—the rescuers were to be Father, Evrek, and a woman named Ilura whom I knew only slightly.

Father had been on leave status, of course, and he had been looking forward to the family reunion, too, not having been back to the world of his birth since before he married Mother. But he was the only unassigned agent on board qualified for such a command; that's the way it goes in the Service. He had chosen his assistants from among the members of the survey teams aboard. Actually, he had asked for volunteers; this in itself should have told me that he meant what he said about the expected dangers. But all I could think of was finding a way to be included. It didn't occur to me that to try to get around a Senior Agent's decision regarding a sensitive mission was hardly the ideal way to start my career. When it's your own father, you naturally think that he overprotects you and that it's fair enough to outwit him.

You don't argue with Father, however. I would have to figure out some other course of action. Meanwhile, I turned back to the text that I had been studying:

> It is by now a well-known fact that the human peoples of the universe have similar histories—not that the specific details are similar, but the same patterns emerge on every home world. Each must pass through three stages: first childhood, when all is full of wonder, when man admits that much is unknown to him, call-

ing it "supernatural," yet believing. Then adolescence, when man discards superstition and reveres science, feeling that he has charted its realms and has only to conquer them—never dreaming that certain "supernatural" wonders should not be set aside, but understood. And at last maturity, when the discovery is made that what was termed "supernatural" has been perfectly natural all along, and is in reality a part of the very science that sought to reject it. . . .

But I don't want to read about all that, I thought, I want to see it! What sort of people are down there on Andrecia? What sort of emergency is it that's taken us off course and is serious enough for a team to be sent in—for them to risk contact, maybe, or even their lives?

Contact is a thing that's seldom permitted, except under very compelling circumstances. Younglings are not allowed to know that the Federation even exists. That's the most unbreakable rule we have, because a Youngling culture could be irreparably damaged by that awareness. You have to be willing to die rather than make an illegal disclosure; in fact one of the provisions of the Oath binds you to do just that. So contact, when it's necessary, requires a cover of some sort. And any mission involving this can be very risky indeed.

I canceled out the text and instructed the computer to give me all the facts it had on Andrecia. It didn't have many. There had been a survey not too many years before, but the Andrecian culture was a rudimentary one; there was no technology to study. The people of the area that had been most closely observed fit into a pattern that was familiar enough: medium height, predominantly light-skinned and fair-haired so far as physical characteristics went, and as for their society, I guess you would call it feudal. Not very advanced; it would be many, many years before the Andrecians, left to themselves, would have developed far enough to give the Service any worry. But they were a very vulnerable people . . . Andrecia was a good planet, a rich one. *Too* rich! It didn't take much imagination to guess the nature of the current trouble.

I'm ashamed to say that to me the idea of our having to save this world from a takeover was a pleasantly exciting one. We're really going to do something, I thought—not just observe, but act! I didn't understand very much in those days. I thought of Younglings as interesting but exotic beings, not as *people,* people with feelings like my own. I had never known any, you see. The whole thing, even the hint of danger, seemed like a game. And I didn't see how my presence could imperil the mission; sworn or not sworn, I knew the rules. Surely Father didn't think that I couldn't be trusted! No matter what we got into. . . .

I knew, with my mind if not yet with my emotions, that the danger could be real. You might think that no Youngling could be much of a match for a Federation citizen, but any field agent knows better. The thing is, you can't always use your advantage. It's not only that the use of non-native physical weapons is prohibited—some of the psychic powers are too revealing, too. There's a rather well-known case where an agent made a small slip, and then had to let herself be put to death for witchcraft rather than go on to an actual disclosure.

You know about things like that, but they don't really scare you. They're too far removed from your experience. Then there are other things that you don't know about . . . not in First Phase, you don't. Only of course, if you happen to have gotten so far as to be on board a Service starship, you think you know everything.

I thought so, certainly, when I joined the Andrecia

party by the simple expedient of sneaking into the small landing craft that the team was to use and hiding myself in the supply compartment.

I won't dwell on that incident; it is not an episode that I am proud of. I've since been told that initiative and daring are prized in an agent and that you have to be able to go out on a limb, even against policy, when circumstances justify it. They did not justify it in this case, however, and what's more I had absolutely no conception of what was at stake.

Anyway, if some of what happened to me on Andrecia wasn't too pleasant, I can't say I didn't ask for it.

The Imperial Exploration Corps had founded many colonies, but this one was better situated than most. It was in the northern hemisphere of a rich new planet, near the coast of a large and fertile continent; moreover, it lay at the western edge of an impressive stand of timber. Not that the trees were in themselves of any value, since they must eventually be cleared. But the area served as a temporary buffer between the base camp and the nearest native village. Most natives, it had been learned, were afraid of this forest. They believed it to be haunted.

On a spring afternoon when the building of the colony had barely begun, the apprentice medical officer, Jarel, stood in the clearing and watched the rockchewer charge again and again at the stubborn perimeter of the woods. It was still being used to burn off surface growth; excavation wouldn't be started for some days yet. The racket was muffled by his pressure suit's helmet, and the cold flames darting from the nose of the big land-clearing machine looked incongruously fierce. It wasn't normal for anything so lethal to seem so quiet! A rockchewer was a monstrous piece of equipment shaped rather like some huge prehistoric beast, and it generated an ear-shattering noise.

So this is how it feels, Jarel thought. This is how it feels to be on a new, untouched planet, light-years from our own star; a planet that will soon be an outpost of the Empire because of our work here. All through medical school, this is what I wanted; I never even considered any other sort of internship. Well, now I've got it.

It was too bad that the land must be cleared. This was kind of a nice planet, green trees and grass and stuff. It was the third planet of a yellow sun, even: in that, as in other ways, it seemed just like home. But the place was crawling with alien bacteria; not only must pressure suits and helmets be worn until immunity was established, but every inch of ground must be sterilized before any construction could be started. Burn off the trees, level the ground—how else could you take over a hostile world?

There was no other safe way. The first load of colonists had already arrived: a dozen couples, plus their kids, in addition to the fifty or so Corpsmen in the original survey party. They had plenty of hard work ahead of them, and no time to waste regretting the destruction of the native vegetation. But it did seem a pity.

It was a pity about the native population, too.

The natives were pretty primitive, of course. They had no technology to speak of, sort of a feudal setup, no real government, not even any cities—and they weren't widespread. They weren't using a fraction of the good land. Certainly they weren't dangerous. It was rather pathetic, the way they'd been venturing into camp two or three at a time, brandishing swords and trying to look ferocious. One of the temporary barracks had been unpressurized for use as a lockup, and any natives that showed up were being held prisoner. There were, after all, women and children among the colonists, and it was best to be on the safe side. There would be time enough when the colony was set up to see about arranging for a treaty and a reservation. Anyway, Captain Dulard seemed to think so.

You couldn't really expect Dulard to give a second thought to a bunch of savages that did not represent a potential danger, Jarel realized. As commander, he had enough else to worry about; so long as the natives weren't strong enough to rise against him, he was satisfied. It wasn't as if the original inhabitants of this world had any rights under the Charter. If they were anywhere near to that level, the planet wouldn't have been chosen, but they were not. They were merely humanoid animals. It being Empire policy to avoid wiping out native species where possible, they would be granted tracts of land. Some of them might even prove to be trainable; there was always a labor shortage in a new colony.

Well, that's the way it goes, Jarel thought. The Empire has to expand; new worlds are needed—and the worlds are taken. He had come to learn how it was done, hadn't he? He had wanted to take part in the shaping of humanity's glorious future among the stars?

Only he wished, somehow, that this was an uninhabited world.

No one knew I was aboard the landing craft until we were actually down to the planet's surface. Hidden as I was, they couldn't detect me any more than I could see or hear them, and of course I had been very careful to keep my thoughts strictly to myself during the descent. Sometimes Evrek and I communicate too well, and the rapport between Father and myself is even better—not that they can probe my mind, since your full consent's needed for that, but I still tend to transmit involuntarily when I'm excited. I don't yet have full conscious control over any of my psychic powers.

A few moments after I felt the ship settle gently to a landing, I came out of hiding. The others were already outside; I had to recycle the airlock. When its outer door slid open I stood there breathing in marvelously free air and sunlight, and I called to them. What a child I was, poised on the threshold of my first new planet, with my happy-go-lucky expectations of grand and glorious adventure! Sometimes I think of it, now that I'm wiser and know that worlds are not playgrounds; I remember how carefree I felt and I'm wistful, for it will never be that way again.

The place where we had come down was an idyllic one, a pastoral spot in which the metallic sphere of our ship seemed almost incongruous. There was a meadow, starred with clumps of yellow flowers, and a fringe of dark woods. Nearby within the forest was a river; the murmur of it could be heard clearly, though the trees hid it from view. The sun, low in the sky, shimmered through a lacy veil of cloud. An alien sun—the first I'd ever seen—yet it didn't look alien. Dimmer, perhaps, than the one of my home solar system; I could look straight at it as the clouds blew past. But it seemed natural.

On the grass near the ship stood the members of the landing party; all three of them turned and stared at me, and I stared back. Nobody said anything, though I caught Father's swift thought: *Oh, no, Elana!* Father and Evrek wore ordinary field outfits, clothes more or less like my own, but Ilura was dressed in a long, full skirt, a style that I could only suppose was Andrecian. (Service starships carry all sorts of odd supplies, like homespun cloth, for nobody can predict what a survey team will run into.)

When I stopped to think about it, I realized that she was of a race very much like the Andrecians, physically, and that she could conceivably pass for one of them—which of course the rest of us could not, our coloring and features being quite different. But it was startling to see her so disguised.

Evrek, I think, was the most upset by my appearance—Evrek, who I'd have thought would be secretly glad to see me! "Are you crazy, Elana?" he demanded as I joined them in the meadow. "Did you think we were going on a picnic or something? It's a critical mission, and risky. You could get hurt."

Evrek is funny sometimes. Looking back, I realize that he was truly afraid for me and because he didn't want to show that fear, he let it out as anger. And I didn't help matters any. "Oh, that's silly!" I said impatiently. "Father won't let any of us get hurt."

Father agreed firmly, "Not if I can prevent it, I won't. And in your case I can. You're going right back with the landing craft."

"To the starship? But that would leave you stranded here!"

"We are going to be stranded anyway, until our job's done. Did you think we'd keep a ship around for someone to find?"

I did not really know many of the details of how a field team operated, I realized. The landing craft could, of course, be returned to the starship's orbit under automatic control and recalled later, but somehow I hadn't expected them to do this. It seemed rather drastic, in a way.

Well, in any case, I'd had a glimpse of Andrecia; it hadn't all been wasted effort. "This is a beautiful planet!" I burst out.

"Yes," said Ilura. "No wonder the colonists want it."

"Colonists?" I didn't have any actual information about what was going on here, other than my own guesses; the official announcement aboard the starship had been very noncommittal.

"You might as well know," Father said. "There's another ship here, a ship from a quite powerful young Empire. They're clearing land for a colony."

"And we're going to stop them?"

"We hope so. There are plenty of uninhabited worlds they can colonize. But they're a formidable people, Elana."

"But still Youngling," I said. They were at a high level, I knew, if they had achieved the stardrive—not too far below us technologically. There could be no other Younglings significantly superior to them. Still . . .

"Yes, Youngling—of course," Ilura told me. "And they have no command of psychic powers at all; their gods are machines. All the same they're dangerous, and there are nearly a hundred of them here, I'd say."

"Come on, let's get busy," Father interrupted. "Elana, you can help us to set up camp, but when I send the ship back you'll be in it."

We crossed the meadow and selected a place near the river, among tall, majestic trees, for the base camp. Naturally we couldn't put up any sort of shelter that would not seem indigenous to the surroundings. But there were plenty of fair-sized stones strewn around nearby—apparently the river was sometimes higher than at present—and from them Father and Evrek erected a small, windowless stone hut. This was done quickly and silently, and, I believe, psychokinetically, though the stones rarely left anyone's hands and conventional plastics were used for cementing them. I know that Father has more ability along these lines than most of us; I could not, with my own mind, have moved one of those stones two feet without emotional stimulus. Perhaps, of course, the urgency was more apparent to him. The fact remains that the hut went up much more rapidly than it should have, if there had been anyone there to watch.

While the hut was taking shape, Ilura and I unloaded the supplies and carried them to the edge of the woodsy clearing. When we were almost finished Father said to me, "Go aboard now, Elana. Leave the last few things in the meadow, and we'll pick them up. I've got to get that ship out of here."

A breeze rippled the new spring leaves of the trees; I took a deep breath, and the air seemed alive with a faintly alien scent. A Youngling world: a lush, green world full of mystery and promise. What might lie hidden in this unearthly forest? I'd had a look at it, anyway—that was something, though perhaps it was only tantalizing. I started reluctantly toward the meadow and the waiting ship. And then, in one brief instant, the first real turning point of my life came; and now nothing will ever be the same as it was before.

There was no warning until, just as I was about to step out from the shelter of the trees, Father grabbed me and pulled me back. Directly across the clearing from us I saw a flash of metal. Two men were emerging from the forest, and they could not be Andrecians. They wore pressure suits and helmets; Andrecia's atmosphere—or its bacteria—must be poisonous to them.

"The ship!" Evrek cried out.

Father must have been aware of what was happening before the rest of us were, for the ship had already begun its swift, soundless lift from the meadow. The invaders couldn't have spotted it as they came into the clearing; a large clump of thick-foliaged trees had kept it out of their direct line of sight. They now had their backs to it, but if they turned within the next thirty seconds they could not fail to see.

"A clear disclosure!" murmured Ilura. "They'll know what an alien ship means! It's the worst thing that could happen, for the Imperials to—"

I understood her. A spherical, noiseless ship—a ship without visible means of propulsion—they'd know it for the earmark of a civilization more advanced than their own. So the danger wasn't just to *this* world. It could change the course of their Empire's history if those men saw and were believed.

The thing happened so fast that I could scarcely take it in. Father and Evrek could do nothing; for them to be seen, undisguised, would have been disastrous. But Ilura wore the dress of an Andrecian woman. Physically, she could pass as Andrecian. As the invaders started to turn toward the rising ship she ran forward with a terrific yell, snatched out the Andrecian-type knife she'd had concealed somewhere—and threw it.

"What's she *doing*?" I exclaimed, horrified. "She wouldn't *kill* them? She couldn't, even if she wanted to, with that, not with them wearing suits."

"No," Evrek said softly. "It was a diversion. The ship's gone, they didn't see."

The ship had indeed disappeared, silently, into a pink-tinged bank of clouds. The Imperials were facing Ilura. Though the knife had fallen harmlessly to the ground, one of them raised his weapon.

It was a laser of some kind; it made no sound, and the flash was unbearably bright. When I got my eyes open again, Ilura was gone. Just—*gone!*

"Her Shield!" I whispered numbly. "What happened to her Shield?"

Evrek faced me. "She didn't use it. The Shield would

have given her away; the Imperials would have known she was alien."

I froze there, overcome by stunned disbelief. They had meant what they were saying. It was not a sightseeing trip, not a picnic, not a game. The things that happened here would be *real*.

The two invaders had turned back toward the forest and were disappearing in the direction from which they had come; apparently they were not in the mood to take on more hostile natives, not knowing how many of these there might be. Still Father stood motionless, his face marked by pain that was more than the shock of a mere observer. I looked at him, suddenly seeing a man who was not my father at all. *You and Ilura were—communicating!* I asserted mutely.

Of course.

Was it her idea . . . or yours?

It was hers, Elana.

But he could have stopped her, I thought. She was under his orders; whether it was her own idea or not, surely he could have found some other way. . . .

Evrek put his arms around me, and I clung to him. Soundlessly I cried, *Oh, Evrek! Why did Father let it happen?*

Elana, he is sworn! They were both sworn; what choice did they have?

Around Evrek's neck hung the Emblem, the multi-faceted pendant symbolizing the Oath, that every agent wears; now, with my cheek against his shoulder, I saw it as if for the first time. All my life I'd accepted this as a standard article of dress; even my mother had worn one, and no doubt it had first caught my eye during my infancy. Certainly one of my earliest memories was of sitting on her lap and turning it over and over in my hands. But I had not truly grasped its significance before.

Evrek, too, was sworn! If he had been the one disguised as a native of this world, he would now be dead. My mother herself had been killed under roughly comparable circumstances, though at the time I'd been too young to understand. The Oath was more than a colorful ritual to which, if you happened to want a Service career, you looked forward all through your schooldays; it was more than a decision that you made once, for all time, about the vocation you would follow. It was a thing you lived with continuously, during every moment you spent on an alien world.

We stayed hidden until we were sure that the Imperials would not return; then, without speaking, we picked up the supplies and carried them into the hut. It was cold there. I dropped my load in a corner and went outside again, into the fast-fading sunlight.

Father followed me and put his arm around my shoulders, but I pulled away. He came after me. "Things like this happen," he said gently. "It's part of the price we pay."

"For being here?"

"For being what we are. For our knowledge."

"I know . . . only it—it wasn't real, before."

"There's always a moment when it becomes real. I'm sorry; I'd rather you had been older."

"I'm all right!" I knew that the situation was one to which I'd have to adjust if I really was old enough to be here. But one thing was still troubling me. "Father, would they have known for *sure,* from the Shield?"

"It was too great a chance to take, considering that we had only a few seconds for a decision." He hesitated, then went on, "Elana, I'm going to be very honest with you. In this particular case, they might not have. In fact, if they had recognized it for what it is—a mental power instead of a physical one—a demonstration of the Shield might actually have been helpful to us; that makes this doubly hard to bear. But they probably wouldn't have recognized it, for they are conditioned to see such things from a materialistic viewpoint. They would have investigated and found us. Even if they hadn't found us, their suspicions would have been aroused, and we'd have lost our only chance to help the Andrecians."

"Why would we?"

"For reasons too complicated to explain right now, reasons having to do with our plan of action." Father shook his head sadly. "No agent can ever be *sure*. Here, we were confronted with a very real possibility not only of starting a chain of events that would have led to the failure of our mission, but of disclosure to the Empire. Two Youngling civilizations, Elana! They would both have been hurt—"

"Hurt, if she'd merely used the Shield?"

"The more power you have, the greater the consequences of the little things."

I looked up at the tall conifers silhouetted against the soft glow of Andrecian sunset. Behind me, the sound of the river seemed to grow louder. There's just such a river near Grandfather's summer place on my home world; I used to hear it from my bedroom whenever I woke at night. How many rivers, I thought, on how many planets . . . in the whole universe? How many of them will I see? Beside how many of them will I stand when something like this happens?

But you don't want anyone, least of all your father, to think that you aren't mature enough to face reality. I turned to him and said steadily, "What happens now?"

Father looked at me thoughtfully. "Elana," he began, "you know that for you to be here, unsworn, is illegal."

"Yes. I—I'm sorry."

"Really?" He met my eyes, and I saw suddenly that he

was not angry with me at all. There was something there that, if it had not been for Ilura, would have been a smile. "You haven't lost your enthusiasm or your nerve, have you?" he asked quietly.

"No!" Realizing what he was leading up to, I added, "You're not going to recall the ship, are you?"

"No, I'm not. I don't dare to recall it right now, and even if I did—well, I've had an idea, Elana." He paused and then said slowly, "You're not really ready. You won't understand everything that happens. But I need someone to fill Ilura's place, and it's too much of a risk to wait for another agent to be brought in at this point."

"Ilura's place? *Me?*" I hadn't dared to hope he'd let me play any real part.

"Yes, if you want it."

"Of course I do!" I said, my excitement returning. After all, I'd known all along that an agent's job is at times perilous, and I wasn't about to let that stop me.

Evrek had joined us just in time to hear this. Glaring at Father, he protested, "Elana can't pose as a native, as Ilura was to have done!"

"No. None of us can, so we've got to revamp the plan. But I've something in mind for which Elana's well suited."

Turning to me, Evrek said quietly, "Elana, you don't have to agree. You don't know what you're letting yourself in for."

"Are you going to try to protect me, too?" I laughed.

"Of course I am! I love you! Don't you see the responsibility you're accepting?"

I followed his glance toward the spot where Ilura had stood just minutes before, and it did give me the shivers, I'll admit. Not that the same circumstances would arise again, but it was true enough that an agent's role would, in principle, entail an agent's obligations; the fact that I was not yet sworn was only a technicality. There are some kinds of training that you don't get until Third Phase. The Shield, for example, is a more or less automatic mental reflex to which you are conditioned from childhood. You can't control it by an act of will unless you've been specifically taught to. Would I even know *how* not to use it?

But if I had any doubts on that score, I certainly wasn't going to let Evrek suspect them. I told him, "I guess I accepted it when I came down here in the first place, didn't I?"

"I guess you did," he admitted reluctantly. Drawing me to him, he added, "But oh, Elana, if anything happened to you—"

Just then Father broke in hurriedly, "Someone's coming. Get inside!"

We retreated into the hut and, staying clear of its uncovered opening, peered out through a chink between the rough stones. More Imperials? To my astonishment, I began to feel a sort of sick, icy fear that was not at all familiar to me.

"Andrecians," Evrek said. "Peasants—woodsmen, maybe—on foot, and unarmed. They look harmless."

"They're coming over here!" I whispered. "They'll find us!"

Father was silent for a few moments, then made a fast decision. He smiled at me and said softly, "Yes. We're going to let them."

"Contact? *Now?*" Evrek demanded, sounding somewhat horrified. "No investigation? No preparation—"

"This isn't a textbook case! There's no time to explain now, but I think we've got to take a real plunge. Maybe no one else will be by here for days, and I'd rather do it this way than seek them out."

You don't question your Senior Agent's strategy.

Besides, not having made a contact before, Evrek was eager. "Can I go out with you?" he asked.

"No. I'm not going out; there's a better way." Father met my eyes with a measuring look. "Elana, are you really serious about wanting to be in on this? Can you follow directions?"

"Yes," I agreed, though I felt less confident all of a sudden.

"Then step outside and let those men see you."

"Alone? And undisguised?" I protested incredulously. Evrek was aghast, as I was, but a look from Father silenced him.

"It's all right," Father told me. "They won't recognize you for what you are, as Imperials would. You won't be revealing anything you shouldn't."

Evrek had hold of my arm, and he didn't release it. "You're surely not going to let Elana make contact all by herself!"

"We'll be communicating, and I'll guide her. But she must be the one to talk to them."

"*Talk* to them?" I wavered. "How can I? I don't know their language!"

"Use ours. The actual words you speak won't matter; only the thought behind them."

"But Younglings can't use telepathy!"

"Not between themselves. With us, most of them can." Abruptly, he slipped to the soundless level of communication. *Don't be frightened. That's very important, because if you are they'll know it.*

But what shall I say to them?

I'll tell you, when the time comes.

I felt he could at least give me a little more information than that. Then I sensed an exchange between Father and Evrek and knew that they were communicating privately. At that moment, Evrek gave me an encouraging grin and dropped my arm. So that's how it is, I thought. They're testing me.

Well, I had gotten myself into this, I thought grimly, and I was not going to back out now. The Andrecians were within a few paces of the hut. I could see them clearly; there were four of them, all fairly young men, wearing belted smocks and hose of a coarse brown fabric. They did not look hostile. One of them, in fact, was whistling a bright, lilting tune. Mustering all my determination, I stepped into the open doorway.

The Oath

Though the Enchantress in no way resembled any woman the woodcutter's sons had seen before, she was in her own manner quite beautiful. She was tall, as tall as Georyn himself, and she was clothed all in silvery green; and her garments were not women's garments nor yet men's either, but were unique. Dark and shining was her hair, and it fell not to her shoulders, but rather made a soft halo of waves around her face. And that face was a strange elfin face, yet radiant, and Georyn knew without question that whatever magic she practiced was good magic.

"Whither do you travel, my friends?" asked the Enchantress, and though the tongue in which she spoke was unknown to them, the brothers had no doubt as to her words' meaning. It was as if, coming from her, any language in the world would be understood; for there was a charm upon her speech.

"We go to ask the King's blessing, for we plan to slay the Dragon and claim the King's reward," Georyn replied quickly.

"Dragon? Tell me of this!" the Enchantress exclaimed, seeming somewhat surprised.

The eldest brother began, "It is a terrible monster, and its mere breath is fire, and many men have been lost in the attempt to kill it; yet *we* shall surely conquer the beast."

But Georyn took a step forward, asking: "Do you not already know of the Dragon, Lady, and are you not simply measuring us? For it is my guess that you know much that we have not even glimpsed."

The Enchantress smiled. "You have guessed truly. I have indeed heard of this Dragon; perhaps I have heard more than you would care to know. Let us speak no more of it. Tell me, what reward do you desire, if you succeed in this quest?"

"I shall ask the King for many servants," answered the eldest brother.

"And I," added the next, "shall ask for chests of gold."

The next brother said, "I shall ask that a fine lady may be my bride."

There was a pause, and turning to Georyn the Lady asked, "And you, what do you seek of the King?"

Georyn hesitated. "I seek knowledge, that I may be the wisest man in the kingdom." He had never admitted this openly before.

"I must warn you," the Enchantress told the brothers, "that if you persist in this venture, you will be in constant danger and will meet with many misfortunes; and it is likely that you will perish."

"That does not frighten us," said the eldest brother, with unconcealed pride.

"When the time comes, you will be afraid."

"Not so!" cried the brothers in protest. "We shall never know fear!" But Georyn knew that the Enchantress spoke truth, and he said to her, "We will be afraid, yet still we shall defeat the Dragon."

And thereupon the elder brothers turned to go; but Georyn did not wish to leave without knowing more of the Enchantress, for he found himself drawn to her as he had never before been drawn to any maiden. Moreover, he was sure that whatever she knew of the Dragon, he *would* care to know, if he was to fight the beast. "Lady," he said boldly, "have you any advice for us, as to how the Dragon may best be overcome?"

She paused, and her eyes were far away, as if she listened to some silent voice that no one else could hear. At length she said, "I can tell you nothing, now. But I will make you a promise. If a time ever comes when you can proceed no further in this quest without aid, return to me, and I may then be able to help you. For I have knowledge of many things that are hidden from your people; and if you are indeed the ones destined to rid the world of this Dragon, that knowledge may be of greater value to you than anything the King can give."

The woodcutter's sons offered their thanks to the Enchantress, but underneath they smiled, for who can balance the worth of wisdom against the wealth and power of the King? Only Georyn believed that magic is not to be scoffed at, and he said, "I will remember your promise, Lady, and I will make you one of my own: I will surely return when the proper time has come."

So with these words to the Lady, Georyn continued on his way; but as he went into the trees he looked back at her, and he hoped that the time would be soon.

Just after sunset, we went out into the meadow and stood in the place where Ilura had stood, ankle-deep in the fresh green grass of Andrecia. Though the actual memorial rites would be held aboard the starship when we returned, the brief, formal words that we of the Service say on such occasions could not be left unsaid. These are resolute words, designed to close a door firmly and with haste. For in the field there is no time for mourning. You must put it out of your mind and go on with the job. Anyone who is experienced in such matters knows this; Ilura herself would have been the last one to question it. But to me it seemed cold and unfeeling, and my eyes were wet with tears that rose as much from indignation as from honest grief. Not that the others were unmoved; Evrek looked more stern and withdrawn than I had ever seen him, and I noticed that as Father spoke, he fingered the Emblem.

Later, when we had eaten something and had set up housekeeping, so to speak, in the hut, we went outdoors again; and there, on the stony slope beside the river, we built a small fire. Dry wood was plentiful in the outskirts of the forest; Evrek and I gathered armloads in only a few minutes. Apparently few Andrecians came here. Our woodcutters must have been far from home.

We sat down close to the warm solace of the flames. It was nearly dark now and the woods seemed gloomy and a little forbidding. "Are we safe here?" I asked. "Won't anyone see the fire?"

"I doubt if the Imperials will stray this far from their camp again," Father said. "Certainly they won't at night. And anyway, if they do come here, our hutful of equipment is danger enough." He did not add what I now know to be the truth, that a quick means of getting rid of the hutful of equipment was continuously at his disposal.

"What about Andrecians?" I persisted.

"If *they* find us, it won't be a disaster."

For a while we didn't talk much except to make brief, inane comments on our surroundings; I guess nobody wanted to be the first to broach the subject of what lay ahead of us. Avoiding even mental contact, we concentrated on the look and feeling of the alien world. Your first night on an unfamiliar planet is always an experience in itself. I've been told that this is true even to those jaded by journeys to the far reaches of the universe.

Then, abruptly, Father grinned at Evrek and at me and said cheerfully, "One tired old agent, one brand-new one on his first mission, and a trainee who isn't even sworn! It looks like a hopeless cause, doesn't it?"

We laughed, sensing that that was what he wanted, though I'd been thinking in pretty much those terms with less levity. And it cleared the air a bit, enough for Father to go on, "All right. There's a lot to talk over. We have some plans to make, and—well, an important matter to tend to, later this evening. Because tomorrow morning we've got to be ready to take constructive steps."

"What can we do without Ilura?" asked Evrek. "She was the essential link."

"I've got some ideas," Father assured him.

"I won't like them if they include Elana," Evrek commented darkly. "Can we ask, now, what that contact was all about?" We hadn't discussed my adventure with the woodcutters; Father had made it plain that he preferred to wait.

"It was just a little experiment to see how well Elana can communicate with the Andrecians," he told us now. "That's something I had to know." Turning to me, he explained, "The original plan depended on Ilura's ability to pass as Andrecian. Now we've got to feel our way, improvise. But that's usually how these things end up, anyway."

"I'm afraid I don't understand anything that's going on," I confessed. "I don't even see what we're aiming for.

What can we do against all those invaders if we can't use weapons or let them know we're here?"

"Elana, there's one point you've got to get straight right away," he said curtly. "We're not *against* the colonists. Though we're here to save Andrecia, we can't do it through violence; all Younglings have equal rights to our protection."

"I know . . . but then what *can* we do? The Andrecians themselves haven't a chance to repulse them, not with spears and arrows and swords against what the Imperials have."

"No. So the aim is to make the colonists leave of their own free will."

"Can we talk them into that?" I asked doubtfully. It sounded rather unlikely to me from what I had seen so far.

"We can't talk to Imperials at all without disclosure, you know that! And even if we could, they'd only think we were trying to claim Andrecia for ourselves."

This was true, and as he went on with the explanation I began to grasp it. There was absolutely *nothing* we could do directly. The Imperials would turn an armada against us rather than give up the "right" to claim one small planet out of the many that were open to them. They'd believe that we wished to compete with their Empire. They had undoubtedly met peoples near their own level who were trying to do just that.

So there was only one course we could take. We'd have to give the natives power advanced enough to impress the invaders, to scare them off. But possession of that power couldn't be allowed to disrupt the Andrecian culture; it must be made to blend so imperceptibly into the natives' own background of beliefs that it would not even be noticed by their future historians. Neither side could ever know that there had been intervention.

Impossible? It seemed so to me, at first. But there's a way to handle such cases. Variations of it have been used before, I'm told, and will be used again. The chances of its working under conditions like those with which we were faced aren't very large, but if it fails you're really no worse off than before.

My first reaction was, "The invaders must know as well as we do that the natives are no match for them."

"Because the Andrecians have no technology?" Evrek asked me.

"Certainly."

Father said to me, "Elana, suppose the Imperials were to discover that the people of this world have something that they themselves *don't* have—something that's frightening because they don't understand it?"

"Wouldn't they be suspicious? I mean, if it's that far ahead of their own science, they'll know the Andrecians couldn't have developed it without help."

"Yes, but what if it were something they couldn't identify as being ahead of their science, something they thought the natives came by naturally?"

"Like what, for instance?"

"Like magic."

I laughed. "You're joking!"

"No. Not at all."

I looked from Father to Evrek and back to Father; both of them were dead serious. Even in the dim firelight I could see that. This place is changing us, I thought; it is drawing us into its spell. We've come far back in time as well as in space. This is a primeval forest, and the fire's but one of the many primitive campfires that must have burned on countless worlds where human races have been born.

My hand rested on a small, smooth stone; I picked it

up and shifted it from hand to hand, scarcely noticing what I was doing. Mystified, I began, "Here we are, with science that's far, far ahead even of the Empire's, and you're saying—"

"That we believe in magic?"

"But we don't! Science and magic are opposites."

"It depends on what you mean by magic, doesn't it?"

"Isn't magic what prescientific cultures believe in? Cultures like—well, like this world's?"

"Exactly. That's the point."

"But it's only superstition!"

"No. That's a Youngling viewpoint, a very adolescent one. If you think it through, you'll find that you know better."

"Wait a minute," Evrek interrupted. "I understood the original plan. Ilura was to pose as a native and scare the daylights out of the Imperials with some spectacular feats of psychokinesis and such, which would be 'magic' to them, and therefore very upsetting. But we can never do it; they'll know we're not like the other natives, even if we can avoid revealing what we actually are."

"There's another method, Evrek," Father said slowly. "We can work through an actual native."

Evrek frowned. "Is that really feasible? I've heard of it, of course, but—well, isn't it pretty chancy?"

"Chancy, yes, but impossible, no. Not in a culture like this one, which is very favorably disposed toward it."

"Perhaps not," Evrek said. "But I don't envy the man we choose to throw an interstellar expedition off a non-mechanized world, single-handed. Why, even if he succeeds, he's bound to suffer for it—"

I turned to Father. "Do you mean to tell me that you're going to send only one man to scare off a whole shipload of invaders? One *Andrecian*?"

Father smiled. "I know it sounds pretty fantastic."

"But he won't have any chance at all, no matter what weapons we give him! If he acts hostile they'll simply kill him, won't they, as they did Ilura?"

"Possibly, though I doubt it. What happened this afternoon was unusual; normally they merely use stunners. I'm not saying there won't be danger. But he will have a chance, Elana. He'll have an advantage over them because the weapon we're going to give him will be very frightening from their point of view. More so from theirs than from his."

"How can it be, when they know so much more than he does?" I demanded.

"About some things they do," Father said. "But you're aware, aren't you, that Younglings in an adolescent stage of civilization have a blind spot? They're very powerful so far as their machines are concerned, but they know nothing at all of the powers of the mind."

I nodded. I'd been reading about it only that morning, back on the starship. It was hard to visualize. What would it feel like to be unable to reach anyone else's mind? To be unable to exert any psychokinetic power over things, even if you *needed* to? To have no Shield? It would indeed be like blindness; yet Younglings have none of these abilities. They do not even know what they're missing!

"But if psychic powers are too mature, too advanced, even for the Imperials," I protested, "certainly no Andrecian knows anything about them."

"He will have an open mind, though," Evrek told me. "He'll be too naive to be afraid."

"I suppose so," I admitted. "Especially since he'll probably believe in magic in the first place. But we can't just hand such things to him, as we could a physical weapon. Younglings don't have the capacity."

"You're wrong there," said Father. "Under certain conditions they do. Our job is to set up those conditions. It won't be easy, and we'll have some failures. If it doesn't work with the first man we try, we'll have to use someone else. But it's the only way open to us now, so we have to take it."

That first night, I didn't really understand the scheme; it wasn't till much later that I began to get a feel for it. On the surface, it didn't look as if one man, however well equipped with "magical" power, could be a very formidable obstacle to people like the invaders. But that wasn't the point. *No* obstacle can faze Imperials, for they thrive on obstacles. But here, it was their method of dealing with obstacles that was to be threatened. He whose strength is in his machines wants no part of psychokinesis. Imperial colonists would not want this planet for long, once they began to suspect that its inhabitants were . . . different. And in the face of that suspicion, they would generalize too easily; what they saw in one native, they would think to find in all, since all were alike to them. The question of deception would never enter the picture, for that which they would see could not be faked.

Of course, carrying this off was not going to be simple. "Set up the conditions," Father had said. But that's a thing easier said than done, because the conditions aren't concrete ones. You can't train a Youngling to release his latent psychic powers by the methods through which you learned yourself; he just doesn't have the same background you do. So everything depends upon a very elusive quality: faith.

In the colony the night air was cool and sweet. Jarel took a deep breath, savoring its freshness. It was a great feeling after weeks of being cooped up in a pressure suit and helmet. He didn't envy the men who still had to wear suits whenever they stepped outside; he would gladly have volunteered to take his off, even if he had not been ordered to do so as the junior member of the medical staff. After all, tests had already proved the adequacy of the new vaccines, though it was a wise precaution, certainly, to try out a few men's immunity to the local bacteria before exposing everyone.

The only trouble with being in the experimental group was that he would no longer be allowed inside the sealed shelters. He and the other guinea pigs would be bunking in one room of the barracks used for native prisoners until the rest of the buildings were opened up. And Dulard, never one to waste resources, had decided to kill two birds with one stone by assigning them all to guard duty on top of their regular work. Not that Jarel minded that; he welcomed the chance to get a closer look at the natives, as a matter of fact. But he did not much like Dulard's policy toward these prisoners. The use of stunners, for instance. The paralysis resulting from a stunner jolt at low intensity might not be bad after you got over the first fright, but still—well, it seemed cruel in a way to keep the poor creatures physically helpless so much of the time.

Of course, if he had his way they wouldn't be locking the natives up at all, Jarel realized. "What harm would it do just to let them loose?" he asked aloud. "Does Dulard really think they'd organize a full-scale attack on us? As I see it, their society's not geared for any kind of mass action."

"No sense in taking chances, is there?" replied his bunkmate, a technician named Kevan. "Do 'em good to learn respect for us, too. It'll make it easier to herd 'em off to a reservation when the time comes."

Jarel frowned. He did not like Kevan and would never have chosen his company had they not been required to bunk together. It did seem as if the Imperial Exploration Corps ought to be more choosy about the guys they turned loose on new worlds. The colonists themselves were for the most part decent enough, though they were understandably more concerned with their own safety and their kids' than with the treatment of the natives. But a few of the Corpsmen seemed to go out of their way to hurt any wild thing that crossed their path. Men like Kevan, now. What excuse was there for taking off on an unauthorized jaunt into the woods and coming back more proud than sorry at having had to kill a "savage" native woman? Dulard had not raised any objections; to him, what men did in their off-duty time was their own business, so long as they did not start any trouble that would be costly to subdue. But Jarel couldn't look at it that way.

"We're doing a great job of earning their respect, all right," he said bitterly. "No one can say you haven't done *your* bit."

"Now, look——" Kevan began.

Obstinately, Jarel went on, "I still don't see why you had to blast the woman."

"She attacked us!"

"Sure, she threw a knife at you. A knife that would've bounced right off your suit, except that it didn't hit even close. Some attack!"

"There were probably a dozen more natives back in those woods, armed with spears. What's the matter with you, anyway? Do you think we're here to play kids' games, or what?"

"What's the matter with *you*?" retorted Jarel. "You could have stunned her; that's what Dulard ordered in the first place——stick to stunners where we can."

"Dulard's too soft," Kevan declared. "We've got to make an example sometimes, put these devils in their place—or else sooner or later somebody's going to get hurt."

"Hurt? Wasn't *she* hurt? Or don't you put murder in that class?"

"Look, blasting a savage isn't murder, and you know it," said Kevan angrily. "Murder's a word that applies to human beings."

"And these natives aren't human, of course."

"Come off it, Jarel. I know you medics are great ones for getting sentimental over the aborigines, but *human*— that's carrying it a bit too far. 'Humanoid' maybe, but they're not *men*. They're way below the level of men. Any fool can see that."

Technically he was right, Jarel knew. So why should it seem so important? He guessed it all depended on how you defined "men." Perhaps he was a fool. Perhaps he should never have joined the Corps. Once he had had ideas about what a fine thing it would be to explore the stars, to open the universe to mankind . . . but it didn't seem quite such a high destiny now. Planets like this one were getting along quite well before the Empire came.

Jarel suspected, suddenly, that he might not be cut out for the taming of primitive worlds.

The fire was dying down; we piled more wood on it, for the night was chilly. I stood close to the blaze, shivering, while Evrek went to the hut for our cloaks. The stone I had picked up was still in my hand; I held it out to the light and looked at it. It was rather an odd stone, more or less egg-shaped but with a smooth-worn hole through the middle, and its color was lovely: a muted, blended shade of brown and red. River-polished, it shone on my palm, and not wanting to toss it aside I slipped it into the pocket of the cloak that Evrek put around my shoulders.

"So where do I come into all this?" I asked Father, as we settled ourselves again.

He looked at me appraisingly. "Elana, what impression did the men you talked to this afternoon get of you?"

I thought about it. They had been rather in awe of me, I felt; and with most of them, I'd been able to establish very little rapport. But one had been bolder than the others: a tall, blond, rather handsome young man. He hadn't seemed as I'd have expected a Youngling to be at all. In fact, if I'd seen him at the Academy in other clothes I might have taken him for a fellow student; I'm used to meeting people from different worlds, after all, and they vary widely in appearance. This man's mind and mine had touched in an almost exciting way, a way that made me hope we would meet again. Even in those few moments he had become a personality to me, an individual.

"Well," I began, "they knew I was strange—different—but they couldn't have had any conception of what I really am, not knowing anything of space travel."

"That's why it was a safe contact, of course. But how did they fit you into their scheme of things?"

"I guess I don't know."

"I'll tell you, then." Father smiled. "They thought you were an enchantress."

"A *what?*"

"An enchantress. A sorceress, a witch. Undoubtedly they thought you could put a magic spell on them—that you *had* done so, in fact, since they understood your unfamiliar words."

"I don't know whether to be flattered or insulted," I said, laughing.

"Be honored. Because this is an impression that we are going to foster."

"Now wait a minute!" Evrek broke in. "Why does it have to be Elana?"

"Because I have some other plans for you," Father told him. "And also because, telepathically, she is more adept."

Evrek put his arm around me, protectively. I realized that he was still unconvinced, and I couldn't see why. How could he not want me to take part, when he loved me? I'd be taking no greater risk than he. And wasn't I in danger anyway, whether I played an active role or not?

Well, it wasn't entirely a matter of the danger. Evrek had guessed what we were in for. And, under the guise of a stiff-necked devotion to the letter of the law that was not at all like him, he made one last try to save me from it.

"She hasn't taken the Oath," he protested to Father. "It's not right for her to participate, unsworn! She shouldn't even have made the contact this afternoon."

Father nodded. "That's true, and I hadn't forgotten it. But it's easily remedied; in fact it's the matter I mentioned earlier that we must take care of."

Stunned by the way his ploy had backfired, Evrek burst out, "You can't be serious! *Here?* On the spur of the moment, when she hasn't full knowledge of the implications?" Holding me close to him, he told me, "Elana, darling, you mustn't do it."

"But I want to!" I hadn't dreamed they would let me go this far, but it was an exciting suggestion.

"I withdraw my original objection," Evrek said quickly. "If we must stretch the law, let's go a little further and let her work here unofficially. Leave her free to change her mind."

Surprisingly, Father defended me. "Look, Evrek," he

said, "Elana's not going to change. She chose the shape of her life years ago, as a child. She was born to it, as you were not; she has no other world to renounce. And she has the talent for it as well as the vocation. I know; I've seen her test results."

He reached for my hand and squeezed it, but went on addressing Evrek as though I weren't even present. "For her to be invested here—tonight—isn't merely a matter of the law, and of this mission's safety; it's necessary for her own protection."

Evrek flushed. "It's too soon," he said obstinately. "The Oath's too hard, too demanding."

"It's been made so in order to keep out people who might try to use our power over Youngling worlds to their personal advantage. But underneath, the Oath is meant to make the job easier, not harder. It lifts the burden of decisions that would otherwise be impossibly difficult."

"You wouldn't expose Elana to such decisions!"

"Not deliberately, but they may come to her as they may to all of us." Father poked the fire with a long branch, sending a burst of sparks up into the darkness. Soberly, he went on, "Just by being here, we're in a position to change the course of history for two Youngling peoples, not to mention what we may do to the individuals we contact. You're right when you say that no one should take such responsibility, uncommitted. The weight of it would be unbearable."

Though some of this was over my head, I had a rough idea of what they were talking about. The laws and rituals of the Service didn't just happen; they were devised by psychologists who knew exactly what they were doing. When you intrude upon a planet not your own, you play with forces beyond anything with which your personal experience of right and wrong has equipped you to deal.

And it's true enough that you can get thrown into a spot where if you weren't bound, if you had to stop and debate as to which was the lesser of two evils, you might go all to pieces.

Yet you don't think of the Oath that way when you look forward to it. You think of the investiture: of the great hall of the Academy lit by torchlight, and the glistening, silver-trimmed white uniforms, and the triumphant beat of the anthem sending shivers up your spine . . . and of course, of the Emblem—of how you'll feel when its chain is dropped over your head and you know that after all the years of study and preparation you've earned the right to wear it. Never in all my wildest imaginings had I pictured this as taking place beside a small campfire in the wilderness of an alien planet, with only Father and Evrek there to see.

It was a thrilling idea but a rather scary one, too, and the cold tingle I began to feel wasn't entirely pleasant. Not that there was any doubt in my mind about wanting to go through with it eventually. Only this *was* rather sudden, rather more of a plunge than I'd been thinking of when I'd so blithely stowed away on the landing craft that morning. For the first time, it occurred to me that I had *not* earned the Emblem and that perhaps it wasn't quite right to take such a shortcut. Not that I wouldn't have to complete my training anyway, but—well, wasn't it akin to getting your diploma before having taken all the courses?

Hesitantly, I said as much to Father. "That needn't trouble you, Elana," he told me. "The Oath concerns the future, not the past. You earn its Emblem not by your success in passing exams, but by your free acceptance of the responsibility an agent must carry, your consent to the ordeal of that responsibility."

That was a solemn thought, and sometimes you shrink

from solemnity. I laughed lightly and said, "You're making it sound ominous!"

Father was not amused. "It's not a thing to joke about!" he said sharply. He gripped my hand, and his voice was very stern and very intense. "Elana, there's one thing I want to be sure you've got straight. Once you're sworn, I won't give you any more protection than I would give any other agent; if we get into a situation where I have to involve you in something unpleasant, I'll do it. If you don't believe that you can be hurt, don't take this on. For you will be hurt, inevitably, in one way or another." He sighed. "Maybe Evrek's right; you still have too many illusions."

"No, I haven't," I said quietly. "Perhaps I did when I forced my way into the landing party. But now, since— since this afternoon, I understand."

"I wonder if you do? You're thinking of Ilura and picturing yourself in her place. Have you pictured yourself in mine? Have you imagined a situation where it was a Youngling that was killed before your eyes, and you were answerable? Or not killed, perhaps, but changed, less happy?"

He stared down into the fire: a breeze stirred, and the coals pulsed red. The smoke blew into my face, and it was a strange-smelling smoke, for Andrecian trees were not those I had known. Father went on sadly, "Of course you haven't. You can't, yet. So you've no comprehension of what I mean when I tell you that the price of power can be rather more terrible than what you saw this afternoon. But then, perhaps if we knew beforehand, none of us would ever take the Oath."

Determinedly, I declared, "Yet if we didn't, how could we ever accomplish anything good? You can't scare me that way, Father."

He smiled and took my hand again, pulling me to my feet. "No, and I don't want to. I don't want to make you afraid, Elana. Because it's not all grim. There can be some pretty wonderful things, too. If the price is high, that doesn't mean that it isn't worth paying. We've the freedom of the universe, and it's a fascinating universe. You'll see much that's good, and you'll never be faced with boredom. And there are great satisfactions. If we can save the people of this world from slavery, for instance—"

Evrek got up and threw another log on the fire; then he turned and opened his arms to me. "I'm sorry, darling," he whispered. "Why do we always underestimate the people we care for by trying to shield them?" With the forced levity that he always uses to cover his more emotional moments, he went on, "After all, I might not love you if you *weren't* willing to go through with it!"

"Mightn't you?" I laughed.

He held me tight. "Well, I would," he admitted. "I'd always love you. But you wouldn't be the same girl."

"Come on, you two!" Father broke in. "If we're going to do this, let's forget the somber side of it and make it the happy occasion it's supposed to be. We can't celebrate as we would under different circumstances, but let's at least give Elana the good memories she deserves."

"Can we really do it here?" I asked. "The whole ritual, I mean?"

"Of course. Agents have been invested in the field before and will be again."

He took me aside for a few minutes to go over what I'd have to do, and to make sure that I understood what I'd be swearing to. None of it was new to me; the Oath, as you probably know, is very straightforward. Reduced to its most essential element, it's simply that you will hold your responsibility to the Service, and to the Youngling peoples with which you're involved, *above all other consid-erations,* though it does contain a number of specifics such as the absolute ban on disclosure of the Federation's exis-tence. I assured Father that I had no misgivings, and then we went back to the campfire and the three of us sat close around it, on the ground; and it seemed a natural, fitting thing, not like a makeshift ceremony at all.

To me, in fact, it was even more beautiful than it would have been in its usual setting—though I suppose you are always more moved by your own rites than by those you observe. No ceremonial torches, no white uni-forms, no music: only the flickering firelight and the dark shapes of the trees and the exotic, pungent smoke fra-grance . . . and far away, rising above the rush of the river, the cry of an unknown bird—an Andrecian bird—that was different from anything I'd ever heard before. I shall remember that bird's shrill, eerie call forever, I think, no matter how many planets I go to.

It is a long ritual and a complex one, but Father knew it thoroughly, even the telepathic parts, the secret parts that the spectators never hear. Certain portions of it are frightening, for your mind is probed more deeply than is usual in telepathic communication and your inborn ten-dency is to fight that. It is not anything terrible, however, so long as you really are sincere in what you are promis-ing and have nothing to hide. Of course it was easier for me with Father, whom I loved and trusted, than it would have been with some dignitary from the Academy; and this was not entirely proper, because there's a point at which you are supposed to be scared. It's a sort of test. More than that I can't say, for the details, by tradition, are not spoken of.

Once you've passed that point, though, something very wonderful happens to you: a glorious feeling of certainty and of conviction. Dedication, I suppose you could say. All my life I had heard people in the Service speak of investiture as a high spot of their experience, and I had always supposed that they were talking about the outward trappings—the pageantry and the festivities. How naive I was! Those things haven't anything to do with it at all. What matters is that you are given something to draw on, a solid core to come back to over and over again, for as long as you live. Whether this comes to you telepathically or simply from your own commitment, I don't know; but I suspect that it's a little of both.

The climax of the ritual is, of course, the repetition of the Oath itself, aloud, and the presentation of the Emblem. We stood; the firelight threw our shadows tall against the backdrop of foliage. Perhaps my voice wasn't audible, what with the river and all, but if you have telepathic contact anyway you can't always tell the difference. *". . . And I, Elana, swear that I will hold this responsibility above all other considerations, for as long as I shall live. . . ."* That's the heart of it; it doesn't seem very difficult or very dramatic, but there's more to it than you might think. You don't see, at first, how many other considerations there can be.

Naturally, when it came to the Presentation there was no actual pendant available for me, and Father was about to do it symbolically, with an improvised garland of leaves; but Evrek took the heavy, gleaming metal chain from his own neck and handed it to him instead. ("Wear it until you get yours," he told me later, when I tried to return it to him, it being a thing that no one should be expected to part with for very long. "It's rather a thrill at first, something I wouldn't want you to miss.") So the rite was complete and perfect for me, and it will always be one of my happiest memories.

Afterwards, when it was over and we had put out the fire, we walked back to the meadow, shivering in the chill breeze of Andrecian spring. Overhead, unfamiliar constellations glittered; I looked up at them, wondering which stars I would someday see as suns. Evrek's arm was strong around my shoulders, the Emblem that was both his and mine hung warm against my heart, and we were on a brand-new planet whose people we would surely save through some heroic deed . . . in that moment, anything seemed possible.

"Is it a good feeling, Elana?" Father asked me.

"'Good' is too mild a word," I told him. "It's more overwhelming, I guess. I feel—well, safeguarded, somehow."

"I'm glad," he told me, pressing my hand. And then, wordlessly, *So glad, Elana! You'll have need of that, before we're through here.*

The Task

The next morning, my first on Andrecia, dawned blue and cloudless. Just after sunrise I went down to the river to wash; there was a low-hovering mist, slowly dispersing, over which the tops of the fir trees on the opposite bank seemed to float. The swift-flowing water was sparkling clear, but cold—colder than any I'd ever put a hand into, that's for certain! I splashed some over my face and arms; it was an awful shock, but afterwards I felt wonderful.

During breakfast Evrek and I tried to get something more out of Father about his plans. What he'd told us the night before had been pretty general, and neither of us had any real idea of how you might teach a Youngling to do the things we had talked about. But Father simply said that he'd have to think the situation through a while longer. Then he questioned me at great length about my encounter with the Andrecian woodcutters, making me describe in minute detail every thought that had come into my head about them as well as what had actually happened; though it seemed to me that since he'd observed the whole thing with an experienced eye, he must already know more about it than I did.

Finally, Father stood up and said, "First of all, I want to do some exploring. Come on, Evrek, let's be on our way."

"How far are we going?" I asked, wondering just how much of a hike he had in mind.

Quietly, he said to me, "You're not going anywhere. I want you to wait for us here at the hut."

"All by myself?"

"Yes." He gave me a funny sort of look.

"Now, wait a minute!" I protested. "I thought you were making me a full partner in this! I don't care if you are about to try something risky; I'm not going to stay behind."

"Yes, you are. That's an order, Elana!" he said sharply.

"An *order*?" Though Father could be obstinate at times, he'd never spoken to me in just that way before. I'd almost come out with an angry retort—for I'm not one to be dictated to—when it dawned on me what he meant. He was Senior Agent now, and he spoke in that capacity, not as a parent. I was therefore pledged to obedience for as long as we were in the field. With chagrin, I realized that he might have had more motives for investing me than he had mentioned.

"All right," I agreed good-naturedly. "But just for curiosity's sake, what would happen to me if I disobeyed it?"

He smiled. "Nothing, in the way that you mean. We're not a military organization; we're bound by the Oath, not by discipline."

I paused thoughtfully. "Father," I said, "what if an agent disobeyed in a—well, a serious matter? What if he broke the Oath?"

"I hope you never have occasion to find out. Vital

orders are enforced, Elana." He went on, abruptly changing the subject, "There are a few things I must show you
before we leave."

These things proved to be details such as how to contact him in an emergency—for I was forbidden to use a
communicator otherwise—and how, in the case of an ultimate emergency when I could not contact him, to signal
the starship. I nodded and assured him that I understood
everything; but inwardly, as he talked, I was getting more
and more nervous. I was sure that no matter how perilous
this "exploring" turned out to be, it would be much easier
for me to go along with him and Evrek than to stay behind
and worry.

It never occurred to me that he might be perfectly
well aware of that.

To be alone, really alone, as I was after Father and
Evrek left, was a new experience for me. I'd scarcely ever
been out of the city on my home world—and there I was
in the wilderness of a strange planet, where it was anyone's guess what might come charging out of the forest.
Looking back, I know that I was not in any great danger.
Although there was some chance of more Imperials coming by, Father considered it a small one; and after all, I
could have used the Shield against most other perils. But
at the time I didn't have much idea of what I was up
against, and I had plenty of leisure to give my imagination
free reign.

At first it wasn't so bad. The elation that had come
from my investiture was still with me; every time I looked
down at the Emblem, I thought of how thrilled I felt to be
wearing it at last . . . and of how silly it was for a full-
fledged agent to be hesitant about staying alone in the
woods. The day was simply gorgeous, and the area around
the hut was a lovely one to be in. It should have been very

pleasant to relax and enjoy myself for once, without having to study.

But I couldn't enjoy it. As the afternoon wore on, I became increasingly conscious of a nameless, overpowering dread. Always before, the concept of physical fear had been an abstraction to me. I'd been apprehensive, naturally, during the grimmer phases of Academy entrance testing; but in such tests you remain aware that you won't actually be harmed. *Real* fear is different. When dusk drew down it was an abstraction no longer, and by the time darkness came I was so scared that every small forest noise made me want to scream.

Father hadn't really said how long he and Evrek would be gone, but he had implied that it would be only a few hours. Surely they couldn't do much exploring after dark—and anyway, I couldn't imagine him staying away at night without telling me. If they had been delayed, wouldn't he let me know? I kept my communicator at my side, willing it to come alive with Father's image or at least his voice, but it did not. I resisted the temptation to call him, for my instructions had been very definite on that point: I was not to break silence unless I was in serious trouble. But I was beginning to believe that something must be terribly, terribly wrong. What if they had encountered Imperials? What if—?

Eventually, in desperation, I attempted telepathic contact. And you know how worked up I must have been to even try, since it isn't practical over such a distance without very strong emotional impetus indeed. But there was no response either from Father or from Evrek. So I huddled miserably in the hut as the hours crept by, not daring to peek out at the blackness of the woods, and tried to face the possibility that something awful had happened and that I was literally alone on Andrecia.

Why, *why* had I gotten myself into this? I wondered. I hadn't had any conception of what it would be like to be stranded in such a situation. Father had forbidden me to signal the starship for at least five days, no matter what the circumstances; for that length of time I'd have to get along, knowing that almost certainly the two people I most loved had been killed in some horrible fashion and that the same thing could confront me at the very next moment.

Strangely, the planet's rotation seemed much slower than I'd noticed at first. The sun did reappear finally, but it wasn't much of a comfort.

Needless to say, I hadn't slept.

It was almost noon before Father and Evrek showed up, perfectly safe and cheerful. When I first saw them, I was torn between a wild impulse to throw myself into their arms, and a sense of outrage that made me want to lash out at them with the bitterest words I could think of. How could they have had so little regard for my feelings? Didn't Father know what I'd go through when I didn't hear from him? And with no apology—scarcely a greeting, even—he said to me, "Evrek and I only came back to pick up some supplies. We'll be leaving again in a few minutes; we're on our way to set up a second camp."

"I'm coming, too!" I burst out. This time, I was *not* going to be left!

"No," he said levelly, "I've got a plan worked out now, and it means that you'll have to stay alone here."

"For how long?"

"Eight or ten days, maybe."

I was flabbergasted. "Is that an order, too?" I asked slowly. Giving me a searching look, he replied, "No, it's not. You are being asked to volunteer."

"Then I—I don't think I want to do it."

"You've got to, Elana!" Evrek said urgently.

I stared at him, puzzled. "Got to? You've certainly changed your ideas since the day before yesterday."

Evrek shook his head sadly. He and Father had had a long, serious talk that past night, and he was doing his best to live up to what had been asked of him. "I don't want to see you pushed into anything you'd rather not do, you know that," he told me. "But you have no choice now; you're sworn."

It wasn't till then, I think, that I really took in what it meant! Oh, they are fine words, glorious words. And the feeling you get during investiture is very overwhelming. But it's not until it makes its first real demand of you, against your personal wish, that you understand what the whole thing's about. "Above all other considerations" means exactly that; it's just as true of small considerations, like being truly afraid for the first time in your life, as of big ones, like the decision Ilura had faced.

I was silent for a long moment. Then with a forced smile I said, "Well, I guess if it's part of the job, I'm willing to give it a try."

Father broke into a grin and hugged me. *Good girl!* Aloud he told me, "I hated to be so rough on you, Elana, but if you were going to panic, we had to get it over with fast. Once we start this, it'll be too late for you to decide you can't do what's required."

"I was on the edge," I admitted.

"I know. The worst part's learning how it feels. You're through that, now."

Why, that's true, I realized. It won't ever be bad in the same way again! Oddly, the main result of that awful night was that I'd found I *could* handle fear and anxiety—and that I could trust Father not to get me into anything I couldn't handle.

For he'd frightened me deliberately. He knew that,

whatever happened to me on Andrecia, I was in for a series of rude awakenings; he also knew that the more closely he could control the time and place of these, the better off I'd be. Learning to cope with being scared while you only *think* you're in a tight spot is much better than waiting until you're actually in one! Father was stuck with me, an ill-prepared trainee in an agent's role, and he had to give me a crash course in the fundamentals to make up for some of the training I hadn't had. And one of the real fundamentals of an agent's makeup is being able to function when he's alone and afraid in a situation that he doesn't thoroughly understand.

I went from Father's embrace to Evrek's; Evrek kissed me, soundlessly pleading, *Forgive me, darling?*

For what?

For withholding response, when you called . . . it was the hardest thing I've ever done!

My long-distance telepathy had worked: I hadn't been sure; you don't have any real idea of what your mind can do under stress until you've been taught to harness your emotions. The Academy gives much more thorough training in psychic control than the average school, because a field agent just can't afford to be without it. I was now beginning to see a little of what the process involves. My eyes met Father's, and this time the smile I gave him was genuine.

Returning it, he said briskly, "Well, I think we're ready to take action, so let's get on with it."

"Am I allowed to know anything about this mysterious plan before you go?" I asked.

"All the details. Cheer up, it's not so bad as I let you think. The Imperials haven't the equipment to pick up transmissions from our communicators, so you'll be able to keep in touch with us. But you'll have to make some contacts with Andrecians entirely on your own."

My enthusiasm came rushing back. Contacting Younglings in the role of an "enchantress" might turn out to be fun! So it was with renewed optimism that I listened to Father's plan, the wild scheme we would use to choose an Andrecian and to endow him with "magic" powers.

These natives were *people*! Jarel thought fiercely. Someday, left to themselves, they might even develop a true civilization. What right did the Empire have to take their future away from them just because they were not civilized now?

He had come to this startling conclusion after several days of guard duty, days during which he'd watched the captives closely, trying to figure out what sort of creatures they were. He'd tried desperately to remember what little he'd read in scientific journals about the findings of the Center for Research on Humanoid Species, which had made detailed studies of the natives captured on many other worlds. But it seemed to him that that august institution was more concerned with clinical analysis of the primitive mind than with intangibles such as human hopes and feelings, which he now suspected these people possessed in full measure.

Of course, he didn't really know anything about their culture. He hadn't seen them in their natural habitat; they had a village beyond the forest, he knew, but he hadn't much idea of what it was like. His notion of primitive life was pretty vague, as a matter of fact. He'd never even read much ancient history.

But the men being held in the barracks had impressed him. Looking into their eyes, he'd seen a manlike awareness and dignity there. What must they think of us? he wondered. With our pressure suits and helmets and all, we must look like some kind of monsters! The natives must think we're not human. It was a good thing that those who were guarding them weren't wearing suits anymore. It must be bad enough for the poor savages, just being in the vicinity of that rockchewer.

He had observed that the natives were scared silly of the rockchewer, especially when it was throwing out flames, and he could scarcely blame them. It did look rather formidable. And it made enough racket to unnerve anybody who might suspect that it was coming after him. To an aborigine who'd never seen any kind of a self-propelled machine before, it might even seem alive. Why, Jarel thought, no wonder they came singly or in small groups. They weren't after the colonists, they wanted to stop the rockchewer. Rumors about it must have spread. Those guys were genuine heroes, and look at what happened to them. It was no picnic to be paralyzed.

The prisoners were not totally paralyzed, of course; once locked up, they were given only enough stunning to forestall any attempted escapes. The treatment in itself was not painful, and it was very efficient; so far, the only man who'd got away had done so before being taken inside. That had happened that afternoon, when Jarel had accidentally-on-purpose set his stunner to "neutralize" during the capture. He'd gotten a dressing down for it from Dulard, naturally, and he knew that he'd be watched from now on. But somehow he felt good about it.

For Jarel, the hardest thing to take was the captives' burning hatred for him. He wished there were some way to let them know that he didn't like what he was forced to do. But of course, they couldn't understand a word he said, any more than he understood their jabber. So every time he stepped inside the room where the men were confined he was met with hostile stares; it was getting so that they followed him into his dreams. He had become a doctor to alleviate suffering, not to inflict it, and the whole business disturbed him more than he cared to admit.

It would be different when the rest of the colonists got there, he thought hopefully. He'd be so busy with the clinic that he wouldn't have time to think of anything else. But underneath he knew that there was a deeper problem than the question of the work he was assigned to perform.

When at length Georyn and his brothers came before the King, they vowed solemnly that they would not fail to challenge the fearful Dragon; whereupon they were given swords and armor, and were told that if they should chance to vanquish the beast they should possess all they had dreamt of, and more. "But," the King warned, "it is not likely that such will ever come to pass. No man who has ventured against this monster has ever been seen again, and I fear that the same fate awaits all of you." And with that word he dismissed them. Yet the brothers laughed as they left the King, and they set forth in high spirits.

Presently, they came to a path that led through the fringes of the Enchanted Forest. Then they ceased their laughter and their shouting and went softly, not knowing what manner of evil spirits they might encounter; and their gleaming swords seemed less invincible, and even the creatures of the forest seemed to be mocking them. But the brothers did not slacken their pace, and Georyn was troubled, for he knew that it would take more than courage alone to overcome the Dragon.

When dusk drew down they paused to drink from a bubbling spring; and as they were returning to the path, they came upon another stone hut and knocked upon its door, asking shelter for the night. Within they found an old man. He appeared to be old, certainly, for his hair was white and his face was not the face of youth; but he was nonetheless strong and exceedingly tall. And although he was clad in the garb of a peasant, he would have looked more natural in king's robes.

That this stranger was a magician, the brothers knew well, for there was a charm upon his speech even as upon that of the Enchantress whom they had met earlier. They understood him clearly, although the words he spoke were of a strange and unfamiliar tongue. "I will give you food and lodging," the man told them, "but in return you must promise to pay whatever price I ask of you."

The woodcutter's sons were weary, and they had had no food all day except dry bread. Over the old man's fire hung a large pot, and from that pot there arose the irresistible odor of rabbit stew. On the morrow, perchance, they would meet the Dragon; and how can a man fight well if he is hungry and has had but little rest?

"We would accept that offer," said the eldest brother, "but we have no money."

"I will not demand money," said the stranger. "But I will tell you no more than that in advance; you will have to trust me."

Now Georyn knew that it was foolish to promise a payment that he could not even guess at, but his brothers were eager; and when he looked into the old man's eyes, he found them honest eyes—unfathomable, perhaps, but surely honest. He did not believe that this man would cheat anyone. So he gave the promise required of him, and enjoyed a good supper and a warm place to sleep.

But in the morning, when the brothers would have set out once more upon their quest, their host detained them, saying:"You have eaten my meat and slept before my fire; now, in payment, you must serve me for three days."

"But we cannot!" cried the brothers, "for we have sworn to fight the Dragon and vanquish it; and we must not tarry, lest another should precede us and claim the reward."

It chanced that as they spoke thus, there burst forth from the wood a rough-clad fellow, a villager, who was pale and trembling with fright. The eldest brother called out, "What is the matter, my good man, that you flee with such haste?"

"Alas!" cried the villager, "I have been bewitched by evil spirits, and I fear they pursue me still."

"Then take cheer," said Georyn, "for you have reached the edge of the Enchanted Forest and are now safe. Where met you these demons?"

"Many miles hence; they attend the Dragon, and have the power to turn men into stone!"

The brothers gasped, for how could one fight the Dragon if one were turned first into stone? And Georyn questioned the villager, who told them: "They are indeed fearful demons, who have the form of men, yet are larger than men, and wear no clothing; and their skins are of a glistening silver, and very hard, so that no sword can cut them. And these demons have no faces, but only round globes for heads; nor do they speak—but they cast spells, and those to whom they point are turned into stone, yet live. I too was bewitched and would presently have been fed to the Dragon; but for a moment the spell weakened and I escaped."

"Did you *see* the Dragon?" Georyn asked.

"Certainly I saw it, and heard it, also! It is huge, ten times the size of yonder hut, and it is covered with silver scales. Its head is higher than the treetops, so great is its neck's length! And when it has no men to devour it feeds upon the foliage; whole trees disappear into its maw, and all around the very earth is seared and blackened. There is a clearing larger than the King's own grainfield where no grass will ever grow again. Never will that beast be slain by any mortal, I think, and our one hope is that we may find the means to appease it."

"Surely, this man must be mad!" announced the eldest brother. "We must be off, if we are to put an end to these foolish fears and gain the treasures the King has promised us."

"Go, then," said the owner of the hut. "I will let two of you depart; but the other two must stay to be my servants, for know that without my good will you cannot hope to win what you are seeking."

At these words Georyn bethought himself that the old man might know of magic that could be used against the Dragon, and he told this to his brothers; but they only laughed and said, "If there be indeed such magic, why has not the magician killed the monster himself and claimed a half of the kingdom? We shall place our trust in strength and prowess and in our sharp swords, not in spells, which cannot be predicted or measured."

So Georyn let the two eldest brothers go on ahead, telling them that he would follow. But the next-to-youngest brother, whose name was Terwyn, said: "I too will stay, for though I doubt that this man's magic can help us, I will not break my promise to him."

Then for three days did Georyn and Terwyn work, cutting wood for the old man and tending his fire; and during that time Georyn perceived that their master was not only good, but was also exceedingly wise. On the last morning of their service, he called them to him and told them that in return for their faithfulness he would grant them any boon that lay within his power. And Georyn forgot all about practical matters, and asked hastily the thing that was closest to his heart:

"Sir, I pray that you will tell me the source of your wisdom!" The old man smiled and said, "Why, my wisdom has come from the stars; for they hold secrets beyond imagination, and I have seen them."

"Is that then the way to knowledge, to be a watcher of stars?" Georyn asked dubiously, for he too had seen stars; often on clear nights he had lain upon the grass and gazed up at them for hours on end. Often too had he sensed that there was more to be seen than he could understand, but that was not exactly the sort of wisdom for which he had been looking.

"That is part of it, Georyn," the Starwatcher said kindly, "but as I am sure you have guessed, it is not so simple as that. So I have not really given you an answer, and you must ask me something else."

Thereupon hope rose within Georyn, and he asked: "Have the stars told you by what means the fiery Dragon may be overcome?"

"Yes, even this they have told me: the Dragon cannot be overcome by ordinary weapons, but only by magic."

"So I have believed!" cried Georyn. "Ah, if the stars would but show how such magic may be understood, and used!"

"This too have they done," said the Starwatcher slowly. "But I cannot give you that secret until you have performed certain tasks that shall be set you."

"Gladly will we perform these tasks," said Terwyn, with enthusiasm. "For if our brothers have not already killed the Dragon—and I fear they would have returned ere now, had they done so—I am ready to agree that our swords alone will be of little use to us."

The Starwatcher looked back and forth between the two brothers, holding their eyes in turn. "The tasks are not easy ones. They will require wit and courage."

"That is to be expected," said Georyn. "Tell us what we must do."

"I have heard," the Starwatcher said, "of an enchanted disk that I should like to have. This disk is no bigger than the palm of my hand, but it is very magical, for within it appear clear images of things as they are—images that move and speak, even as do the people that they represent. Were you to look into such a disk, Georyn, you could see me from afar, and hear my voice; and so too could I see and hear *you*."

"Only tell us where this marvel may be obtained," cried Terwyn, "and we will get it for you."

"I cannot tell you where to find the enchanted disk," declared the Starwatcher. "You must discover it for yourselves."

"It is indeed a difficult task," whispered Georyn, nearly overcome. "But we will attempt it, if that is the only way to the Dragon."

"It is the only way that can offer you even the smallest hope of success," the Starwatcher said firmly. "Go now, and do not return without the disk."

So Georyn and Terwyn went forth into the wood, and for a while they wandered aimlessly in despair, for they knew of no place where they might even begin to search for an enchanted disk in which the images of living men might be seen. Surely not even the King himself had ever heard of such a wonder! "I do not believe that the thing exists," said Terwyn. "The Starwatcher is making sport of us."

"I do not deem him a man who would do that," said Georyn thoughtfully. "Nevertheless, it may well be that there is no enchanted disk and that he is simply trying to spare us death in combat with the Dragon, knowing that only through trickery can he keep us from challenging the monster. But I do not really think that is the way of it. I believe that we are meant, somehow, to accomplish this task."

"Perhaps so," Terwyn conceded, "but when? Ere we find a magical disk such as the one he desires, the Dragon may die of old age."

Georyn nodded. To search without direction would, he knew, be of no avail; and besides, they had been told that the task would require wit. That could only mean that the key to its accomplishment lay within their present knowledge. Yet what did they know of enchantments? All at once it struck him: perchance there was indeed some-one from whom they might learn where the disk was hid-den, the Enchantress who dwelt on the other side of the forest! For the Enchantress had promised that she would aid them if the time came when they could proceed no further alone, and surely that time was now.

With renewed hope, then, the brothers pressed on until they came to the river; and they followed it to a ford from which, by late afternoon, they were able to reach the place where they had met the Enchantress. And the Lady stood there under the trees before the stone hut, with the last rays of the sun shining upon her silvery garments, and she was even more beautiful than he had remembered, Georyn thought.

Yet there was an indefinable difference about her, too. Spirited she had always been, beneath the calm dignity of her manner; but now there was a strength and an assur-ance in her bearing that caused Georyn to wonder how he dared think of her as he had, in his secret heart, begun to think. And as he looked at her he perceived the reason for the change, for about her neck on a silver chain there hung a brilliantly gleaming pendant of many facets, and he knew beyond all doubt that it was enchanted.

The Enchantress, following his gaze, raised her hand

to the pendant and touched it; both Georyn and Terwyn stepped back in awe. "Lady, I see now the source of your power," said Georyn respectfully. "I am dismayed before so potent a charm as that."

She seemed quite startled, as if she had not been expecting him to recognize the thing for what it was. (But surely she knew that he was not so foolish as to think that any mortal woman, whether she were lady or princess or even queen, could possess such an ornament!) Smiling, she let the pendant drop; and as the light of the sunset touched it, it appeared to glow. "Fear it not!" she said to them. "It is indeed the Emblem of my power, but it works only for good and cannot be used to harm anyone."

"I am very glad to hear that," Terwyn said, "for I think now that your power is far vaster than I had dreamed."

"Though the Emblem is mighty," she told him, "but little of its force is at my command; for its power is not an easy one to wield." Her voice was melodious, but her words were, as before, only meaningless sounds in themselves; the brothers heard them through their minds more than through their ears. "And you, Georyn?" she continued. "Do I surprise you, also?" But she did not say how she knew his name.

"No, Lady," Georyn replied, and as he said it he knew it for the truth. "Neither you nor your enchanted Emblem is any surprise to me, for I have known since I first beheld you that in you is a thing that I have looked for all my life; and to learn your secrets shall now be my only goal and hope."

It's hard now for me to recall just what did happen during that first real exchange with Georyn. Your feeling for a person who has come to mean something to you colors all your memories, so that you can't describe them objectively. But I'm sure that right from the start I thought of Georyn not merely as a Youngling, but as someone whose friendship I would value. Even at the beginning I could communicate much more easily with him than with his brother; Georyn's telepathic ability was just naturally greater; or, I suppose, he may already have been backing it with emotion.

The past three days had done a lot for me. I wasn't bothered by being alone any longer; and the nights, although dark and lonesome, had been nothing like that first one. I was enjoying my leisure. The weather was bright; the river, although too cold to swim in, was beautiful to see; and I was becoming well acquainted with a family of squirrels that lived in the tree outside my hut. Though I knew, theoretically, that there were more challenges ahead, I had no anxious forebodings.

When, on the fourth day, the two Andrecians came to ask my help, I met them feeling pleasantly excited but in no way afraid. I knew that Father would not have sent them unless he was thoroughly satisfied that they were decent and trustworthy young men, as well as good candidates for the task of confronting the invaders. And of course, he had already told me their names and as much as he could of their background.

Father and I had talked frequently by means of our communicators, and I had been carefully briefed as to exactly what I was to do and why. It was a complicated scheme. You can't just say to an unsophisticated Youngling, "Now I am going to teach you to move objects by the power of your mind!" It requires a good deal of buildup. First, he has to believe that you do indeed have "magic" at your disposal and that it lies within his reach; to him, such things as a video communicator and a battery-powered arc light are just as magical as psychokinesis, so that's easy.

That's not all of it, however, and the other prerequisites are much harder to arrange.

There were parts of the arrangements that I didn't like too well. When I first heard the plan, before Father and Evrek left to establish the second camp, I objected to the testing that our protégés were to undergo, some of which would be decidedly disagreeable for them. "Do we have to scare the poor men to death?" I protested. "Must we have all this 'prove your worthiness' rigamarole?"

"Elana," Father said, "if you want to train a man to do something difficult, you start by finding out how he reacts to difficulties. Aside from the fact that that's something you've got to know, it's the greatest favor you can do him, because you're giving him a chance to make sure that he really wants to be in on the deal."

"We don't intend to trap anybody into this!" said Evrek. "It will change his whole life, Elana; whether he wins or loses it will. The man we use has got to be a genuine volunteer, and we mustn't delude him by making it seem too enticing."

He seemed surprisingly grave, almost sad. "And so it's kindness to turn it into an ordeal?" I asked.

"Think of all we went through to get into the Academy," he reminded me. "That wasn't made easy, was it? Well, the principle's just the same."

"Yes, and as a more immediate example," Father went on, "why do you think I had you make that first contact alone, before you were even sworn, and why did I force you to stay by yourself under circumstances that I knew would be frightening to you?"

He had me there. Because I could see, once I thought about it, that before I'd been asked to commit myself, I'd been given a taste of experience on which to base my choice.

"There's more to it," he continued. "For one thing, this sort of testing builds up a person's self-confidence, and they're going to need confidence."

"Builds it up? I should think it might have the opposite effect!"

"Not if it's done right. Of course, you have to have grounds for believing that a man can succeed in a test before subjecting him to it, because if he fails and suffers from it, that's as much your fault as it is his."

"I'm not sure that I can make that kind of judgment," I said uncertainly.

"Of course you can't, and you won't need to. I'll make those decisions, Elana. All you have to do is help carry them out."

"Be glad you don't have my job," Evrek said grimly. "You'll at least play the part of a good witch, and I've got to appear as a cruel one."

"That shouldn't be too hard for you!" I began, in a bantering tone. But I stopped short, seeing his face. This was not a thing he wished to joke about.

"As a matter of fact," Father said, "to project, telepathically, something opposite from what you feel—in this case, to threaten—is just about the hardest acting job there is. Evrek's role is brief but very demanding, for he's got to be convincing enough to make these men really afraid of him."

"I suppose so," I conceded. "But it still seems heartless."

"Elana," Evrek pointed out, "all other reasons aside, no inexperienced Youngling can do anything much in the way of psychokinesis without there being emotion back of it. For that matter, can you?"

"I could if I had to!"

"But not if you didn't have to; that's just the point."

"We've got to build in some urgency," Father said. "At first, we'll simply be teaching them to believe in our magic, but they've got to be emotionally involved right from the beginning, and fear is the most powerful emotion we can arouse."

"You're so cold-blooded about it!"

"That's not true!" he exclaimed heatedly. "If I've given that impression, it's got to be straightened out right now. If we don't approach this with warmth and compassion and faith in these people as human beings, we haven't a chance of succeeding."

"But won't we be tricking them, setting up threats deliberately?"

"No," Father assured me. "There will be no deception. You and I will tell them nothing that we aren't perfectly sincere about." He smiled encouragingly. "Elana, fear isn't necessarily a bad thing. It's a natural result of aiming high."

"Don't forget," Evrek added, "we're going to give them something good, something they'll want very much to have. Like everything else, it has its price; but they'll pay that price by their own choice."

It was rather hard to get used to the idea that I could tell a man that I was giving him "magic" to help him defeat a "dragon" and still be perfectly sincere about it, but by the time I'd had several encounters with the Andrecians I understood what Father meant. The language of symbols is no harder to learn than any other foreign language. The fact that Georyn literally believed the colonists' land-clearing machine to be a dragon never interfered with our communication at all, and I never told him any lies, either. Nor did I lie to him about myself; he simply interpreted my thoughts according to his own framework of beliefs. If he credited me with "supernatural" powers, it was only because his definition of "natural" was narrower than mine.

Yet there were problems, problems I could never have anticipated. I expected, you see, to be playing a game of make-believe with the Andrecians. During my briefings as to the sorts of explanations that would be meaningful to Georyn and Terwyn—which Father gave me via the communicator, just as fast as he could learn what concepts they understood—I got the impression that I would be simply acting out a part in a fairy tale. It didn't occur to me that I myself would be affected.

Not that Father didn't warn me. "Elana," he told me, "one of the first things you'll learn when you start working with these people is that they are fundamentally no different from other people you know. The fact that they are Younglings in terms of their culture does not mean that they are in any way childish as individuals. Any man who is capable of doing the job we are going to give him will be a strong, self-assured person, and you will not feel toward him as you would toward a child."

This turned out to be something of an understatement. But it was a while before I realized it.

The Light

Now when Georyn and Terwyn told the Enchantress of the magical disk that the Starwatcher had demanded of them, she told them: "This task is much simpler than you know, but it is at the same time more difficult."

"Simpler?" questioned Georyn. "Can you, then, tell us where the disk is to be found?"

"I can do better than that," said the Enchantress, "for I myself have the thing that you seek." So saying, she went into the hut, and to the amazement of the brothers she brought forth the enchanted disk even as the Starwatcher had described it. There did indeed appear an image within the disk—an image of none other than the Starwatcher himself, as tall as a man's finger—and it moved as though it were a living thing! Furthermore, the miniature figure spoke to them in the Starwatcher's own voice; but the words were strange, and they took no meaning from them.

"This is a great marvel," said Georyn. "I had not thought that such a thing could be!"

For a long time they stared into the disk; and it showed them not only the Starwatcher himself, but also the interior of his hut, and his table, where only this morning they had sat to eat, and even the red glow of his fire. Then Terwyn said, "Why, Lady, since the disk is now before us, do you say also that our task will be difficult?"

"Alas," said Georyn, "I fear that the Lady means that she will not give us the disk."

"Oh, I will give it to you gladly," the Enchantress told them. "But there is a condition."

"Name it," declared Georyn, for he was willing to agree to any condition that was honorable, and he could not imagine the Enchantress setting one that was not.

"It is simply this: if I give you this thing, you must solemnly promise that you will allow it to be taken from you by no one but the Starwatcher, even if you must die defending it."

"That is no condition at all," exclaimed Terwyn, "for we would not let anyone else have it in any case." But Georyn knew that the Enchantress did not make statements that had no meaning, and that if she said the condition was difficult, it most assuredly would be. Nevertheless, he promised her that he would defend the disk with his life, and Terwyn did also.

So it was that the brothers, having thanked the Enchantress for her aid, took the magic disk and started back the way they had come. And as before, Georyn looked back as he left the clearing, and he hoped that he would have occasion to seek the Lady again; for to him she was far more than the possessor of enchanted objects.

The sun had sunk below the horizon when they set out, and within the wood it was already almost dark. The tops of the trees were lost in gloom; their many trunks seemed to be crowding closer as the remaining light faded. "We can go no further tonight," Terwyn said. "We must stop to sleep, for we cannot travel in the dark."

Georyn agreed, and they began at once to seek a good place to build their campfire. But in the next instant the brothers froze with fear, for a dark figure loomed ahead of them, a figure that was approaching noiselessly, blocking their path.

No mere mortal threat was this; the stranger could not be a villager nor yet one of the King's huntsmen, for he was taller than other men and his eyes had an alien look. And indeed the eyes were all that could be seen of the man's face, for the hood of his cloak covered it almost completely. This cloak was of a gray stuff that, though it hung in folds, was more like to metal than to cloth, and it shone—not softly, as did the garments of the Enchantress, but harshly.

Yet the stranger's appearance frightened Georyn but little beside a more fell circumstance. For though the figure was totally silent, its thought was all too understandable. And that thought was this: *You must give me the enchanted disk.*

"We will not," said Georyn, for the demand had been made as clearly as if it had been spoken aloud, and it required an answer. Terwyn too stood fast, making no move.

If you do not give it, then I will take it; and I will make you sorry. You cannot stand against my power.

Georyn knew that this was the truth; they were helpless before such a thing as this. For the stranger was clearly an evil spirit or a wizard of some sort, and one cannot fight wizards as one can fight men. Yet having given their word to the Enchantress, they were bound to resist, whatever evil might befall them. "The condition was in truth a real one," he murmured to Terwyn, "but we accepted it, and we must now hold to it."

"What an ill chance!" exclaimed Terwyn.

"I do not think it was chance at all," Georyn told him. "For I am sure that the Lady knew exactly what would happen. Do you think, Terwyn, that enchantments are easily bought? If it were so, all the evils of the world would have been vanquished long ago; there would be no Dragons left!"

The dark figure moved toward them. Georyn and Terwyn drew their swords, but it was to no avail, for they were disarmed within seconds. As if they had life of their own, the weapons flew out of their hands and landed on the path, out of reach. The stranger had not touched them; his hands were still hidden under his cloak.

Georyn closed his fingers tightly around the precious disk, and drawing a deep breath, he waited. By all normal logic they were in the power of an evil spirit and were about to die; but he suddenly found that he did not believe their doom to be a certain thing. For two reasons he did not believe it: first, the Enchantress had *known* what would happen, he was positive of that, and he was also positive that she would not have sent them to a sure death; and second, there was the matter of the enchanted disk. If this wizard could by magic obtain their swords, then he could surely obtain the disk in the same fashion; yet he did not do it, and it was therefore obvious that the disk itself was not the thing at issue.

So Georyn faced the stranger and he said, "We will not give you the disk, for if we were truly powerless against you, you would have it by now. Instead, you have offered us a choice, and our choice is to keep it—so stand aside and let us pass."

And as Georyn and Terwyn walked forward, the dread demon did indeed stand aside! The brothers went on, swordless, and they did not look back; and though they camped for the night only a little distance from that place, they saw no more evil spirits.

Evrek contacted me that same night, after his encounter with Georyn and Terwyn, since I had insisted that I wanted to hear the outcome just as soon as the thing was over. (The communicator I'd given the brothers had been a spare one; I still had my own.) I'd hated to send them off like that, knowing as I did what they'd meet. Of course I *had* warned them, and I was sure that Georyn, at least, had fully understood.

"It went surprisingly well, darling," Evrek said. "They showed a lot of spirit, and I think I managed to get them pretty scared, too. I could hardly keep from letting them sense my admiration. That Georyn is a sharp one; I wasn't expecting him to reason his way out of it the way he did."

"Georyn goes right to the heart of the matter every time," I agreed, thinking what a surprise it had been to discover that intelligence has so little to do with background. Georyn was definitely not a person you talked down to.

"We've been lucky in finding those two, all right."

"Evrek," I said thoughtfully, "aren't we taking some awful chances? I mean letting Andrecians have a communicator, even temporarily. What if they were captured and the Imperials found it?"

"It would be bad," he said soberly. "But we've got to take chances if we're to accomplish anything at all. This next business, with the light, is particularly dangerous; the thing can be seen for miles, but of course they'll keep to the middle of the woods with it, and they'll have it for a very short time."

"Too short," I said. "Do you have to take it from them?"

"You know I do, Elana. It's not going to be fun, though." He sounded tired and, I thought, rather dejected. To my chagrin, I realized that I hadn't offered much sympathy. I hadn't meant to sound as if I were blaming him; I knew his job was much harder than mine. His role as "evil spirit" wasn't all of it, either. I got the shivers, thinking of some of the other things he and Father were doing.

They had been to the nearby village more than once, dressed as peasants. Fortunately the invaders were steering clear of settled areas. If they had spotted one of us in local dress, they would have had no reason to suspect us of being alien, of course; they'd simply have gotten the idea that there was another *native* race. However, they might then have started a real investigation of Andrecia's inhabitants, something we weren't anxious to have them do. After all, for our scheme to work, they had to keep on believing that one native was like another.

It had been necessary to visit the village not only to gather information, but also to get supplies. Father was now feeding Georyn and Terwyn as well as the rest of us, and we were saving our concentrated food for emergencies. Buying things had proved no problem; the unminted silver with which a survey team is normally equipped was very acceptable to local shopkeepers. But I could not seem to get any details about that village out of Evrek even, let alone out of Father. I wanted desperately to go too; but when I pressed the subject, Father said that I had had "insufficient preparation." And anyway, I had to stay put in order to do my own job.

It had also been necessary to do some scouting of the invaders' camp. Evrek had gone while Father was working with the brothers; I had not been told of the venture until it was over, but I suspected that this first trip was not the last. There were all too many occasions on which I was unable to contact Evrek. Naturally we had to know what the colonists were doing, and we had to have specific details on which to base our instructions to our "dragon slayers" when the time came. But the thought of what could happen if Evrek were caught was a thing I had to keep pushing from my mind.

Meanwhile, Father felt that the brothers were surpassing his highest hopes and that it had been little short of a miracle, our happening to find men so well suited to the job as quickly as we had. "I was expecting them to stand up to Evrek," he said the morning after that first trial, "but Georyn did more than that; he showed an ability to think fast under pressure that may be a very big bonus so far as any encounter with Imperials is concerned."

I didn't answer. Somehow, the thought of Georyn being sent to confront Imperials was more disconcerting than it had been at first.

"Of course," Father went on, "the next test is quite a bit more demanding." He reviewed the procedure in greater detail than he'd done before, and the more I heard the less I liked it. To me, it seemed entirely *too* demanding.

"Won't it be awfully discouraging to them?" I protested.

"Yes, it will. But if they can't face that and keep trying, what chance will they have of dealing with the invaders? I'm willing to bet that there will be plenty of discouragement *there*."

That, I couldn't argue with. And this was more than a test; it was an essential part of the leadup to the instruction we were going to give. Georyn and Terwyn had to learn that courage, while essential, was not in itself enough, and that magic can be challenged only by more powerful magic. Yet still I hesitated.

"It seems like such a dirty trick. I hate to have any part in pulling it on them, that's all," I complained.

"We all do," Father said. "But if they're going to back out, it's better to find out now than later." He paused, then continued, "Do you know how to give the right kind of encouragement, Elana?"

"I think so. I'm supposed to make them feel that I want them to succeed, that I believe they can, and still scare them a little with my warnings."

"That's right. Try not to give away the happy ending, not even after you can see they've earned it. Let it come as a surprise."

"Are you sure there'll *be* a happy ending?"

Father smiled. "For this episode, I'm almost positive. For the whole venture . . . well, as we've known all along, it's a long chance—but I've got a strong hunch that these men can achieve one, if anyone can."

With glad hearts, the brothers took the enchanted disk to the Starwatcher, and he said to them: "You have done well, and I am very pleased to have this thing. But before I can give you the secret that will overcome the Dragon, you must perform another task for me."

"We are ready to try it," said Georyn, "and this time, you do not need to warn us that it will be difficult!"

The Starwatcher smiled. "It may indeed prove so; but I have no doubt that you are equal to it."

"What must we do?" asked Terwyn, in haste to be off.

"Bring me a piece of the Sun, so that in my hut there shall be no darkness, though the fire be cold and night envelops the forest."

"But that is impossible," faltered Georyn. "No man can touch the Sun."

"Nevertheless, you must obtain a piece of it," returned the Starwatcher. "Go, and do not return until you have done so."

So Georyn and Terwyn went again into the forest; and they were joyful no longer, for they knew that any attempt to reach the Sun itself would be quite useless, and they could scarce believe that a piece of it had ever been imprisoned anywhere upon the earth. Georyn doubted that even the Enchantress could do such a thing.

Yet it was his belief that in her lay their only hope. Accordingly, the brothers set out once more for her hut, although already the time drew on to nightfall. Dusk was deepening ere they came to the place, and a chill wind sighed in the tops of the towering firs; and still Georyn and Terwyn continued on their way, all the while looking up at the blazing stars and wondering how the Starwatcher had been able to glean their secrets. And when at last they approached the abode of the Enchantress, therein was light, not soft and ruddy, as is firelight, but white and dazzling, like that of the Sun.

And the Enchantress met them; and when she learned their task, she put the light into Georyn's hands, confined within a small globe of glass, with a handle by which to hold it, that he might not be burned; and there was yet more light, in another globe, which she kept. And Georyn accepted the gift with reverence, for he knew now that she must be custodian of all life's secrets if she could hold the Sun itself and bequeath it unto her friends.

"You command great powers indeed, Lady," he said to her. "But surely you cannot simply give us this marvel. What shall we do to earn it?"

The Enchantress replied, "You are right, Georyn; for this too, there is a condition."

"We will meet it willingly," said Terwyn.

"It may be harder than it seems," she warned, with a gentle smile.

"So was yesterday's condition," Georyn told her. "I would not expect it to be otherwise."

"Well, then," said the Enchantress, "here is what is required of you: if I give you this thing, you must promise me that you will return to the Starwatcher with it tonight, without pausing for food or rest, and that you will let no one touch it but him."

"That will not be hard!" cried Terwyn. "For we are already in haste to complete this task, and we shall not mind traveling at night with this to light our way." But the Lady did not reply, and Georyn knew that the condition would be hard. Still, both he and Terwyn promised her that they would not stop to rest until they reached the Starwatcher's hut, and that no one would be allowed to touch the light.

"Know also," said the Enchantress, "that were this light allowed to burn by day, it would be outshone by its parent Sun and would expend its fire to no purpose; therefore, since the dawn may come ere you reach your destination, I must show you how to extinguish it."

"But if it is extinguished before we come to the Starwatcher," Terwyn protested, "how then shall we have fulfilled the task that he set us?"

She laughed. "Have no fear; the Starwatcher will know how to make it burn again." And she guided Georyn's hand to a tiny ball at the base of the globe, saying: "Turn this, and the light will be darkened."

"I understand," said Georyn. "I will do as you have told me."

Then the Enchantress said to them, "I can show you a shorter way to the Starwatcher's hut, which will save you some hours; but it lies through the heart of the Enchanted Forest."

"Lady," said Georyn, "I must tell you that I know little of the Enchanted Forest except wild tales that I have heard, and those tales have not been encouraging. But I believe you have knowledge as to the truth of them; so I will ask you directly whether you think that this route is a safe one for us to take."

The Enchantress hesitated, and then she said, "I will not tell you that the Forest holds no peril. But I believe that this particular path, on this particular night, is the proper one for your purpose."

Georyn looked at her closely. "That answer is less direct than my question, Lady."

"My answer was not meant to be direct—which you knew, when you framed that reply to it," the Lady said quietly.

Thereupon Georyn was sure that her advice had been intended not as a suggestion but as a challenge, and for that reason he could not refuse it. What a strange thing, he thought, that after all the years of avoiding the Enchanted Forest, he should be obliged to set out into it in the dead of night, with no real knowledge of what he would meet except for a clear hint that it would be something frightening!

But he kept a cheerful countenance as the Enchantress showed them where they could cross the river and pointed out the path on the opposite bank that they must take. And when they reached the other side of the log bridge Georyn looked back; the Lady stood at its far end, holding her own light aloft so that it shone upon her, turning her Emblem into a brilliant, flashing star. And this time, he raised his hand in a gesture that was more a pledge than a farewell.

I stood on the riverbank watching Georyn's small light disappear into that great dark forest that he truly believed was enchanted, and it was all I could do to keep from calling out to him. What if there really *was* peril there . . . peril other than the all-too-terrifying ordeal we had prepared for the brothers, which was in itself bad enough? What if they should lose their way? Suppose something unpredictable happened to them. We'd be responsible!

Holding my own light in front of me, I started back along the now well-worn trail toward the hut. Then suddenly I stopped and switched it off for a moment, deliberately letting the darkness close around me as I had not done on any night since I had been alone. My eyes, dazzled by the former brilliance, could see nothing. It *was* scary! A little of the panic I'd felt during that first fearful night hit me, though I knew how to squelch it now. Of course, I reminded myself, I was still unused to the wilderness; I had grown up in a world where light was normal and essential. To the Andrecians it was an unheard-of miracle, and they had undoubtedly been in dark woods plenty of times before. But not in the Enchanted Forest. Not without a campfire, without starlight even, fresh from an encounter with an "evil demon" that had ended in a disheartening defeat.

All at once I was struck with a fantastic idea—was it possible that they *wouldn't* be defeated? Could they turn the tables on us and really overpower Evrek? It was two against one, after all. To my horror I realized that I was half-hoping that they could. Evrek, after all, was protected by the Shield and wouldn't actually be harmed. Of course there wasn't any danger of such a thing happening; Evrek was quite capable of keeping the upper hand.

I hadn't heard from Evrek all day long. I'd thought that being with him on Andrecia would bring us closer together, but it didn't seem to be working out that way. The gulf between us was widening, not closing, despite the fact that I too was sworn. Our nerves were on edge, and we just weren't communicating as well as we once had. Maybe it was because we were afraid for each other, and we were both trying to conceal it. Or maybe it was simply that we were wrapped up in our new and awesome responsibilities.

I turned the light back on and carried it into the hut. Determinedly I sat down and opened a book, but I could not read it. Instead of printed characters I saw Georyn's face. Why, I wondered, should it haunt me so? Georyn was quick to grasp ideas, but I'd met lots of smarter men at the Academy. He was bold, courageous, but in my Service friends I'd come to expect that as a matter of course. And as for looks, well, I'd known at least ten classmates who were far more attractive than Georyn.

He suspected that I was testing him, I was pretty sure. But he wouldn't be expecting me to put him through the sort of experience that was waiting for him tonight in the depths of those woods. He'd be stunned by it, and hurt. He might stop believing in me. Father didn't think so. Father thought the brothers would come back to seek my aid again. He felt that if they didn't trust me that far, if they hadn't that much regard for my trust in *them,* then our relationship couldn't be good enough to support what was to follow. Maybe he's right, I thought. Maybe if I've done my job right, there's no question . . . maybe it's *my* success or failure that's at issue here.

And I *mustn't* fail with Georyn! He had been afraid, yet he had smiled and waved to me. Terwyn tended to discount danger, to believe that nothing could possibly happen to him. Georyn was more realistic; he had gone into the Enchanted Forest with no illusions at all, unless his faith in me was an illusion.

All along I'd known that, in theory, I would not want

to see anything unpleasant done to Younglings, whether it was for the sake of their own world's future or not. But there was nothing theoretical about the way I felt now. I knew that I was not going to be able to do anything except sit and worry until my protégés were safely back again.

Dulard kept close tabs on what was going on in the colony, and usually made the rounds of the camp each night before turning in. One evening, when he stopped to chat with Jarel and the other men quartered in the prisoners' barracks, he seemed disturbed about something.

"You've been hanging around these natives a good deal," he remarked to Jarel.

"Isn't that okay?" Jarel asked.

"Sure, go ahead, so long as you don't let it interfere with your job. If you can pick up any of their lingo, it'll be useful when it comes to moving them to a reservation."

"I don't think," Jarel said, "that they're going to be very cooperative about that. Are you sure it's practical, sir?"

Dulard sighed and Jarel sensed that he was the source of the disturbance. But strangely, Dulard didn't seem hostile. Jarel almost had the feeling that Dulard sympathized with him, although he couldn't say so. Of course, for him the safety of the colony had to come first.

"You medics are all alike," Dulard said. "Sometimes I think you'd like to pull out whenever we find that a planet's *got* natives. Jarel, these savages haven't a chance."

"I know."

"Then what the devil are you worrying about? Since when can't we arrange a simple treaty without starting trouble? They aren't strong enough to fight us; if they were, we'd never have picked this planet in the first place. An undeveloped base isn't worth men's lives."

"Men's lives? How about *theirs*?"

"We're not killing them off, are we? They'll get a whole tract of free land."

Jarel laughed shortly. "Yes, free—on their own planet. Maybe two or three percent of the surface. Of course, it won't be the most attractive two or three percent, but—"

"Good Lord, Jarel. You talk as if they were human."

"Maybe they are. Not by our standards, naturally, but maybe by theirs. Sure, they're not too bright and they haven't got civilization—anyway, not as we define civilization. But someday! What might they have become someday, if we'd kept out?"

Dulard insisted, "You can't look at it like that. That's like looking at ancient history and saying what might other primitive tribes have become if the more advanced nations hadn't taken over new continents."

"It's not the same," Jarel argued. "There wasn't any independent future for separate cultures of the human race, *our* human race. Isolation was impossible on a single world; they had to merge or stop developing. But we don't have to come *here*. In the long run it won't make a bit of difference to the future of the Empire if we don't claim this particular planet."

"In that case," put in Kevan, "I should get me a soft job back home and breathe *real* air."

Dulard glared at Kevan and at Jarel both, but he spoke to Jarel. "I might say that you are hardly an addition to the morale around here."

"I'm sorry, sir," Jarel said stubbornly, "but I can't turn off my feelings just because the inhabitants of this place don't look exactly like us and therefore don't have any rights under the Charter. I've watched them pretty closely, and they're *people*. They didn't walk into this camp just to gape, you know. They came to defend their village.

They haven't much idea what they're up against; they think that the rockchewer's alive, that it's a—well, sort of a dragon."

"A *dragon*? Like in those old myths?"

"Sure, like in those old myths our own people had once, before we ever heard of spaceships or 'civilized' planets."

"Say!" exclaimed Kevan. "I read some of those when I was a kid. The dragon's always demanding that the people bring him a beautiful maiden so's he'll leave the village alone. I'll bet if we—"

Jarel scowled at him. "The dragon," he said stiffly, "usually gets slain."

"Well, these would-be heroes aren't about to slay *us*," Kevan stated flatly. "They haven't any weapons besides spears and arrows and those crude swords."

Thoughtfully, Jarel said, "I wonder."

"Now look, Jarel—" Dulard began. He paused a moment, then went on. "The natives are *not* human, after all, and for more than one reason it would be a bad thing if any of you started thinking of them as if they were."

"I know," Jarel answered. "They've no firearms, no nerve poisons, nothing like stunner rays. By the way, do we have to go on using the stunners?"

"Why not?" demanded Kevan. "They have no permanent effects, and it saves putting bars on the place."

"How would you like to be shut in there unable to move around of your own volition? Sure, I know, it's painless. Animals don't care. But what if they aren't animals, Kevan? What if they turn out to have something we don't know about? Something big?"

"Such as what?"

"I'm not saying there's anything beyond future potential. But what do we really know about intelligence?

Maybe technology isn't everything; maybe there are races in the universe whose minds work differently. Maybe this one's on a higher level than we think."

"You don't believe that," asserted Dulard.

"No," Jarel admitted. "I think I understand these people; I think I see where they fit in with the primitive species that have been studied at the Research Center. But I'm not *sure*. Suppose for example, and I'm not saying this is possible, but just suppose that a race discovered how to use ESP, or something of that nature."

"ESP—mind reading? Ghosts and mediums and stuff? You're kidding," Kevan guffawed.

"Maybe. But maybe it's not 'supernatural' at all. There may be all kinds of things we haven't discovered yet. And who's to say what kinds of forces a people will discover and put to use first?"

Dulard shook his head. "Jarel," he said, "I don't know how a guy like you got into this kind of work. But if it makes you feel any better, let me tell you this: the day your friends in there start reading minds, or doing things with forces we don't understand, we'll get our ship out of this solar system so fast you'll hardly know we were ever here."

The Enchanted Forest was darksome indeed, for the trees met overhead, hiding even the stars from view. So thick was the undergrowth that the path was hard to follow despite the globe that Georyn held before him, the globe containing the wondrous piece of the Sun. The light made a safe circle around the brothers, illumining the ground at their feet and the nearby tangle of branches. But beyond that sanctuary, beyond the curtain of mist that encroached upon it, were black and unknowable things.

"What if the light should fail?" whispered Terwyn. "What then would become of us? For to be here without it would be unbearable."

"I do not think," said Georyn, "that the light will fail of itself; for it can be no less faultless than she who gave it to us. But we are dealing with enchantments, so we must be prepared to meet something unexpected. We cannot hope for our task to be straightforward. That is not the way of such things!"

At that moment, the brothers sensed a movement on the path ahead, a dim suggestion of a tall, dark shape! "Hold up the light!" Terwyn said urgently. Georyn did so, yet still they beheld but little that lay before them. No need had they to see, however, for the same soundless speech that had challenged them on the previous night again flooded their minds. *You must give me your piece of the Sun.*

"We cannot do that," said Terwyn resolutely. Then, to Georyn, he said, "Let us go on, as before; no doubt the result will be the same as it was with the last evil spirit we encountered."

"I am not so sure," replied Georyn, "for we meet him here on his own ground, and his power may be the stronger for it; not for nothing is the reputation of this Forest so black. Nevertheless, we must try."

But ere they could make any move, the ominous thought of the wizard came again, more insistently. *This time, I am not giving you a choice! I will take the light, whether you consent or no.*

With terrifying certainty Georyn knew that this was no bluff, for the thoughts of the demon were not like words, which might or might not have true meaning. It was very clear to him that while last night he had been offered a choice, tonight he would receive none; if the wizard could get the globe, he would do so. "We have but one hope," he whispered to Terwyn. "If we put out the light, perchance he will not find it."

"But we may not be able to make it burn again!" exclaimed Terwyn. "We would then have to travel through this Forest in the dark. We could not even build a fire, for we have promised not to stop."

"That cannot be helped now," Georyn declared, and he turned the ball at the base of the globe firmly. As the Enchantress had predicted, the light was instantly extinguished. There was not even any glow, as with fading coals; it was as if there had never been any piece of the Sun at all. The world around them was now totally obscured; yet still the brothers felt the demon's presence, and they were aware that he was moving toward them.

There was no sound. Georyn clutched the darkened globe, and together he and Terwyn walked forward in the desperate hope that at the last moment the wizard would step aside as he had done before. And the cloaked figure must indeed have either stepped aside or dissolved into nothingness, for at no time was it within touch of them. Yet as they had been bereft of their swords by sorcery, even so was the globe wrenched from Georyn's hands; and to their great dismay it disappeared into the impenetrable shadow of the Enchanted Forest.

Blindly, then, did Georyn and Terwyn charge ahead, intending to fight this demon at whatever cost to themselves; well they knew that loss of the thing that had been entrusted to their care would be a defeat past bearing. But valor was useless, for neither the wizard nor the globe was anywhere to be found! The chilling thought assailed them: *There is no use in searching, for you will not find it. You will not find me, either. You must accept your failure.* And with that, the evil spirit departed; its very thought was gone from the place, and thus was Georyn at last convinced that they were now in truth alone.

The brothers were overcome by despair. They had not really believed that such a thing could befall them. Though for some time they continued the search for the vanished globe, in their hearts they knew it would avail little. And all the while Georyn was thinking, This is a riddle that has no answer. She would not set us an impossible task. For he could see no way in which he could have withstood the magic that had been used against him, if willingness to die in defense of the light had not been enough. And that meant that the Enchantress must be either less well-intentioned than he had thought, or less omnipotent—but neither of those could he believe.

"Terwyn," he said, "There is but one thing we can do now. We must return to the Enchantress and tell her what has happened."

"But she may be very angry," objected Terwyn. "That Lady has great power, Georyn, power past our understanding. Though she seems gentle, I have no doubt that she is dangerous if her wrath is aroused. Even more dangerous than demons in dark cloaks, perhaps."

Georyn knew that if he had misjudged her good purpose, this might very well be true. As an enemy, the Enchantress would surely be formidable; logic told him that to walk into her trap, if it had been a trap, would indeed be rash. But this was not a matter for logic. "We still must go to her," he told Terwyn. "We cannot return to the Starwatcher without the thing for which he has asked, and we will not find it here by hope alone. Besides, she trusted us with the light, and I will not deceive her."

"Nor will I," admitted Terwyn. "You are right; it is the only course we can take if we are to continue with this quest. Let us camp here, and set out at first light of dawn."

"We must return *now*," Georyn declared firmly. "To wait for dawn would be a violation of our promise."

"But the condition has already been violated."

"Not by our will. And it must not be, if we are to hope for any further aid from her."

So the brothers stumbled back through the darkness, retracing the way they had come. If following the trail had been difficult before, it was almost impossible now, and they proceeded very slowly. More than once they blundered off the path, but the undergrowth was so dense elsewhere that they were able to feel their way back to it. At last a welcome sound swelled before them and they broke out of the forest onto the stony riverbank. The log bridge was barely visible and the crossing of it was hazardous; yet they pressed forward and met with no mishap.

There was still a light within the Enchantress's hut; resolutely Georyn and Terwyn approached the doorway and stood just outside it, looking in. The Lady's dark head was bent over an awesome thing that could be naught but a book of magic spells; Georyn could see that its pages were covered with strange markings, and he was overcome with wonder. Yet at that moment she looked far more like a mortal maiden than a witch. He deemed her to be entirely innocent of any ill intent, and he knew also that he desired her friendship more than he had ever desired anything.

She looked up, startled, and to the brothers' amazement her face beamed with unmistakable delight at their coming; but then she turned solemn, as if she had suddenly remembered that such a thing was not seemly. "Why have you returned, and where is the piece of the Sun that I gave you?" she demanded coldly. But Georyn knew that underneath she was not cold, nor was she angry.

They entered the hut, saying: "No longer do we have the light," and thereupon told her how the globe had been taken from them. "We would have fought this demon to the death, had he not disappeared as he did," Terwyn concluded. "Is there a possibility, Lady, that he can ever be found?"

"You may do with us as you will," Georyn added, "for we do not ask your mercy. But if there is any means through which we can recover the light, we would like to know of it."

The Enchantress rose and stood before them. "I told you," she said calmly, "that the condition would be hard. But I did not say in what way it would be hard."

Georyn stared at her. "Did you know all along, then, that we would fail?"

"That is something that no one can ever know; there is no magic that can foresee the choices of men! And even if there were, you have not failed yet."

"Not failed?" exclaimed Terwyn bitterly. "We made you a promise that we did not keep."

"Oh? Is that in truth what you believe?"

Slowly, Georyn said, "No, perhaps it is not. A promise is only a choice made beforehand; we did not change our choice, for we were offered none."

"Then the promise was not broken!" the Enchantress declared.

"There is something else," Georyn went on. "You told us that no one was to touch the globe. But the wizard who took it from us did *not* touch it, any more than he touched our swords, yesterday."

"I wondered if you would think of that," said the Lady, and there was approval in her eyes.

"Then you *did* know."

She gave him a searching look. "It is true that I expected

you to encounter magic too powerful for you to combat. That is one of the first things to be learned about enchantments, Georyn, and if you are to deal with them further you will have to face it."

"Am I to believe, then," Georyn answered, "that you consider me fitted for such learning?"

Seeming strangely sad, suddenly, she told him, "You are very well fitted for it; but it is going to get still harder as it goes along, I am afraid."

"I will try it in any case," he replied. Then, thoughtfully, he added, "This magic whereby objects move without the touch of men is a very wondrous thing, Lady."

"Very wondrous," she agreed, and she did not call it an evil one. Turning to Terwyn, she then asked, "Do you want to continue, too?"

"I do," Terwyn said. "I swore to kill the Dragon, and I will not turn from it now."

"So be it," said the Enchantress; and she went on steadily although, Georyn thought, somewhat reluctantly: "I cannot help you to recover the piece of the Sun; I can only tell you that you must now reenter the Enchanted Forest by the same dark path, without it."

And although this chilled Georyn's heart, he nodded his assent; for he believed that her ways were inscrutable and that his best hope lay in trusting to them. Then all at once the Lady broke into an irrepressible smile and said, "I will not tell you where or how, but in time, if you travel that path bravely, you will regain what you have lost."

And with these words she bade the brothers depart; but Georyn turned, saying, "Lady, would it have happened so, had we not told you of this thing?"

And the Enchantress answered, "No, Georyn, it would not; but of course, you knew that." And her face told him that she was very glad that he had known.

So Georyn and Terwyn again went forth from the Enchantress, and though it was hard to turn their backs on the lighted hut and pass beyond even the reach of starlight, they did not hesitate. And after a time, a faint point of light appeared in the depths of the Forest far ahead of them, and they followed it; but it moved before them so that they could not approach. Then finally as dawn was spreading up out of the east, they came upon it, where it had been set upon a rock in the midst of a small glade; and as they reached out to take it, the first ray of sunlight pierced the trees. And though the globe still contained a piece of the Sun, it was no longer of fiery brilliance, for its parent Sun now outshone it; so Georyn extinguished it once more as the Lady had bid them. But a light now waxed within him at the knowledge that such wonders as he had been shown could exist.

The Cup

In the morning, the brothers came to the Starwatcher and said, "Here is the piece of Sun for which you have asked; and though it is dark now, we have been told that by your magic you can make it burn again." And he replied, "That is true, for I have an understanding of enchanted things. But you must perform one final task for me before I can give you magic that will enable you to stand against the Dragon. It will be more difficult than the others; do you wish to hear of it?"

Georyn and Terwyn assured him that they did indeed so wish, although by this time they viewed the difficulty of such tasks with a great deal of respect. However, since they were nearly spent with hunger and weariness, having been required to travel for a day and a night without food or sleep, the Starwatcher told them that they should rest before setting out again. Thereupon he himself went off into the forest, and they did not see him until the morrow.

"I have no doubt that we will be forced to seek the aid of the Enchantress again," Terwyn said to his brother as they were finishing their meal. "But I hope that she will not put us into another such situation as we met last night. I do not care to be made a fool of more than once."

Georyn said, "She was not making fools of us, Terwyn. I cannot fathom her full purpose, but I know that there was more to it than a test of our loyalty to her. Somehow, I had the feeling that she did not enjoy all of what she did. I—I pitied her, in a way."

Terwyn frowned. "Have a care, Georyn! A witch, having no heart, will have little regard for yours; and though she seems very fair, her fairness in itself may be perilous. Who is to say that she charms only lifeless things, and not men?"

"I will not have you speak so of her!" exclaimed Georyn angrily.

"I meant no harm by it, for I myself am fain to trust her. But whether her purpose be good or ill, brother, she has little need of sympathy from *you*. You will never get even a glimpse of what goes on in such a mind as hers; and as for the wisdom that you are always seeking, think not that she will impart it to you. The wisdom of enchanted folk is not for the world of mortals, nor will it ever be."

"I do not agree with you," insisted Georyn. "Must a man then live always as his fellows live, and never reach beyond? There is more to knowledge than you dream of, Terwyn, and if it lies in some enchanted realm—well, I think that there is a door to that realm. And I think that the Enchantress knows where the door is and can open it."

"Perhaps; but will she leave it open? Think, Georyn: even if she should let you look through such a door, the time will surely come when it will be sealed again; and when that happens you will be not on her side of it, but on ours. How will you feel then? Let us accept her help against the Dragon, but no more—for we are men, not wizards."

"I am not sure," said Georyn, "that there is such a difference between the two." Well he knew that however unwarranted Terwyn's first warning might have been, this last one was all too pertinent. Yet just the same he intended to pursue the secrets of the Enchantress, both for love of her and for their own sake.

Early the next morning, when the brothers presented themselves to the Starwatcher, he said to them, "This time, all I ask of you is that you shall bring me a cup. But it is no ordinary cup: rather, it is a very remarkable one; for the cup I seek can float upon the air with naught to support it, and yet spill no drop of water."

"Remarkable indeed," said Terwyn. "But no more so, surely, than an enchanted disk that holds images that move and speak!"

"Nor than a piece of the Sun that can be darkened or lighted at will," added Georyn. But to himself he thought, "It is very near to being as wondrous as a sword or a globe that moves without anyone's touch."

F ather and Evrek came to the base camp to talk over the next phase of the operation with me in detail. "This is the big step," Father said. "If Georyn and Terwyn get along as well as they have so far, we're in business; but it's going to be very tricky."

"I have to hand it to them," Evrek remarked. "Every time, they come through with a little more than we have them figured for. Deliberately turning out that light took nerve! I hope this time I'll be able to let them win."

"So do I," I agreed fervently. "But Evrek, do you think they'll really be able to counter your 'magic'? If they can, I want to see it!"

"You won't, I'm afraid," he told me. "It's got to take place off in the middle of the forest again."

"I'm sorry," Father said, "for if it comes off they'll get a tremendous lift from it, and it should be pretty thrilling to watch."

"Couldn't she follow them?" Evrek suggested. "After all, we'll be joining forces anyway if they succeed."

"I don't see any harm in that—so long as you keep out of sight, Elana, until it's over." He smiled. "You can bring us something to celebrate with. A canteen of soda pop ought to seem literally marvelous to them."

"I guess it will! They won't have tasted anything like it before, certainly."

"First, though," he reminded me, "you've got some 'magic' of your own to perform. Let's have those cups, Evrek."

Evrek opened his pack and got out two wooden cups with elaborate, intricately carved handles, obviously native handcraft. "Two genuine enchanted cups," he declared. "The best the village has to offer."

"Enchanted? How?"

"You should know"—he grinned—"since you are going to cast the spell on them."

"What do you mean, spell?"

"An incantation that will make these cups float in the air without anything touching them," Father told me. "It should be something very dramatic. Pick anything you like in the way of poetry. In our language, of course. You don't want to convey meaning with it; it should sound like gibberish to the Andrecians, only be rhythmic and easy to memorize."

"I'll think of something," I promised. "But why all this hocus-pocus? Why not just do it?"

"Because the concept of controlling objects by conscious mental effort is beyond the Andrecians, while that of casting a spell is not. And to them a cup, even a floating cup, may be less magical than a disk containing moving images or a 'piece of the sun;' so it needs to be made impressive."

Less magical? I thought, suddenly, of how the colonists would react if presented with such a comparison. Well, even naïveté has its advantages—not that the Imperials had lost much naïveté, but theirs was the cynical variety. We couldn't teach *them* to use any psychic powers; their so-called scientific attitude would get in the way.

But I saw what Father was driving at. If I gave Georyn and Terwyn a magic spell to pronounce, they would believe in the spell. They would be fully convinced that it would be as effective for them as for me. But would it? I'd always simply accepted psychokinesis as a fact; I'd never analyzed its prerequisites before. Now I had to know some of the theory.

Father told me, "There are three important factors; but the first, the belief, is the most essential of all. If we've given them that, the rest will be easy."

"It still seems incredible," I said.

He laughed. "The human mind is incredible. It can do nothing without belief, yet practically anything with it. In our society, belief in this particular ability comes naturally; a child learns it from his parents, as he learns language. Here it is not natural, so we've had to lay a foundation for it. I think now that that foundation is strong enough."

"But if they can't do it at first, won't they stop believing?"

"Yes, so we have to be very, very careful. This is the most difficult part of the whole business, Elana, knowing at what moment it's safe to let them try. Because they must succeed the very first time. When you teach them the 'spell,' you'll control the cup yourself; they'll only *think* they're doing it. The crucial part, the transference of control to them, I'll handle. At that point, of course, they'll be under great emotional stress, which is the second of the three essential factors."

"I know it's a principle of psychic power in general, and psychokinesis in particular, that emotion helps," I said. "But I don't really understand why."

Father hesitated. "I'll try to make it clearer," he said. "But first, let's practice this a little. We've got to make absolutely sure that you can do what's necessary."

He held out one of the cups to me and I took it, feeling somewhat doubtful. You can't control your powers easily if you haven't had special training, because while you believe in them, you also know that failure's possible: the very thing the Andrecians would not be allowed to learn. At the time, I had never before had a real need to use psychokinesis; I'd only played around with it in the way that any child does. Sometimes when I was in the right mood, I was quite good at it; but could I count on that? Keeping a small object like a cup motionless a few feet off the ground is pretty elementary, of course; but still, what if I should drop the thing, or something?

I held the cup before me with both hands and tried to concentrate, but I was suddenly very unsure of myself. I couldn't seem to bring myself to let go of it. I just couldn't pick a moment when I was ready for the attempt. How awful it would be if I *couldn't* control it well enough to do the job.

"Go ahead!" Father said sharply.

Drawing a deep breath I parted my hands. The cup lurched, hovered for a moment, and then crashed to the ground.

Impatiently, Father burst out, "What's the matter with you, Elana? Can't I depend on you for a simple thing like that?"

"I was doing the best I could," I said miserably.

"Apparently that's not good enough! I'm sorry now that I let you have any part in this."

I stared at him, incredulous. It was not like him to be so unreasonable. Glancing around, I saw that Evrek's face was impassive; he did not seem inclined to jump to my defense. "Let me try again——" I began.

"No! I'll revise the plan," said Father, his voice hard and angry. "I can't take a chance on you; anyone can see you're too young to take this much responsibility."

"I'm *not*!" I said furiously. I'd show him! I picked up the cup, thrust it out in front of me, and quickly drew my hands back. It stayed put, as it was supposed to. "I *can* do it, if I'm given half a chance!" I declared.

He grinned. "When you're mad enough, you can," he agreed amiably.

"Oh——!" I sputtered. "You and your—manipulations!"

"Elana," Father explained, "that illustrates the point pretty well, doesn't it? When you are angry or frightened or wrapped up in some other strong emotion, you don't stop to worry about whether you can do the thing or not. You just go ahead and do it, because you *have* to."

"I guess I see," I said slowly.

"When Georyn and Terwyn do this for the first time, they'll be under a lot of pressure," said Evrek. "They'll be outraged because I've already defeated them once without letting them fight; yet they'll be afraid, too, because I'm going to make some very ominous threats, threats that, after the lesson I taught them last time, they'll have no reason to doubt! And they will know that mastery of this 'magic spell' is the only chance they have to save themselves."

"But will they know how to master it, when their minds have never worked in this way before? I mean, if it's possible, Younglings should be able to do it any time the belief and the emotion happen to be present."

"You're right; naturally, there has to be more to it," Father said. "There's the third factor I spoke of. Psychokinesis is centuries ahead of anything they could develop for themselves. So the initial knowledge of 'how to do it' has to be passed to them telepathically."

"Can they understand that kind of knowledge?"

"Not in words; they have no such words in their language. But there's another level, you know. I've got to be the one to do it, since you and Evrek haven't yet learned to transmit in that way."

I began to see. Of course, he wouldn't try to explain the thing. He'd simply give it to them, just as he had given me an overwhelming, undefinable feeling of elation at my investiture. They would never understand the skill consciously in the way that we understand it. And so, of course, they would always need immediate, raw emotion in order to use it at all.

Not that I seemed to be very much more advanced than that. "How am I going to manage the demonstration?" I asked nervously. "I won't be either mad or scared, at least not scared in the helpful sort of way—"

"No, but when the time comes you'll be aware of how much hangs on your doing it perfectly," Father assured me. "For you, it will be stimulus enough just to know that if you slip, this whole scheme will very likely fail and Andrecia will be lost to the invaders. You do know, don't you, that we probably won't get a second chance?"

I shuddered. "You make me feel so—so accountable. So weighed down with it, as if the fate of this world was in my hands."

"That's how I want you to feel," he said gently. "You can't afford to take it casually. But Elana, don't worry about it. If I didn't have complete confidence in you, I wouldn't dare to give you a key role."

He wouldn't, I knew. Under the Oath, he could consider neither his own personal feelings nor mine. You might think I'd have found this cold comfort, but Father never made it seem cold. Instead, he managed to give us confidence that something wonderful was going to come out of all this, something that would be worth whatever we had to go through.

Once more the brothers set off for the hut of the Enchantress; and they took the shortest way, through the Enchanted Forest, for Georyn declared, "This is not a time to shrink from whatever there may be in the place. We are going to encounter plenty of magic, both white and black, before we are through; and we might as well get used to it."

The sun was yet high in the sky when they arrived at the hut, and the Enchantress was nowhere to be seen. But on searching, they came to a meadow, and she sat there in the grass amid clumps of yellow flowers; and though again she held the book of charms before her, she was not looking at it.

Seeing the brothers, she got to her feet and ran toward them; and the smile with which she greeted them was not hidden, this time. "What a lovely day it is!" she exclaimed happily. "Oh, this is a fair world, touched by such sunlight! Do you not think it so, Georyn?"

"Fair indeed, Lady," he agreed, but the beauty of the sunlit meadow was not in his mind. And he was moved to wonder whether it was invariably true that a witch had no heart. For surely, such feeling as he saw in her could be naught but genuine.

Yet as he and Terwyn told the Enchantress of the cup that the Starwatcher had sent them to find, her gaiety faded and she said, "As you have guessed, I have such a cup; in fact I have two of them, which are a pair and must not be separated. But——"

Georyn smiled at her and said, "But there is a condition, which is harder than it seems? Do not look so downcast, Lady. That is not such a woeful thing. It would be a poor enchantment indeed that had no price."

"The risks but add interest to the game," Terwyn declared stoutly.

"So I too once thought!" the Lady said. "But alas, it is not a game." She looked out over the meadow toward a break in the rippled grass—a trampled spot—and it was almost as if she saw something there that was, to them, invisible. And with one hand, as she spoke, she twirled the magical Emblem. "Georyn, are you and Terwyn very sure that you want to confront the Dragon? It will not be easy. Even with the Starwatcher's magic, and mine, it will not be easy!"

But Georyn knew that if somewhere the enchantment existed that could make it possible, he did not care whether it was easy or not; so his heart was light as he said to her, "We are absolutely sure."

"Why? Because of the reward the King has promised?"

"Indeed so," began Terwyn; but Georyn said: "No, Lady, for the King himself has not such knowledge as can now satisfy me, having glimpsed that of the stars."

And at this he perceived that she felt sorrow, though he could not divine its cause, for why should there be grief in *her* concerning his desire for such unattainable wisdom? And not wanting to dwell upon that which disturbed her, he continued, "Now, let us see these marvelous cups."

They walked back to the hut, and the Lady brought forth two carven cups, cups that did not look very different from many that the brothers had seen before. "In fact," murmured Terwyn, "if I did not know better, I should say that they had come from the woodcarver of our own village."

The Enchantress took one of the cups, and from a tall, cylindrical silver jug she filled it with water. Then, holding it carefully between her two hands, she said: "This is not quite like the other magic that I have shown you. For this, it is necessary to use a charm." And as the brothers watched in awe, she raised her voice and began to repeat the words of a spell—strange, musical words that differed from her accustomed speech in that they carried no intelligible meaning. Slowly, then, she stretched her hands out in front of her and parted them. And the cup remained poised in the air where she had placed it, motionless, and no water spilled from it; and the Lady dropped her arms and backed away.

She was silent now; there was no sound anywhere except, in the background, that of the river. Still the cup floated, and neither of the brothers could turn their eyes from it. Then, though the Lady's lips did not move, Georyn heard her voice as if from far away, saying: *Georyn, take the cup!* And he stepped forward and put his hands around it. As he did so, the cup settled into them, so that he seemed to be holding an ordinary vessel such as those from which he had often drunk. And when he looked up again, the Lady was laughing. "Do not drop it," she said. "For the charm is broken now, and you would have wet feet."

Terwyn was still staring as if bewitched. "That is the strangest thing I have ever seen," he said at last. "For the cup looks too plain to hold so strong an enchantment."

But Georyn said, "It is in my mind that the magic of this is not in the cup at all, but in the spell. Is it not so, Lady?"

"You are already wise, Georyn! You see beyond your experience."

"I have had experience," he said with a troubled frown. "As you well know, I have seen something of this sort before. For two nights past it has been used against me. How then am I to distinguish between a good spell and an evil one?"

"That is a good question," the Lady admitted, "but not simple to answer. For good and ill are in the uses and not in the nature of things."

"Yet if this is related to the magic practiced by the evil demons of the Forest——"

"There are no evil demons. There is peril, surely, but that is not the form it takes."

Terwyn protested, "But we ourselves have met them, twice."

"I am quite certain that you are mistaken," the Enchantress said, and her tone seemed almost to be one of amusement.

"Were you then, through your own magic, testing us?" asked Georyn, for he had suspected this all along.

The Lady answered gravely, "I am not permitted to say." But as to what authority such as she might serve, she did not tell them.

"Even if what we saw was not an evil spirit," persisted Terwyn, "there are many that attend the Dragon; we have met a man who was turned into stone by them."

"That is another matter," said the Enchantress. "The servants of the Dragon are not demons, either, but men who have been bewitched. They are a danger to you, but they are not in themselves evil."

"Have they truly the power to turn men into stone?" asked Georyn skeptically.

"They have indeed." Hesitantly, the Lady went on, "Perhaps I should tell you that when you meet the Dragon, this will undoubtedly happen to you, and you must be prepared for it."

"We will be turned into stone?" cried Terwyn, horrified. "How will we be able to fight, then?"

"There will be a way, for you will not be defenseless. But you need not worry about that now. For the moment, you need only to learn this charm."

Georyn exclaimed joyfully, "You will teach us to use it, then? I had feared that the Starwatcher alone——"

"I will teach you, for you have earned it. But you must promise never to use it except as I shall direct you. It is not as safe as it seems."

"I am sure of that, Lady, and I will promise gladly," said Terwyn. So both the brothers gave the Enchantress their word that they would never repeat the charm save in her presence, or the Starwatcher's. "Or," she added, "in one other instance, which I shall describe to you presently."

With that, Georyn took up the cup again, and Terwyn took the other; and the Lady taught them the spell. And the cups did indeed float steadily wherever they were placed, as each of the brothers repeated the strange words. At length, when they had proved that they knew the words and would not forget them, the Enchantress said, "Now you must return to the Starwatcher; for again I shall require you to journey without pausing, and I am sure that you do not want to wait for dark."

"We do not," said Terwyn grimly. "Is there any other condition, Lady?"

"There are two," she said slowly.

"I will venture to say," Georyn declared, "that one of

them is that we must not allow these cups to be taken from us; and I have no doubt but that we will be put to the test. Have we any reason to suppose that we shall fare better than we did last night?"

The Enchantress's dark eyes measured him. "What do *you* think, Georyn?"

He hesitated, then said thoughtfully, "I believe that this charm that we have learned is intended to be used as a counterspell against the magic that overpowered us before; and I also believe that if we fail this time, it will be a real failure, for which we will be answerable."

"That is indeed the way of it," she agreed. "You may use the charm in defense of the cups; but I warn you that merely to recite the words will not be enough. For the best of spells requires the control of a firm will."

So Georyn knew that this final test would be the most difficult of all, but he nodded confidently and said, "And the other condition?"

"Oh," the Enchantress said, "it is simply that in return for what I have given you, I would like your promise that if you succeed in this task, you will come to see me again. For I—I would like to advise you in the matter of the Dragon."

"But Lady," exclaimed Georyn with warmth, "that is no condition at all! Rather, it is a reward."

She turned away hastily. He could not see her face well; and yet, if she had been anyone other than who she was, he would almost have said that she blushed.

When the brothers had gone, I went straight back to the hut and contacted Father. I was shaking, not only from the strain of my performance being over, but from something else. Inexplicably, my eyes stung as if with tears. Oh,

Georyn wanted knowledge, all right! He wanted it too much; and on top of that he had begun, all too obviously, to want some things that he was never going to get.

"What is it, Elana?" Father said anxiously. "Did anything go wrong?"

"Not with the magic charm," I told him. "That went beautifully. I'll give Georyn and Terwyn a good head start, and then I'll be along to meet you. But that's not why I called."

He was silent, waiting for me to go on. Father has a way of projecting his sympathy that comes through even over a communicator; I didn't hesitate to speak my mind. "Don't you see what we're doing?" I burst out. "He's perfectly well aware that we've got a lot more knowledge than we're revealing. He wants it—and we're deliberately tantalizing him, making him reach for something we don't intend to give!"

"Of course we are," Father admitted gravely. "It's unavoidable, since we're raising him above the level of his culture."

"But it's cruel."

"Perhaps it is. On the other hand, Elana, I don't think that sort of reaching is a bad thing. A certain amount of it's the normal price a man pays for an inquiring mind. How else can Youngling peoples evolve?"

"He'll be hurt, though."

"Do you suppose he doesn't know that?"

"How could he know? He hasn't all the facts."

"No one ever has all the facts. All a person can do is to choose a goal that seems worthwhile and commit himself to it. That's as true for Georyn as it is for us."

"But we're responsible for him," I insisted. "We should protect him!"

"Like a little child . . . or a pet? Now you're thinking of him as the invaders do: as less than human."

"Of course I'm not! He's a person, a person I care about." It was rather a shock to me to realize, as I said this, just how much I did care.

"Then grant him the right to suffer for a cause of his own choosing," said Father slowly. "He did choose it, you know. This cause—call it a quest, if you like, as he would—is a deadly serious thing from his point of view; it is as serious as your Oath. If you care about him, don't belittle it by trying to make it easier than it is."

"Oh, but he thinks he can save the world by slaying a dragon! With the help of a magic spell!"

"And he must think that. If he ever stops thinking it, it will cease to be true."

"Are you saying it's true now?"

"Elana," Father said soberly, "if we don't believe that it is, we might as well give up right now and go back to the starship."

He was right and I couldn't deny it, so I signed off. I wasn't any happier, though. Somehow, when I became an agent, I hadn't pictured quite this sort of responsibility.

I stood in the doorway of the hut and watched the sun sink slowly into the low haze of Andrecian afternoon. The tears brimmed over, my first for Georyn. What would become of him? Suppose this crazy scheme did save Andrecia, suppose the whole thing was a glorious success. Whether he was acknowledged as a hero by his own people or not, the local king would have very little to offer.

And there was something else about which I felt even worse. For I hadn't been wholly frank with Father. The truth was I could hide from myself no longer the fact that Georyn was not interested in me solely as the holder of magical knowledge. What was more, I couldn't say that I was so absorbed with Evrek as to be totally oblivious to

Georyn's interest. Were he not a Youngling, I thought, nor I an Enchantress, we might easily come to like each other simply as boy and girl.

J arel walked a little way into the woods, away from the depressing sight of the ravaged clearing. He looked up at the stars, thinking that it had been a long time since he'd seen them through evergreens that way—a long time, and a long jump through space, too. It reminded him of the way he used to stare longingly up at them when he was a kid, dreaming of the day when he'd be old enough to go out there. Maybe that was what was getting him about this planet, its likeness to home. Maybe that was why whenever he looked at the natives he got the feeling that he was way back in time, instead of here on a new world where people seemed like people and yet weren't, really. Back in time . . . that faint, yellowish star over the tall fir tree, that was his own sun, home. The light he was seeing had left there just about the time his ancestors had believed in dragons and all sorts of other crazy superstitions. Were *they* human, those distant men to whom the starlight he now saw had been sunlight? Of course, yet there had to be a dividing line somewhere.

He did not really take seriously the things he had told Dulard, of course, all those wild conjectures about extrasensory perception. He didn't believe in things like that any more than the average citizen did. He had only wanted to shake the guys up a bit, challenge their cool assumption that because the natives were different, they were inherently inferior. Of course they *were* inferior, technologically; but as individuals, were they any different from anyone else? Hadn't they the same feelings, maybe even the same kind of intelligence?

It was too bad there was no way to fool Dulard into thinking that the natives really were more powerful than they looked. He'd admitted, after all, that if there were any reason to fear them, he'd pull out fast. This was a colony, not a military base, and it was meant to be a safe colony. It was meant to be run by inexperienced home-steaders, once the Corps had completed the preliminary construction work. So if the local inhabitants were to show up someday with an impressive weapon of some kind, even if they never *used* it. . . .

Jarel stopped short. He mustn't start thinking along those lines. To speculate about the natives, even to argue with Dulard about them, was one thing; but to side with them against an Imperial colony would be treason. And anyway, there was no way he could manage it. In the first place, he didn't have access to any weapons other than those manufactured by the Empire itself. And in the sec- ond place, it would be quite obvious to Dulard that no superior weapon, even if it was one he'd never seen before, could have been developed by a nonmechanized society like this world's.

Dulard was right about one thing, Jarel realized; he shouldn't be in this kind of work. Not if seeing a prim- itive people overpowered bothered him this much, he shouldn't. Because the Empire did have to move forward, and technology was important, any way you looked at it. Technology was necessary to scientific advance, and sci- entific advance was good. Even with the natives, it was not so much their present culture that he valued, but what they might become. Expansion was necessary, too; with- out expansion, mankind would soon become decadent. If it were a choice, survival of one race or the other, even indirectly. . . .

But it was not a choice. There were plenty of planets

on which no sentient race had evolved. Less suitable planets for colonization, of course, but the Empire's technology could make them usable.

There were planets to spare. There were so many that they were not worth fighting over; the Empire did not fight, in fact. When a planet was occupied by a race advanced enough to resist, the Corps stayed clear of it, and apparently other spacefaring peoples did the same, for though occasionally aliens with starships had been encountered, the Empire had never found it necessary to defend its worlds.

How would *we* like it? he suddenly wondered. What if there were civilizations *above* us? Sure, we've never run into one, yet it could happen. Would a superior people think *us* too lowly to be worth preserving?

Well, Jarel sighed, there was no use losing so much sleep over it. Nothing he could do would make any difference. The natives' interests were going to be sacrificed whether he liked it or not, and from the prospective colonists' viewpoint it would happen in a good cause. He knew he shouldn't blame men like Dulard, who were doing the best job they knew how to do. But it would be nice, he thought, if there *were* such a thing as telepathy, just so he could give those poor captives in the barracks some idea of what it was all about.

Though the Enchanted Forest by daylight was not nearly so fearsome as by night, still it was a place of gloom, and no sunlight could penetrate its heart. The brothers were assailed by dread as they proceeded further and further into the wilderness of moss-shrouded trees. It was a fine thing to be told that there were no evil demons; but the creature that, to their certain knowledge, they must confront again had the *feel* of a demon and last time, he had won.

At length, when twilight was upon them, they judged that they must be near to the abode of the Starwatcher, yet still no enemy had challenged them. Then abruptly they came to a place where they could no longer see the path. It simply stopped, as if the trail they had been following led nowhere at all; they found themselves in the midst of an impenetrable grove that had been untouched for untold years, and the only way out was the way they had come in. The brothers looked around apprehensively, half-expecting to see that way, too, close behind them.

"I cannot understand it," muttered Terwyn. "We came straight through only this morning——"

"We must expect," Georyn told him, "to encounter things that we cannot understand. Undoubtedly we have been led to this place by design, and you know as well as I what is likely to befall us here." And indeed, even as he spoke this foreboding was borne out. The brothers found themselves faced by a threat more dire than any they had anticipated, for this time there were *two* dark figures!

The two stood side by side, silently, cutting off the only escape from the place. Their hoods covered their faces completely; no expression could be seen. The thought of one of them was as overpowering as before: *You must give me the cups!* But though the other communicated nothing, the menace of his presence was all the stronger for it; the brothers sensed some great, immeasurable strength there that was only awaiting the proper moment to assail them.

Do not attempt to resist me! came the dark command. *Until now I have been merciful and have not punished you for your defiance. But it will not be so if you refuse me for a third time! If I must take the cups by force, you will suffer for it.*

Both Georyn and Terwyn knew full well that although they were being tested, there might in truth be a dreadful penalty for failure. The Lady had, after all, given them clear warning that it was not a game. A means of defense against the fell magic had been provided them, but, Georyn thought, they had as yet no real idea as to the use of that means. For the Enchantress had mentioned a need for control over and above that which they had exerted when they repeated the charm under her guidance, and as to the nature of that control she had offered no clue.

Yet he was sure that she had meant him to succeed in this, *wanted* him to succeed. So there was a way. If simply saying the magic words was not enough—and she had said that it was not—then the other thing would surely come to him, if he looked for it and did not lose courage.

You have ten seconds, Georyn! After that, I will take the cup. Do not be foolish; do not seal your own doom! The Enchantress cannot help you now.

"You cannot have the cup," said Georyn, aloud. And, holding his hands before him, he began to say the words of the charm in a firm tone.

But still, inexorably, the cup was drawn from his fingers; more slowly than with the sword or the globe but all too surely, it was being taken from him after all! Desperately Georyn raised his voice, but while continuing to recite the spell he was thinking, "I *must* stop it! I must, for if I fail now she will no longer befriend me. She will teach me nothing further, and worse, I may never see her again." For it was this, even more than his antagonist's vengeance, that he truly feared. "Oh, Lady," he cried silently, "what is it that is asked of me? Where must I search for the answer?"

Then even as hope was fading, it was as if there had indeed been an answer, though not from her. For Georyn found his mind filled with a glowing presence that was unlike anything he had ever felt or imagined. There were no soundless words such as had come to him from his assailant and, once, from the Enchantress herself; but somehow, from outside, had come knowledge. He could not interpret it; he could not put it into words of his own; but suddenly he *knew* how to control the spell. It was an indescribable thing, a thing like knowing how to lift one's arm, which, if one had not been born knowing, would surely be difficult to learn. Yet this could be learned, he was learning, and he was aware, dimly, that the ability to accept such teaching depended upon the strength of one's desire.

Exultantly, he fixed his eyes upon the cup, and for an instant it wavered, so that if it had contained water, some would have sloshed over its rim. And then it froze! It hung motionless in the air before him, as it had under the control of the Enchantress; and Georyn knew that before, even while he spoke the charm himself, it had been under her control; but now he was holding it by his own will. He was master of the spell now, and the command of the weird enemy could have no effect upon him.

That command had, rather, been turned upon Terwyn; the other cup was now being pulled toward the cloaked figures. Terwyn, his face contorted with helpless rage, repeated the words of the charm in a determined voice; but it was ineffective. Since Georyn's mind was totally occupied with its strange new task, he could give his brother no aid; instinctively he knew that to relax his concentration for a single instant would be to break the spell. And in the end no aid was needed, for all at once Terwyn's face took on a look of wonder as he too received the secret, knowing no more than did Georyn whence it had come.

Then joyfully did both brothers step forward to reclaim the cups; and they felt a great relief, like a rest after some arduous labor, as they took those cups into their hands. But to their dismay the cloaked figures did not vanish into the forest; instead they advanced threateningly.

"If they want a fight," cried Terwyn, "they shall have it, and I for one shall rejoice in the chance! We shall see who is to pay for resistance, now that we are no longer subject to their magic!"

Georyn agreed heartily. Unarmed though he was, he was not in the mood to fear a fight; and if magic of some new variety was to be employed against him, he felt quite ready to face it. However, it did not come to that, for the two figures made no move to attack them. Rather, the one whose thought was unreadable threw back his hood revealing, to the brothers' astonishment, a familiar face. It was the Starwatcher himself!

For a long moment, Georyn stared at him; then finally he went forward with the cup in his hands and held it out, saying, "I see that in spite of my resolve to keep this from you, I must now give it over after all."

"That is not necessary," said the Starwatcher. "You and your brother may keep the cups, for you have proven yourselves fit holders of them. And besides, were you to give them to me, you would want some magical weapon in return."

"Yes, as you have promised us!" Terwyn said eagerly. "For have we not fulfilled our part of the bargain?"

"You have fulfilled it admirably," the Starwatcher told them. Then, impassively, he went on, "But though you have done so, there is no secret that I can now give you."

Terwyn began angrily, "You gave us your word!"

"Wait!" Thus silencing his brother, Georyn met the

Starwatcher's gaze. "There is not," he said with an awe even greater than that which he had felt in the presence of the Enchantress. "There is not, for we already have it!"

"The secret that will overcome the Dragon?" Terwyn exclaimed. "How can that be?"

Georyn turned to him. "The charm is not for cups alone," he said wonderingly. "It is a general thing, a thing that could be extended past imagination—"

The Starwatcher smiled. "Once again you step ahead of my anticipation, Georyn. You are too quick for me; I can keep nothing from you, not even to try your strength of purpose."

"You have been working with the Enchantress all along," Georyn declared. "She chose us to challenge the Dragon when she first appeared to us—even before, perhaps; it was she who arranged that we should be given these tasks."

"Although that is not the precise truth," answered the Starwatcher, "it is close enough, as close as you are likely to get. For we are, as you have guessed, in league; and you have been chosen to confront the Dragon. That, however, will be a more difficult task than you yet know, beside which the tests that you have undergone will be as nothing."

"With the Enchantress's help, and yours, surely we need have no fear!" Terwyn burst out. But Georyn told him: "If there were naught to be feared, why then would she have gone to such lengths to test our courage? For she is gentle and good and would not play with us merely for her own amusement. Is that not so, sir?"

"It is indeed so," the Starwatcher said firmly. "In her goodness, you may have absolute trust; and you may be sure that I would never have sent you to her, were I not sure that she may have equal trust in yours."

As he spoke thus, there was a rustle of leaves behind them, and Georyn turned to see the Enchantress herself standing on the path, wrapped in a glimmering cloak; and in her hands she carried the tall silver jug that she had used before. And the brothers went to her and held forth their cups, and she filled them, not with water this time, but with a rosy liquid that seemed like to wine. Yet it too was magical, for when they drank of it they felt an icy prickle that was unlike the tang of any wine they had ever tasted. At this, Georyn knew a fleeting fear, wondering whether Terwyn might not have been right after all, for who could say what sorts of potions a witch might have to offer?

But the Starwatcher took Terwyn's cup, and drank also, there being not enough vessels for all. And Georyn gave his own cup to the Lady, so that she too might drink. As her hand closed upon it, their eyes met; and in that instant all doubt passed, for he saw into her heart and knew, with a certainty akin to his mysterious knowledge of the spell, that the feeling that now rose within him stirred also in her. Then great was Georyn's happiness, and he was sure that whatever might betide in the end, he would ever rejoice in the wondrous chance that had come to him.

The Awakening

What is it, I wonder, that makes two people suddenly become important to each other? So important that everything else around them just fades away? People have been wondering that since the beginning of time, I guess; to the Younglings it must be even more puzzling than it is to us. Mutual attraction, I suppose they call it. Perhaps, but it's more than just physical attraction. It's telepathy—not the controlled kind, not silent conversation, but the deep and wordless variety. Two minds touch, that's all. Two minds that don't have anything in common in the way of background, and then all of a sudden they have everything in common, because they've found that the essential, *real* things are for them the same.

It was that way with Georyn and me. I suppose you'll find it hard to imagine what I could see in him, a Youngling. Well, at first I was simply touched—touched by the fact that he was facing such fantastic odds with a naive but determined bravery, and even more by the longing I sensed, the groping for something above and beyond the life to which he had been born. But then, somehow, our relationship changed. Perhaps it was in the moment our eyes met over the cup, the night of that final test. Georyn was in high spirits then; the exhilaration of his triumph was in him and his mind had command of powers he'd never dreamed existed. It met mine with strength, not mere hope. And after that there was a current between us that we couldn't have turned off if we had tried.

I guess it happens to you only a few times in your life. Maybe only once; maybe, for some people, never at all. To me it wasn't new; Evrek and I had it. We still do. Only with Evrek I was used to it. It's more overwhelming when it first begins, I suppose: this link, this subconscious sharing between your mind and another person's. Anyway, I was overwhelmed. I don't really remember what day I first dared, in my private thoughts, of course, to call it love.

Father brought the brothers back to the base camp with him for further training, and near my hut, under his direction, they built a small shelter of logs in which the three of them slept. Evrek didn't come; not only was he spending a good deal of time observing the colonists, but he still had to appear nightly in the guise of a menace. "Georyn and Terwyn have to stay afraid of me," he told me ruefully. "They've got to be given more skill, and we don't dare to let them just practice on their own."

"I suppose not," I agreed. "One failure could undo all we've accomplished."

There was an awkward pause. For Evrek too this was a painful subject; he did not enjoy the role he was required to play. But we both knew it was necessary, so he tried to treat it lightly. "By the way," he teased, "whatever possessed you to teach them the words to the Academy anthem for a magic spell?"

"I don't know. I suppose I could have taught them to

count from one to twenty or made up a bunch of non-
sense syllables; but since neither they nor the invaders
have ever heard our language, it can't possibly reveal anything. And they're bound to get it garbled."

"Georyn didn't have it garbled last night. It was all I
could do to keep a straight face when he started intoning
the words!"

"Well, you can't say they weren't appropriate ones."

"You're an incurable romantic, Elana. What if they
teach it to their descendants? The next field team through
here is going to get a shock!"

"So I'll put it in my report. What would *you* have
taught them?"

"Never mind!"

It was true enough that while the brothers no longer
needed to be as stirred up emotionally as they'd been for
the initial breakthrough, they still had to *feel* something in
order to get reliable results from the "spell." So we made
them continue to meet Evrek at night, in the "enchanted"
forest. And now, they were required to go separately, and
to wrest objects from Evrek's possession as well as to keep
him from getting what they themselves carried. This was
far harder on Evrek than on them. Of the three of us, he
alone was barred from meeting the Andrecians as friends;
he had to hide all sympathy, even in thought, and deliberately make them hate him. That's a difficult assignment,
certainly not the kind you normally draw on your first
field mission. Evrek carried it off, but he found it a pretty
miserable business.

Though Georyn and Terwyn didn't suffer in the
same way, it wasn't pleasant for them, either. They knew
we were staging the eerie encounters, of course, but they
were still unsophisticated enough to enter into the spirit
of the thing. Fear of the supernatural dies hard, and they

were more than half-convinced that only their "counter-spell" was keeping their adversary from wreaking dire vengeance upon them.

But if the nights were grim, the days were unexpectedly serene and shining. I shall always remember those days as a sort of bright glade amid the dark woods of our desperate venture. Whenever I think of Andrecia, I'll see in my mind the fresh greenness, the unspoiled beauty of its springtime, and I'll relive the hours Georyn and I spent beside the river, with the pale Andrecian sun streaming down through the trees, talking or simply sitting silent, content with the joy of each other's presence.

We both knew, of course, that there was no future in it. What's more, we were aware that for there to be anything more than friendship between us would be absolutely unthinkable. Georyn, for his part, treated me with a respect bordering on reverence; he never so much as touched my hand. More than once I found myself wishing that he didn't place me on quite such a high pedestal. Yet it was evident enough that although he took an avid interest in anything I said to him, conversation was not his only reason for seeking my company.

As for me, on one hand I was appalled at what I might be doing to him. What right have I, I kept thinking, to open a door through which he will never be allowed to walk? But on the other, I stopped looking ahead and just gave in to the happiness of our shared thought. People who love each other can no more keep from communicating than from breathing, particularly if they are accustomed to doing it on the telepathic level. Naturally, I had picked up some of the Andrecian language by this time and I often used it, but for us the spoken words were still more or less superficial.

I didn't see Evrek often, and I must admit that I didn't

devote a great deal of thought to him. Evrek and I had always taken each other for granted, I guess; ours was hardly the romantic sort of love, and because it was on such a different plane from the thing I felt for Georyn, I never thought about it in a comparative way. It never even struck me as strange that, worried as I was about Evrek's safety, I scarcely missed him from day to day, whereas if Georyn disappeared for an hour or two, I was lonely. I'm thankful now, of course, that Evrek was not there to see what was happening. I suppose he *would* have seen, and that would have been just awful, all the way around.

The thought of our mission was something I kept pushing into the furthest corner of my mind; and when that thought did intrude, it was fear for Evrek and for Georyn that disturbed me. I didn't anticipate any more rude awakenings for myself.

I was still determined to visit the local village. Father didn't want me to; he'd already said so once, and when I brought it up again he was more explicit. "I'd rather you didn't, Elana," he said. "It's not so much a matter of the physical danger as of the fact that you're not ready to understand all of what you might see there."

"But wouldn't I learn a lot? I mean, to *be* here and pass up the opportunity to study this planet's culture—"

"I'm afraid you'd learn some things that you're better off not knowing for the time being. Youngling worlds are unlike ours in more ways than one. There are certain aspects of human nature to which you haven't ever been exposed, Elana, aspects that our civilization has out-grown. A fully trained agent is prepared. You'll get some courses later on that will equip you to deal with what you're inevitably going to run into; but you won't enjoy them. Don't rush that sort of awareness on a mission that doesn't demand it."

Father is an awfully good psychologist, and ordinarily he is expert in managing people, so it's hard to believe that he failed to foresee how I'd react. But, of course, after that kind of buildup, I was more anxious to see the village than ever, as who wouldn't be? Perhaps underneath he did feel that the time had come for me to learn the less palatable facts of Youngling life and was trying to give me fair warning, but somehow I don't think so. I think it's more likely that it was a matter of principle. Father would never order anybody to shy away from reality; he believes too strongly that that's an area in which a person must proceed at his own risk.

I proceeded. And I'm not sorry, for Georyn and I were the closer for it; how could we have truly known each other, had we not found that there were some things about which he was wiser than I? Georyn did not live in a fairy-tale world, and it was just as well that I found it out before I started wondering whether the evolution of Younglings might not be a goal of questionable merit.

So for a time the brothers dwelt with the Starwatcher, nearby to the hut of the Enchantress; and during that time they were more than once required to face fell sorcery, alone and in darkness, and were thus taught much concerning the uses of the magic spell. But although the nights were often filled with dread, Georyn's heart was joyful, for the Enchantress welcomed his company and she did indeed open a door to wisdom beyond his most fantastic dreams.

Those spring days were golden ones; one sunlit morning followed another and though, toward nightfall, clouds often towered over the Enchanted Forest, there was no rain. It did not seem like a world that could contain a fearful Dragon. And in his secret heart, Georyn began to hope that the Dragon had already been slain by someone else, for he had no longer any need to seek a reward from the King. The wisdom of the King and his councillors he now saw as a pallid thing beside that which he had been shown.

Terwyn, however, was impatient to be off. "I am sure that we can overcome the monster with the magic powers we now have!" he insisted. "Why must we waste further time here, while others may even now be trying to claim the glory and the reward?" But Georyn said nothing, for each day that they tarried seemed to him a blessing beyond price.

The Starwatcher often disappeared into the forest on business of his own, of which he told them nothing. As he departed one morning, he mentioned that someone must go into the village that day to buy food; and when Georyn offered to do so, the Starwatcher gave him money and instructed him as to what was to be bought with it. But even as Georyn set forth, the Enchantress came to him, saying: "I have never seen the village, for though I should very much like to, I do not know the way there. Will you not take me with you?"

And Georyn told her, "Lady, I will take you anywhere you desire to go; you have but to name it." So the two of them set out together. The day was very bright, and as they came to the road beyond the meadow, Georyn began to sing. Then the Lady too took up the tune, but the words were strange to her—although by now she often spoke in his language as well as to his mind—so she soon broke off in merriment; and Georyn thought that one would surely think her mortal after all, to hear her laugh.

When they were nearing the village, the Enchantress said, "These garments of mine must not be seen, for I do not wish to be known for what I am. If I am to enter the village with you, you must get me a cloak such as the common people wear; and I will give you silver to pay for it." So they thought for her to hide within the wood while Georyn went to fetch the cloak; but before long they came upon a cottage, and thinking that the folk who dwelt there might be willing enough to trade a cloak for silver, Georyn went to the door and knocked upon it.

There was at first no answer, but then a thin child peeked out, and in answer to Georyn's question said: "We have no cloak, nor even any food, for our mother is dying and our father has been taken away by the King's soldiers." So Georyn entered and saw that the woman was indeed sick unto death, and there were other children who were in no better case; but when he told the Enchantress of this, she would scarce believe him.

"If she is so sick, Georyn, why does no one help her?"

"What help is there for such sickness? People are in fear of contagion, no doubt; and tomorrow she will be dead whether anyone shows her kindness or not."

"And the children, too?" she asked, horrified.

"Perhaps; but I think the children are weak only from hunger."

"Hunger! Has she been unable to cook for them, then? Why, we must stay and fix them some food, Georyn."

He hesitated. "I do not question your magical powers, Lady. If you can obtain food for these people, by all means let us do so."

"It is not a matter of magic, but of ordinary common sense! There must be *some* food in the cottage."

"That I very much doubt. One might hide food, but one would not then let one's sons die from the lack of it."

"Die—from *starvation*? You cannot mean that! Who in the village is responsible for feeding these people if they have no money?"

Frowning, Georyn said, "Now you jest with me, Lady."

She stared at him. "You mean that there is no one?"

"How should there be? Few there are who have any food to spare, and those few have little concern for the likes of these folk."

"Perhaps—perhaps that is true, in this world," she said slowly. "But then surely we could kill some game in the wood. Have they a bow, Georyn, that you could use?"

"They have not, nor have I any liking for such a risk; though if you asked it of me, I would dare it, Lady."

"Dare? To kill a poor defenseless deer? I have not much liking for it either; but if people are in need of food, it cannot be helped. Did these children's father never think of that?"

"Ah yes, he thought of it. That, in fact, is why he was taken to the dungeons of the King; for as you surely know, the game of this wood belongs to the King's huntsmen."

"Georyn, that is a terrible thing!"

"Many believe it so, but few would speak boldly of their thought."

"Well," she said at length, "I would give these folk my silver; but it would seem more to the purpose that we should bring them food on our way back. So let us continue now."

Thereupon they went ahead until they came to another cottage, where Georyn was able to obtain a cloak for the Enchantress. Though the day was warm, she put it on, hiding her own silvery garb, and she pulled its hood over her dark hair; and so disguised she went on into the village.

Once there, the Enchantress gazed around her as if she had never seen any village before. But much of what she saw she did not like, for alas, the people of the cottage were not the only sick and hungry folk in the land.

Georyn bought all the food that he and the Lady could carry; and at the end they had no money left, for the Enchantress gave the last of it to a beggar. This beggar had no hands, and she demanded to know how he had lost them. But when Georyn told her, her eyes widened in unbelieving horror; and thenceforth she was very quiet.

When they had returned to the cottage of the sick woman, the Lady herself insisted upon entering; but before long even she was convinced that there was little she could do save to give food to the children. In this she was bountiful, and would in fact have given it all to them, had Georyn not convinced her that the Starwatcher would be ill pleased if he came back empty-handed.

No more did they sing as they trudged back along the dusty road in the fading afternoon, for the Enchantress was sad and silent; and Georyn too was troubled. It had not hitherto occurred to him that the Lady's magic power could be insufficient to fulfill her every wish, and he was much distressed at the discovery. It was not right that *she* should be unhappy! "No one could have saved the woman," he said awkwardly, thinking to comfort her. "Surely, she was beyond the reach of any imaginable power. It is grievous indeed, but must we not accept such things?"

"But there are charms and potions that can cure all ill-nesses," the Lady cried bitterly, "though alas, I have them not. Oh, Georyn, I am so limited! I am not what you think me to be! I have not all the powers that are known, and many that I do have, I may not use." She turned her face to him, and it was wet with tears.

Georyn put his hand upon her arm. "Lady, do you weep?" he asked incredulously. "I did not think that the heart of an enchantress could be so moved."

She pulled away, and he knew that though she was

angry, it was not because he had dared to touch her. "Am I made of stone that I should see such things and shed no tears for them?" she demanded. "You do me injustice, Georyn, if you think my heart less than human!"

Going to her, he put his arm around her shoulders, and this time she did not draw back. Georyn led her to a large flat stone by the side of the road and they sat upon it, under a wide-spreading shade tree. "It is the way of things," he said slowly. "Men and women are born to hunger and sickness and all manner of suffering; and the plight of those whom you have seen today is as nothing to that of some upon whom the wrath of the King has fallen. But surely you, with all your wisdom, know this? Or perhaps," he reflected, "perhaps it is not so with enchanted folk."

"It is different," she said sorrowfully. "I did *not* know! I was told often that the world of your people was different from my own, but that it should be like *this*! It is unbearable, Georyn! How do men live in such a world?"

He paused, and then said quietly, "We live as anyone does: by hope; for what other way is there? And though of what we hope for, I have never been sure, I now think that perhaps it is that the world itself should be like the enchanted realm one day."

And at that, her face brightened, and she told him: "It *will* be! For that too is the way of things, and we who wear the Emblem work toward that end. Only——" She sighed, and went on, "Only it will not come in your time, Georyn."

"I should be a child indeed if I thought that it would," he said to her. "For it will be a very great change!" There was a silence, while Georyn brought himself to raise an issue that had been troubling him for some days. "You are not of this world, Lady," he said finally, and it was not a question, but a statement.

"No, Georyn, I am not," the Lady replied; and it almost seemed that despite her grief, she was sorry that she was not; but surely this must have been his own wishful thinking, for how could such a thing be? How could one who had known the enchanted realm care aught for the world of men?

"Is it permitted for me to ask why you are here, then?" Georyn ventured.

She nodded. "I am here to aid in the defeat of the Dragon, and for that purpose only; and I must tell you, Georyn, that once the purpose has been fulfilled, I cannot remain."

"Must the fair pass away with the ill, then?"

"I shall not 'pass away'; I shall return to my own world, where there are many wonders beyond your imagination."

"I am glad of that for your sake, Lady; but it seems to me that in this quest I am working to my own ill end, if my success is to mean your departure." Georyn turned away from her and added softly, "I am not so sure that I want to slay the Dragon, now."

The Enchantress reached over and took his hand. "Georyn," she said seriously, "the Dragon is to this world a very great evil, far greater than you know. Though the full reach of this evil is past your understanding, I can tell you this: if it is not challenged here and stopped, there may well come a day when the entire world is consumed by it! On that day there will be no more free men of your people, if indeed there are any of your people left at all."

"Then certainly we must stop it, whatsoever the cost. But who are Terwyn and I, Lady, to challenge such a threat as that? We are only a poor woodcutter's sons."

"You are fit as no one else is, for this task is such that it can be accomplished only by one of your people, one who can wield the powers of enchantment and be unafraid."

"I would never be afraid of *your* enchantments!" he said, smiling.

"That is because you know little of them, then. They are perilous, Georyn; even to you, they are perilous. But there is no other way. Though I can help you, I cannot myself do what must be done. Oh, Georyn, if I could I would do it, and spare you the ordeal you must face! But the Emblem has no direct power against the Dragon; it can only aid."

"To be selected for such aid," said Georyn, "is surely a very great honor; and I shall try to be worthy of it. But I shall not look forward to the hour of my triumph!" And with those words he rose, and they went on their way again.

Why is it, I wonder, that you can accept the idea of deliberate killing, such as I had seen the Imperials perform, as an unavoidable Youngling barbarism; and you can even know the bare facts about Youngling wars in which thousands or even millions of people have been intentionally slaughtered; yet still, you are horribly shocked by your introduction to lesser but more revolting evils? Nothing that I had ever heard or read had prepared me for the sort of thing I saw in that Andrecian village. Suffering of that type is so completely alien to our society that I just couldn't believe, at first, that among Younglings it is natural and widespread.

I don't think I was any more naive than the average Federation citizen. Who other than a specialist in psychology, history, or ancient literature would have any occasion to come into contact with that kind of knowledge? Of course, I would have had to find out about such things sooner or later. All agents do. At the Academy, as Father had told me, you are thoroughly educated as to what to expect and how to deal with it. It is not a First Phase course.

Younglings, I suppose, grow up knowing about hunger and disease and brutality. They can't even visualize a society from which these are absent. Initially, it hurt me to find that Georyn could accept such conditions so calmly; I had thought him more sensitive than that. It was a long time before I recognized his attitude as the normal and essential insulation for living as a Youngling.

I have no such insulation. The image of that handless beggar haunts me still. And yet I had been lucky. I had visited a quiet country village on one of its peaceful days; I had not seen the King's justice perpetrated in the public square, which I am told is a fairly common occurrence.

I won't record all of what Father said to me the night I came back from my unauthorized excursion. He didn't scold me, nor did he once say anything that smacked of "I told you so." Rather, he encouraged me to talk about what I'd seen, and tried to show me how it fit into the known scheme of things. He was very honest, yet at the same time very sympathetic; and though he presented a picture of Youngling cultures that I had never dreamed existed even in my worst nightmares, he did manage to help me come to terms with it.

We sat beside our campfire until long after midnight. Finally, we got down to the problem that was bothering me most of all. "Why doesn't the Service *do* something?" I demanded indignantly. "At least in some cases we could help! Why don't we bring in food and medical supplies, for example, and—"

"That would be a direct violation of policy, Elana. It

would be flagrant interference in the internal affairs of Youngling worlds."

"Father," I said hesitantly, "haven't you ever questioned this policy? I mean, I know we're sworn not to, but——"

"That's a misinterpretation of the Oath!" he exclaimed. "We are sworn to carry out Federation policy, yes, just as a policeman is bound to uphold the law; but that doesn't mean we suspend our own ethical judgment. At times, we *must* question, if we are to be human beings and not robots. This, apparently, is one of those times for you, Elana. All right, don't back away from it."

Having grown up with the Service, I was accustomed to assuming it could do no wrong; that he should so coolly challenge me to examine that assumption was something of a jolt. Yet it was true enough that I now had some doubts that just couldn't be pushed aside. "I——I can't believe it's moral, for the Federation to stand by, having the power to relieve suffering and not using it," I said slowly.

Father smiled, though his voice was grave. "You aren't the first person to react in this way, you know. In fact if you didn't, I'd be worried; I'd be afraid you were too callous to make a good agent."

"If you're suggesting that I'll come around, because everyone else has——"

"No, I'm not suggesting that. I do believe the weight of the evidence is on the side of the policy as it stands; but if I didn't, I wouldn't be here, so in that sense I'm prejudiced."

"Let's hear some of this evidence," I said skeptically.

"I can summarize it. You probably won't accept it, though, until you've had a chance to really study the subject; and that's not going to happen overnight." He paused, deciding how best to make his point. "Do you know why disclosure is harmful?"

"Yes. At least I guess I do. If Younglings knew how far

behind they were, they'd start questioning their own worth, their place in the universe; they might get so discouraged they'd simply give up. Or even if they didn't, they would skip steps in their development, and they'd be hurt because they'd be exposed to knowledge they didn't fully understand. At best their civilizations would become poor copies of ours, instead of keeping their uniqueness."

"Those are the basic factors. It's vastly more complicated, of course."

"But it doesn't explain why we can't devise some way to correct obviously unnecessary evils without revealing ourselves," I protested. "How would that be any different from what we're already doing?"

"There's an essential difference. We are permitted to step in only when nothing else can prevent extinction of the Youngling race; and what's more, protecting Youngling civilizations from each other is not at all the same as attempting to protect them from themselves. But Elana, that's beside the point. The real issue here is the whole concept of 'obviously unnecessary evils.' Who are you to say that human suffering is unnecessary?"

Hotly I asked, "Are you telling me that it *is* necessary? Why?"

"Because people advance only through solving problems; and if there were no problems to solve, no one would get very far."

"But *why* should it be like that?"

"If I knew," Father said ruefully, "I would be a long way ahead of any philosopher I've ever heard of. It's like asking *why* the stimulus of fear is needed to enable Georyn to release the full powers of his mind. You can't answer that directly; all you can do is look at results."

"How do we know what the results would be if we don't ever try to help?"

"From history," he told me. "The existence of these evils is not a chance aberration! The same patterns have shown up on every world that has ever been studied; any attempt to change those patterns—and there were some, in the early days of the Federation—has invariably led not to good, but to an even worse evil: the stagnation and eventual downfall of the civilization involved. It's been learned the hard way that there is a natural progression that can't be tampered with."

He stared thoughtfully into the embers for a moment, then went on, "To Younglings, who don't see the whole picture, it doesn't always look as if there is very much progress involved, but there is. The worlds of the Imperials, for example, have no untreated disease, no beggars, no barbaric punishments. And in time, Elana, they'll outgrow the other social evils, too—such as the problem of the individual citizen being pretty much under the thumb of the Imperial government. Not easily, however, and not without pain . . . it just doesn't happen that way."

"But look," I said, "progress involves people helping each other. For instance, the well-off nations of a world helping the disadvantaged ones. You're not arguing against that, are you?"

"Of course not. But the members of their own species must do it; we can't do it for them."

"Couldn't we sort of speed up the process, though?" I persisted.

"No! You can't give evolution, any more than you can give personal maturity. Could you take a small child and teach him to function as an adult?"

"I suppose not. If you tried, you'd only end up making him neurotic. Yet neither would you let a child grow up without any guidance."

"The cases aren't really parallel," Father explained.

"That's the big danger in drawing an analogy between an individual human being and a planetary civilization; it's apt in some respects, but not in all. Children aren't born independent. And independence is the one thing a maturing species *must* have, not only to hold its own, but to make its eventual contribution toward the development of the Federation itself. We cannot guide toward an end that we can't see."

Well, as he'd warned me, there's a great deal more to it than can be explained in one night's discussion. I still don't fully understand; and I don't expect to, without doing a lot of reading, because it's just about the knottiest problem there is. Perhaps I'll decide, in the end, that I do disagree; honest dissent is respected by the Service and there are channels for expressing it, though the use of them is not a thing to be undertaken lightly.

But there was one more idea I felt I must bring up. "I don't see how it could do any harm," I declared, "for us to—to help a few specific people, people who are ahead of their own time, maybe . . . people who *deserve* it. . . . "

"No harm, to make life easier for the best, the most deserving? Now you're really on shaky ground, Elana! It would be the surest way to mess up the whole process. How do you think a world advances, if not through the efforts of those very people? To take away any of their incentive by artificial means would be a fatal mistake. Besides, the Service doesn't interfere in the lives of individuals as such. We are not gods; we haven't the right even to think of it!"

We are interfering in Georyn's, I thought bitterly. Though not, of course, for his sake. . . . In a low voice I said, "But it's so hard on a person who happens to be born into the wrong age!"

Father put his arm around me. "Of course," he said

quietly. "It always has been, Elana. That's just the way things are."

It is the way of things, I reflected. That was what Georyn had said, too. And yet to him the thought of an enchanted realm where it was *not* the way, even a realm that he could never enter, had seemed less a frustration than a comfort.

Late that night Georyn left his bed and walked out into the meadow alone, and he looked up at the stars as he had done often in the past; but now as he gazed at them he thought of the enchanted realm, for the Lady had told him that it lay somewhere out beyond them. And he tried to imagine a day when *she* would be up there, beyond that black curtain, forever beyond the reach of his thought; and it seemed too hard a thing that he should be required to hasten the day. But he had known from the beginning, after all, that the price of wisdom would be high; and now there was this other thing, the business of a challenge to some mysterious, far-reaching evil, for which she herself had chosen him. So in the morning he went to his brother and said: "I believe the time has come, Terwyn, for us to be on our way; the Dragon will not wait forever."

"I have believed that for some time!" exclaimed Terwyn. "And I am very glad to see that you have finally come around to it. But I knew, of course, that you could not go around with your head in the clouds for much longer, unless you were in truth bewitched."

But when the brothers told the Starwatcher of their intent to set out for the place of the Dragon, he said to them, "The time has indeed come, and the Dragon must be confronted. But there is a condition of which I have not yet told you, and that is that the man who attempts this thing must go alone. One of you must stay behind, so that should the other fail, there will remain a chance that the Dragon can be defeated; and you must decide between yourselves who is to go and who is to stay."

At this, Georyn felt a surge of joy, for he knew that Terwyn would be quick to volunteer; but his face burned with shame at such a feeling and he said firmly, "I will go."

"You will not!" cried Terwyn angrily. "For I am the elder, and it is my right; though I would do much for you, brother, I will not give you my chance at this. I would have been off days ago, had I but known that we could not travel together in any case."

And Georyn, seeing that Terwyn was truly anxious to win the King's reward, conceded to his brother's wish; and his own happiness at this turn of events he hid even from himself.

So in the hour of the next dawn the brothers stood before the Enchantress, and she returned to Terwyn the sword that had been taken from him during his first meeting with the dark wizard; and they did not ask how she had obtained it. And she said to him: "You are going now upon a venture that is fraught with more difficulties than you know, but you must not be afraid! There is a way to victory, although that way is not so simple as you have hitherto believed."

Then she told him more of the hideous bewitched folk who guarded the Dragon, and of how he would be surrounded by them and turned to stone, and how he must then invoke the magic charm to draw their weapons from their hands. "And," she continued, "if there be aught else that you can move by means of the charm, you must do so; for the more magic you show the Dragon's servants, the more they will fear you, and they may in time release you from their spell. But under no circumstances should you use your sword against them."

"As to the Dragon itself," Terwyn inquired, "will you not tell me how best to strike?"

The Lady turned aside and softly answered, "I cannot tell you that, Terwyn. I can only say that you must expect the problems to be very different from anything you have imagined." Then she met his eyes once more, saying: "Whatever may betide, you must be of good hope and trust that in the end the Dragon *can* be conquered, however invulnerable a monster it may seem to you."

"I will trust in that," Terwyn promised, "for I know that your magic will not betray me."

With a troubled frown the Enchantress said: "It will not, but I must warn you that your danger will be real; it is possible that you will meet with some misfortune from which that magic is powerless to save you." She paused, and since Terwyn did not acknowledge the warning she added sadly, "I hope that the reward will prove worthy of the risk!"

"It is not only a matter of the reward," Terwyn replied resolutely. And thereupon he took leave of them; and Georyn clasped the Lady's hand and smiled, for he did not doubt that his brother would be well guarded by her enchantment. Then as they stood watching, the sun rose into a fair sky, shedding a radiance upon the world to gladden their hearts; and Terwyn went alone into the dense shadow of the Enchanted Forest.

This man was different from the rest of his people, Jarel thought. He didn't act as scared as the others. Oh, you could tell that he *was* scared, but he put on a better front than most. He strode into camp boldly, all alone, and walked directly toward the rockchewer, the mere sight of which petrified the average native. Did he too think it was a dragon? Jarel wondered. He almost appeared to be challenging it.

Jarel, Kevan, and another man—one who was still wearing a pressure suit and helmet—approached the native; reluctantly, Jarel stunned him, while the others grasped his arms. This whole business of taking innocent men (he couldn't help thinking of them as "men") into custody was still repugnant to Jarel, and it was clearly beyond the scope of his job as a medical officer. But Dulard had ordered it, and Jarel told himself that he was showing the prisoners more kindness than someone else might. This case was particularly disquieting, though. He admired courage and did not look forward to seeing it eroded, as it inevitably must be, by the psychological impact of the stunning.

The continued use of stunners was Jarel's pet gripe, for it was hardly conducive to a friendly relationship between captive and guard. He realized that very likely he was suffering from this more than the natives, who didn't want to be friends in any event. Still, sometimes he thought that if a man like Kevan ever had a taste of it himself, he'd be less inclined to call it a humane method of controlling prisoners. The possibilities of this idea would have been quite tempting, were it not that the use of a stunner on an Imperial citizen was classed as an assault—a form of antisocial behavior that was not treated lightly.

Once the native's arms had been securely gripped, Jarel freed him from paralysis; they could carry him to the barracks, but it was easier to let him walk, and, Jarel believed, less degrading. The poor guy was in no position to give them any trouble, certainly. As they started across the clearing, however, Jarel inexplicably dropped his stunner. It was as if it had been torn from his grasp, almost. Just as he reached for it, Kevan's stunner too fell to the ground, fell *slowly,* as if under low gravity, or so it seemed. The native was speaking words that did not have the ring of the local language, and his eyes, Jarel noted, were wild with a desperation more intense than the panic of a timid man.

"What the——!" Kevan muttered, bending to retrieve the weapon. At that moment the native wrenched free from the third man's grasp and struck out fiercely with the sword that no one had yet bothered to take from him. The sword made no impression on the tough plastic of the man's pressure suit, but enough harm had already been done. Kevan acted without hesitation. The stunner was still on the ground, but there was another weapon at his belt that he had no scruples about using. The native did not feel his death; he was vaporized instantly.

Jarel, blinded by the brilliance of the flash, yelled furiously, "You fool! What did you do that for? He wasn't any danger to us! I'd have stunned him again in a minute——"

Kevan laughed. "Stick to your own field, medic. Don't tell *me* how to run the war."

"I wasn't aware," Jarel said coldly, "that we were fighting a war."

"Well, we are! You starry-eyed idealists make me sick! We're on a hostile planet here! We've got to fight for every inch of ground we take, and if we ever let our guard down, even once, we'll pay sooner or later. There are women in this colony—women and kids, too—do you want some crazy savage to come charging in here with a sword when *they're* around? No matter what official policy says, a world's not tamed until we've got rid of every last native that can't be domesticated, and anyone who says different is kidding himself. Sure there's a war. That's what colonization is."

Perhaps so, Jarel realized. Wasn't that the name used

whenever men were free to kill other men and walk off without so much as a second glance from anyone? Did the equality of the match really have anything to do with it?

Blinking, the purple afterimage of the blast still before his eyes, he stared at the spot where the needless tragedy had occurred, and it was as if all the goals he had once believed in had been abruptly vaporized, too. It was not fair to put all the blame on Kevan, he thought suddenly, for there was logic to Kevan's argument. Sure, Kevan had pulled the trigger in this instance; but wasn't the guilt shared by the whole Corps, the whole Empire even? Wasn't he, Jarel, guilty too, at least as guilty as the billions of other Imperial citizens whose tax money was supporting the takeover of alien worlds?

We ourselves are no better than savages, he said to himself bitterly. We are on no higher a level than the natives, and we never will be; progress is a myth! If there *are* superior peoples in the universe, it is pure luck—good or bad, depending on how you look at it—that they have never found us. For if they ever do, they will surely consider the Empire the worst disease ever to threaten the galaxy and will deal with us accordingly.

Evrek observed the whole thing from the cover of the woods, but he could not contact us until some hours later; he never took a communicator anywhere near the invaders' camp for fear of being caught with it. His report was brief and to the point, but I could tell that he was struggling hard to seem impassive. Evrek is like that. He doesn't want to let his feelings show.

My own feelings were unconcealable. Terwyn was dead—Terwyn, whom I had watched go with no greater emotion than my relief that his brother was not with him!

I had been half-expecting disaster . . . but not really. Coming as it did on top of my turmoil over the other discussion, it was almost more than I could bear.

Father didn't try to evade the issue. "This is hard to take," he said frankly. "Very hard; yet we can't let it throw us, any more than we gave in to our grief for Ilura."

"But I—I sent him to his death!" I whispered. "He *trusted* me, and because of that he was killed."

"He knew his danger and went to it of his own free will," Father reminded me. "If we had never come here, he might very well have tried to kill the 'dragon' on his own."

"Maybe so," I protested. "But still—"

We were in the hut; he led me over to a bench and we sat down. "I know," he said quietly. "But still, you were responsible. Elana, I've known this moment was coming, as it does to every agent; but I hoped it wouldn't come so soon. No, don't turn away," he went on, seeing how I shrank from consolation. "Now that it has come, you must face it. It's not pleasant, but it's something we all have to go through."

"Are you telling me I'll learn not to mind?" I demanded fiercely.

"Certainly not. If you ever did, I would have you back in that starship within the hour! You will become reconciled, but never insensitive. That's the burden we accept when we take the Oath."

I bent my head. "Perhaps I wasn't ready after all," I said in a low voice.

"Perhaps," he said, "but I think you were. Remember that if this were easy for you, you would never have been sworn at all."

"What do you mean?" I asked, startled out of my determination not to accept any sort of comfort.

"I mean that it's precisely because you find this painful

that you were chosen for it; anyone who didn't would have been screened out by the Academy entrance tests. A person to whom the lives of individuals were unimportant would not be allowed to set foot on a Youngling world."

That made sense, I realized. Someone who didn't care what happened to these people would be a dangerous man to have around, whether his mission succeeded or not. But how could you care and still do what had to be done? *Oh, Father, what's the answer?* I cried silently.

There isn't one! Not the sort you're looking for!

I clung to him. "Evrek was right. The Oath *is* too demanding."

"Elana," he said gently, "it's not. It's meant to help."

"Maybe, if forcing me to ignore my conscience is helpful."

"The life of a man you've seen and talked to is a real, immediate thing," Father said slowly, "against which the welfare of his people hundreds or thousands of years from now can be only an abstraction. The Oath's designed to make this remote, abstract goal more concrete—to give you an emotional handle on the thing you must balance against your natural and necessary reluctance to be responsible for a man's death."

"But how can I be sure I've got them balanced right— in a given case, I mean?"

"You can't. But when you swear to act in the way that will, in your best judgment, be in the best interests of the world with which you are dealing, you make your decision once and for all. You don't have to weigh the goals each time, only the odds."

"Is that what you meant," I asked, "when you told Evrek that I must be sworn for my own protection?"

"Yes. I would not have placed anyone in this position without it, least of all my own daughter."

I protested unhappily, "But isn't that just glossing it over? Playing with words, to make ourselves seem noble? I mean, making a ritual out of it doesn't change the real questions!"

"That's true," Father admitted, "and we'd be very shallow if we thought otherwise. Yet having made the choice in all honesty, we've got to stand by it, for if we didn't, we couldn't function at all."

He stood up and paced to the door of the hut; the sunlight streamed in, and with his back to it I couldn't see his face.

Brusquely, he went on, "Elana, I'm not going to soften this for you. If you don't believe in the essential rightness of what we're doing, you shouldn't be here. Because this case is a very mild instance of the kind of thing to which you may eventually be exposed. You had Terwyn's full consent, and it's not always so."

"Full consent?" I said bitterly. "He wasn't even aware of the issues!"

"He was very much aware of the only one that counts: he was endangering himself in pursuit of a high goal. Give credit where credit's due, Elana! If you consider this cause worth sacrificing for, don't you suppose he did, too? Don't demean his act of courage by seeing him as a mere puppet, with you holding the strings. Respect it for what it was! If you do less you are patronizing, placing yourself on a plane above him; and Youngling though he was, you were *not* above him in the human sense."

What could I say? I had been warned, certainly, that I would be hurt. Yet you just don't take it in, beforehand! Choking back hot tears, I looked down at the Emblem, and for the first time the sight of it didn't give me any sense of elation at all. *Above all other considerations . . .* but I hadn't thought in terms of *these* considerations. Perhaps

I shouldn't be on a Youngling planet! Perhaps taking the Oath had been a terrible mistake. But I had done it, and tomorrow it would be Georyn whom I would have to send into a danger that had now been proven to be even greater than we had guessed.

The Stone

It would be nice to be able to say that once you become an agent, you are always very dignified and mature; but you are not. At least I'm not. The day Terwyn was killed I stayed in my hut most of the afternoon, and I cried harder than I had for years. Agents can, of course, get into much worse situations, situations involving innocent bystanders instead of enthusiastic volunteers. But my eyes had been opened to the possibilities. Besides, there was the prospect of Georyn's venture; and for me, that was a matter of feelings more personal than those involved in my mourning for Terwyn.

When I finally went outside, I saw that the sky had clouded over completely for the first time since we had been on Andrecia; the wind was from the east, and it carried the scent of rain. I wrapped my cloak around me and went to look for Georyn, but he was nowhere in sight. Father, however, came immediately to meet me. He took my arm, and we walked slowly along the path by the river, for a time not saying anything, although I could see he had something on his mind.

Then Father began, "I've been giving some serious thought to where we stand. All along, the worst part has been the fact that I couldn't predict how our Andrecians would react to the problems they'd run into. Now, I've been able to analyze the reasons why Terwyn failed."

"I don't want to talk about it anymore," I told him.

"Elana," he insisted, "we *must* talk about it if we are to see to it that Georyn isn't defeated by the same things." When I didn't answer he went on, "Before Terwyn panicked and used his sword, he tried the 'charm' twice; both times it was a failure. There were three main reasons, I think. First, in spite of the fact that we warned him that he would be paralyzed by the Imperials' stunners, the actual shock of it was too much for him. Second, the sight of so many things utterly alien to his past experience unnerved him; the colonists have all kinds of stuff besides their land-clearing machine, and Terwyn had never seen any products of a mechanized technology before. And finally, he was so busy watching the 'dragon,' not to mention the Imperials themselves, that he couldn't turn the force of his mind to psychokinesis."

"Those sound like three good reasons for calling the whole thing off," I said.

"In the usual case that might be true," Father said. "But with Georyn, I think we can overcome those obstacles. I've figured out a way to prepare him for them. Originally I wouldn't have considered anything of this nature, because the average Youngling wouldn't adapt quickly enough; but Georyn has some special qualifications."

"What way?" I asked, hoping that it would mean putting off the hour I dreaded. "How long will it take?"

"Just tonight. It's rather risky, but I'm going ahead

with it, because I think this is a time when we're justified in gambling." He broke off, seeing the look on my face, and laughed grimly. "Risky for us, for the mission, not for Georyn. I've been in contact with the starship; they're going to send our ship back down."

I was caught between relief and astonishment. "The ship? But why?"

"Because we haven't the facilities to do what needs to be done without it," Father told me. In detail, he described what he was planning to put Georyn through. The idea didn't please me one bit; it involved the use not only of drugs, but of some quite rigorous conditioning techniques.

"That's awful!" I exclaimed.

"It's not awful, Elana. It's merely an adaptation of the methods used at the Academy for the training that's given in psychic control. We'll make it simpler, naturally, since we don't need to give Georyn as much control as an agent needs and we don't have all the proper equipment."

"It will be terrifying, though."

"Yes, and that's exactly what it's got to be," Father agreed. "That's how it's designed, because Georyn must be taught to respond to the type of terror he'll face later in the way that he must respond if he is to survive."

"How many times does he have to prove himself?" I demanded, close to tears again. "Hasn't he been tested enough?"

"This isn't a test. It's training, and more than that, it's a way of helping him learn what *not* to be afraid of, familiarization, so that when he meets the real thing he won't panic."

"I'd rather not send him up against the real thing at all," I said.

"But we must, and he has volunteered for it. He

wouldn't back out now even if we asked him to. So let's give him all the preparation we can."

"*You* can give it to him," I conceded.

"No," he said slowly, "I can't. It must be you, Elana. At least you must be the one to explain it to him and get his consent."

"Why me?"

"Because only you can give him the confidence he'll need. There is a—a bond of trust and understanding between you and Georyn, a bond that will enable you to present this in such a way that he'll know, underneath, that he will come through it all right, no matter how hard parts of it may seem. It's because of that bond, even more than because of Georyn's innate courage and intelligence, that I feel he can adapt to this form of training in time for it to do him some good."

I hesitated. Father's description of the procedure had been full of innocent-sounding technical terms, but I'd had enough experience to know pretty well what he had in mind. "Will you use pain as a stimulus?" I asked directly.

"Yes," he admitted. "It will be mild, though, and of course absolutely harmless. Elana, pain's not categorically bad any more than fear is. Where the aim is to build a person up rather than to break him down, it can serve a constructive purpose."

"But Georyn won't know that!" I objected. "I can't bear to have him think that I'd deliberately let him be hurt."

"He'll agree to it of his own free will," Father pointed out. "I haven't ever asked you to deceive him, you know. You will tell Georyn quite openly that the ordeal will be a grueling one, but that it will be ultimately to his benefit. And that's the truth."

Lowering my eyes, I said desperately, "Don't ask this of me! It's—not just a job, anymore."

Father looked at me rather strangely and then for a long time was silent; we resumed our walk. Finally he said to me, "I'm afraid this may seem hardhearted, and I don't want it to, but I've got to use my best judgment as to what's the right thing to do. So I'm making it an order, Elana."

"What if I refuse it?"

"I'm not going to answer that, since we both know that you won't. If you did and Georyn failed through lack of the support you could have given him, you would never forgive yourself."

There was no argument to that. Resignedly I said, "What sort of explanation can I give him?"

"Simply say that you're going to teach him more magic." With an encouraging smile, Father added, "You know, Elana, the harder a thing is to come by, the more valuable it seems. If Georyn suffers a little to gain 'magical' knowledge, that in itself is going to increase his trust in its power, and he will feel better and stronger for it."

I shivered and pulled my cloak tighter against the chill wind. Father went on, "There's one more thing. Georyn's faith in the 'charm' may be shaken when he hears that it didn't protect Terwyn."

"That would be surprising," I murmured, not without irony.

"So we've got to give him something to replace it, something concrete to hang onto, I think, as a focus for his belief in his 'magic' powers."

"How do you mean, a focus?"

"Oh, some small object, a talisman. Something like a magic ring. Only we can't give him any artifact of ours, since he'll have to take it to the invaders' camp with him."

My hand, warm in the pocket of my cloak, closed on the stone I'd put there my first night on Andrecia, the lovely reddish-brown stone I somehow hadn't wanted to toss aside. "An enchanted stone," I said thoughtfully, drawing it out. "This stone?"

"That's fine!" Father said. He gazed at it thoughtfully and, taking my hand in his, declared, "Who can guess what powers lie hidden in that which is native to this world?"

"Just a minute! Do you mean I'm to tell Georyn that the Stone, in itself, can work magic?"

"Yes, exactly."

"But it can't."

"No, but if he believes it can that's all that matters. And if you present it in the right way, he will believe it."

"Now you are asking me to deceive him," I protested.

"Symbolism isn't deception! People need symbols, Elana. Why else do you wear the Emblem?"

"Oh, but that's different!"

"How? Because you know it's a symbol, while Georyn will believe literally in the power of the Stone? That's irrelevant! In both cases it's the idea that is potent and not the talisman, but knowing this is only a matter of sophistication."

It was true enough, I realized, that Georyn had believed all along that the Emblem was the source of my power. The use of the Stone would undoubtedly make him more confident of his own. Yet it did seem like fakery, somehow.

And there was another point that disturbed me; it had been disturbing me, in fact, ever since I'd let Terwyn go with such vague parting instructions. "We've already deceived Georyn in one way," I said to Father. "We've let him think that eventually he will 'kill' this 'dragon' when we *know* that he won't be able to do anything remotely resembling that. Even if the colonists do leave, it won't be the sort of victory he's expecting."

"Elana, that's a thing we can't possibly explain. He's got to have an immediate goal that he can visualize; without it he couldn't approach the job with any assurance at all. You must not take that from him, even though it is stretching symbolism a bit further than you might wish."

All right, I thought. I can't tell him that he *won't* kill the dragon. But somehow, I'm going to give him fair warning—not only about failure, but about success.

Upon a day of gathering clouds, as afternoon was waning, Georyn was told that Terwyn had been unable to prevail against the Dragon and that in the attempt to do so had been slain. And at these tidings Georyn's heart was heavy, for he had loved his brother; and moreover, despite the warnings of the Enchantress, he had not believed that there was true danger of her magic failing so long as his purpose did not falter. When the Starwatcher assured him that Terwyn had displayed great valor, the quest began to seem hopeless indeed.

Nevertheless, he deemed that it had been laid upon him to continue it without delay, however little liking he had for the job. Unlike Terwyn, who had gone to the Dragon in anticipation of winning a reward, Georyn knew that for him victory might be no less bitter than defeat. Yet his success would be the Lady's success, while his failure would be hers also, and perhaps in truth the world would be consumed if the evil was not stopped; so what choice was there in the matter?

As darkness fell that evening, Georyn went to the hut of the Enchantress, where she sat bathed in the magical white radiance of her captive piece of the Sun, and he said to her: "Lady, I have come to bid you farewell. I will set forth at first light tomorrow, for I must try the thing, now that all depends upon me."

And she answered, "You are right, Georyn, you must. But not tomorrow. For you are not yet ready; the Starwatcher and I have learned from Terwyn's death that the Dragon is guarded by an evil spell that is stronger than we had believed, and the charm that you have mastered is not in itself enough to challenge it."

"What is to be done, then?" Georyn asked. And as he said this, he sat down beside her, for he was no longer in awe of the strange enchanted things within her hut.

The Enchantress bowed her head, and he could see that she was troubled. At last she said, "We are going to give you something else. But Georyn, I will not deceive you, there will still be danger. It is all too likely that if you attempt to complete this quest, you too will die. Even if you vanquish the monster, you may be slain in so doing."

"I would willingly die, if I could free the world of this evil by it; and I know now that enchantments are less infallible than they first seemed. But Lady, I shall not abandon hope so long as I have your good will."

"You will always have that, Georyn," she said softly, and her eyes glistened with tears. Then, hesitantly, she went on, "There is indeed hope that the spell that guards the Dragon may be broken, but the conditions are very hard."

"Lady, I have met such before. Tell me the conditions!"

"They may not all be told at once. They are very complicated and concern the uses of enchantments. Yet I warn you that the final condition is so difficult that we had not planned to disclose it to you, for we feared that you would be discouraged. I now believe, however, that you have the right to know of it; so although the Starwatcher is still opposed, I will tell you, if you wish."

"I wish to know the truth, even if it is not pleasant knowledge," said Georyn, "for I am loath to meet it blindly."

"You still must meet it blindly, for the condition is very cryptic. It is this: he who breaks the evil spell will be required to give up that which he deems most necessary to the triumph of good, and to face what appears to be a grievous failure. But as to how and when this must happen, that will remain hidden, for part of the condition is that the circumstances may not be known in advance."

"But how then can I tell what I must do to bring them about?" Georyn protested.

"You cannot. I have revealed the requirement as a warning, not as guidance, and you must act as if you had never heard of it!" exclaimed the Enchantress. "It is best forgotten, now; but when the condition has been fulfilled, you will know."

Georyn frowned, thinking that this was the most perplexing idea that had yet been presented to him. "It seems a paradox, Lady, that the triumph of good should be brought about through giving up something that appears necessary to that triumph," he said.

"Yes. But it is ever true that what looks like a paradox is merely a thing that cannot be understood by means of our present knowledge. Of this one, I can say no more, for I myself cannot predict exactly what is going to happen." The Lady sighed. "Perhaps the Starwatcher was right, and I should never have mentioned this. Yet I—I care about you, Georyn, and I could not bear to let it come to you as a shock in the end."

"I am happy that you told me of the condition," he assured her. But he was happier still at the other thing she had told him.

Then the Enchantress rose and going to the cloak that lay upon a bench in the corner of the hut, she drew something from its pocket. And she said, "Now I shall entrust to you magic far greater than a simple charm; but I must have your promise that you will never employ it lightly, nor in an unworthy cause, for much evil could be wrought by its misuse. It is meant to serve you only in the most desperate necessity."

Willingly did Georyn give the promise; whereupon the Lady held out to him a small, smooth stone, very like to those found along the banks of the river, a stone with a hole through its center. Reddish brown in color, it shone softly under the dazzling white light. And a wonder came upon him, for despite its commonplace appearance, he knew that it was no ordinary stone.

"It is enchanted," the Enchantress told him, and he could not read her smile. "It looks simple, does it not? Well, I will tell you frankly that it is a thing that learned men of more than one world would find very hard to understand."

"I am honored that you should consider me worthy," said Georyn gravely.

"I fear that it is not a matter of my considering you worthy, but of your proving yourself. I give you final warning, Georyn: if you accept this thing, you do so at your peril!"

"If it were not perilous, it could not be very powerful," Georyn observed. "For does not power always carry some sort of danger?"

She laughed. "Georyn, did you once seek the *King's* wisdom? I think it would have been better had it been the other way around!"

Georyn flushed and quickly asked her, "What powers has this Stone?"

"Many; but they cannot all be released at once. Its strength will grow as you learn to use it."

"Will it ever approach the strength of—of the Emblem, Lady?" Georyn ventured. And he asked not because he wanted such power for its own sake, but because a sudden wild hope had come to him that he might be permitted to share that which was uniquely hers.

"No, Georyn, it will not," she told him honestly. "The Emblem reaches beyond space, beyond time, into another scheme of things; and such power cannot be embodied in any object of this earth. But the Stone will have a power that the Emblem does not have: the power to act directly in this world to save it from evil."

For a long while Georyn stared at the thing; then he took it into his hand, knowing as he did so that he was committing himself irrevocably. One could never cast aside a responsibility such as this, having once accepted it. The stillness of the night was suddenly broken by the echoing cry of a forest bird, and the Enchantress looked up with a startled glance of recognition, or at least of memory. Then her eyes met Georyn's and there was fleeting elation in them. "We have much in common, you and I," she whispered.

He closed his free hand over hers. "Now I am truly honored!" he said, and with a light laugh he added, "If the Stone has so raised me in the first moment of my holdership, to what heights may I not aspire?" Then, serious again, he went on, "What are the terms, Lady? One does not receive power simply by taking a stone into one's hand and setting forth to meet the Dragon in the next instant, whether the stone be enchanted or no."

"No, one does not," the Lady agreed, but as she spoke she seemed irresolute, somehow. "Georyn, do you trust me—trust that I work only for your good?"

"If I did not, Lady," he answered, "I should not trust myself either; for more than once I have placed myself totally in your hands."

Outside, a silent rain had at last begun; the Enchantress looked away, toward the wet veil that had fallen across the hut's open doorway, and with evident reluctance she said: "I am very glad that is the case, for your trust will now be put to trial. Georyn, the powers of the Stone are not easily bent to a man's will. You are strong enough to wield them, I know; but you must learn, and I—I must now bewitch you in order to make that possible. But I warn you that you may not enjoy being bewitched. It will be terrifying; far more terrifying than anything you have yet experienced."

Then Georyn's heart chilled, for the Enchantress had always spoken truth to him and he knew that she did so now. But he was already committed and he did not regret it, so he smiled at her and said: "To be bewitched by you, Lady, is not a trial but a privilege."

The Enchantress then took two cups that were already filled from the table behind her and gave one of them to him, holding the other herself; and she said, "So be it, then. Drink to the success of our venture!"

Georyn raised the cup, and then, seeing something not quite straightforward in her gaze, paused apprehensively. It was all too obvious that the Lady had not yet told him everything.

She sensed his question, and as she answered her voice trembled slightly. "Yes, there is a potion in it; but I swear to you that it is not an evil one, and that it will do you no lasting harm."

Slowly, Georyn said, "If you tell me so, I will believe you; for I know that you would cast no spell over me that would lead me to peril."

"I have never promised that, Georyn. I have told you the exact opposite: this whole affair is perilous, for you and for all of us."

"All of us?" Georyn stared at her with distress, saying, "Surely, Lady, you do not mean that there can be any danger to yourself!"

With some hesitation she admitted, "I am in great danger simply by being in this world, so long as the Dragon remains."

"Had I but known," Georyn said unhappily, "I would never have desired that you should linger here. Now indeed we must make a quick end to the business. I shall drink your potion without fear; but I hope that the conclusion of the quest will not be long delayed by it."

"The ordeal that you now must undergo is necessary to ensure your victory. It will help you to learn the uses of the Stone; but do not expect the learning to be an easy or a pleasant process. It is never so with an enchantment of any great value."

"I am well aware of that, Lady," said Georyn, and he drained the cup without further hesitation. Then, brushed by the first tendrils of real terror, he forced a laugh, asking: "What will happen to me, now?"

The Enchantress put her hand on his, and although it was icy cold he felt a warmth spread through him. "Nothing really bad, but you will not understand it while it is happening. Trust in the Stone, however, and all will be well with you; for the Stone will give you the power to control things in circumstances where the charm alone would be useless." She tried to smile, but all at once her composure broke, and she cried desperately, "Oh, Georyn, do not hate me for this!"

But Georyn did not hear these last words, for an enveloping blackness had come upon him, and he had fallen forward to be caught by the strong arms of the Starwatcher, who had at that moment entered the hut.

The ship came down under cover not only of darkness, but of rain. Evrek joined us; together he and Father took Georyn over to it. Georyn would not be allowed to know that there was a ship, naturally. When he regained consciousness, he would be inside, in an environment that would be totally incomprehensible to him. (This was part of the conditioning; one of the big things he was to learn was how to adjust to a foreign and unpredictable situation.) We were going to keep the ship on the ground for several hours, but it really wasn't such a large gamble; in all the time we'd been on Andrecia, no Imperials had come our way except on that first afternoon.

"I don't want to watch this," I told Father.

"You'd better," he replied. "Otherwise, you'll picture something much worse than the actual trial."

Evrek smiled at me. "It won't be half so bad as you seem to think, Elana," he told me. "Georyn will tell you that himself afterwards. I'll bet almost anything that he will."

"How do *you* know?" I demanded irritably.

"For one thing, because your father just got through trying this setup on me, to make sure it's working right," he said gently. And with a puzzled frown he added, "It's not like you to worry so much, darling."

I turned away. He had not, of course, guessed why I worried about Georyn; and I didn't want him to.

"Look, Elana," Father said, "I'm not going to do anything to Georyn that I wouldn't do to you in similar circumstances. I promise I won't throw anything at him that he can't handle."

"Similar things *will* be done to you when you take your

advanced training in psychic control," Evrek reminded me.
"And you'll find that you won't mind at all. Neither will
Georyn, when he catches on—and he'll catch on fast."

I had to admit that he was probably right. And the plan
was well set up to help Georyn. It even included a drug-
induced paralysis that would simulate the effects of the
Imperials' stunners. I could only agree that it was a good
thing to expose him to that in advance, because though it
doesn't hurt it can really throw you the first time you
experience it; we'd described it to Terwyn, but there's no
substitute for a practical demonstration. Georyn needed
real proof that physical helplessness doesn't affect the
power of the mind at all.

But there was another thing about which I had serious
reservations. "Father," I said unhappily, "why must you
show him this film?"

"It's the only one I could get hold of. I don't know
what he'll make of a travelogue showing the capital cities
of the Federation; but he won't understand enough of it
for there to be any disclosure involved, that's certain."

"That wasn't exactly what I meant. It just—just seems
unnecessarily cruel, that's all."

"Why, Elana, I don't think he'll be unduly frightened
by the film itself. There'll be some bad moments when it
first diverts him from the psychokinetic control he's being
forced to maintain, but that can't be avoided, because
we've got to teach him to split his attention."

"If he doesn't learn to keep control more or less auto-
matically, on a subconscious level, he'll be so overcome by
the sight of the Imperials and their machines that he'll
lose it," Evrek said. "Just as Terwyn did."

Father added, "The use of a film is an efficient way of
giving that lesson; and knowing Georyn, I think he'll
probably enjoy it. He may be sorry when it stops."

I didn't say any more. Father did know Georyn, but not as well as I knew him. Yes, he would enjoy the film, and he would be sorry when it was over. With any other Andrecian, perhaps that would be that. But Georyn, I was quite sure, would go on being sorry for a very long time.

Outside the barracks a dreary rain was falling; to Jarel it seemed of a piece with the mood of despair that had been with him ever since the ruthless killing of the native. He moved the lamp closer and bent over the paperwork on which he was trying to concentrate, but it was no use. Kevan's words kept coming back to him: *A world's not tamed till we've gotten rid of every last native . . . sure there's a war! That's what colonization is.*

That was not what he had thought it was when he joined the Imperial Exploration Corps. He had thought it a noble goal to spread humanity across the galaxy, a chance to do something constructive toward the future. He had thought it self-evident that mankind should reach for the stars, and never once had he questioned the price. He had not really been aware of there being a price. The conquest of space, the growth of the Empire into a grand commonwealth of worlds—ever since he was a kid, he'd wanted to be part of that; it was a hard ideal to give up.

Yet he couldn't close his eyes any longer, Jarel thought. Why, in fact, had he kept them closed so long? Had he sold out? Was he so anxious for an exciting, high-paying career that he could overlook any crime the Corps might commit just to stay in? Was he so crazy about planet-hopping that he was willing to trade his soul for the chance to do it?

It was not just Kevan's callousness, not just the death of a brave young man who hadn't looked as if he deserved to die. After all, Jarel had seen men die before. A doctor saw all kinds of suffering and couldn't afford to be squeamish about it; he didn't expect life to be pretty, on this world or any other. The trouble was not so much that another "savage" had been killed as that Dulard and the others had ignored the incident, as they had ignored earlier ones—ignored them because underneath they knew that what Kevan said was true. Two peoples couldn't share a planet. It either belonged to the race that evolved upon it, or that race got wiped out. Whether it was wiped out by the first shipload of men to invade the place or by natural attrition a couple of centuries later didn't make a whole lot of difference.

If he stayed in the Corps, Jarel knew, this wouldn't be the last native race he would help to subdue. Even if he himself never set foot on another planet that was being grabbed, he would still be supporting the Corps's policy, wouldn't he, if only by default? And he was no longer so sure that the goal itself was a worthy one.

"I don't know," said Jarel miserably to himself. "I just don't know anymore. Perhaps the invention of the stardrive was the blackest mark on our already black history, perhaps truly wise peoples control their population and stay home where they belong."

It would be nice to think that all this was leading somewhere, that there was such a thing as progress after all; but when it came right down to it, he didn't see much evidence for that. In fact, he had a suspicion that the natives were better off than the average Imperial citizen, so long as they were left alone. They were like children, he thought wistfully, no worries. No real worries at all. Oh, they fought among themselves once in a while, maybe, but in between they didn't have to be concerned with things like world problems or visions of lands beyond their own. That village of theirs was probably a quiet, happy place. What they had there was probably worth a lot more than the so-called blessings of civilization. In fact his own people might be ahead of the game if they were still living the life nature intended on their original home world, instead of looking for others to mess up.

If he were a brave man, he decided, he would get out right now. He would walk into that forest, armed with all the medical supplies he could carry, and he would live the rest of his life among those natives. He would let the Empire go where it most assuredly was heading.

He walked to the window and looked out at the rain, thinking ruefully that he didn't have that kind of courage. He was not cut out to be a hero, he supposed. He was not even sure that he would have nerve enough to make a dramatic break if he could save them by it! And of course he couldn't save them; he couldn't even save the ones locked up that he was required to guard. If he let them go, Kevan or somebody would have them rounded up in ten minutes, if they were lucky; and if they weren't lucky they'd get blasted.

Still, Jarel decided, he still had some self-respect—too much to be associated with the Corps now that he'd seen what it really stood for. So he would request transfer to headquarters; he would go back with the supply ship, and then, well, he would resign. It was a great dream, this star roving, but behind the window dressing it was an empty one.

When Georyn came to his senses he knew instantly that he had been transported to some strange castle of the enchanted realm, for he saw naught that resembled the world of his own experience. The room in which he found himself was small and round, and its windowless walls were of a solid blue material, without cracks of any kind. It was a dungeon, he supposed; yet it was not dark. Rather, it was lit with a brilliance not unlike that of the Lady's globe of light, though he could see no such globe.

But the sight of the place was as nothing beside the helplessness that he felt. He was lying on his back upon a soft but unyielding couch, and he could not move so much as one finger. In no way was he bound; there were no chains, no cords, yet his body would not obey his will, and even the attempt to turn his head was of no avail. He was not dazed after the manner of a man waking from some horrific dream; his mind was alive and clear, and he knew with dismaying certainty that he was *not* dreaming, but was in truth immobilized. It was as if he had been turned to stone.

Turned to stone! The Enchantress had told him that he would be turned to stone, temporarily, when he met the servants of the Dragon. Had she then betrayed him into their hands? She would not do such a thing. Yet tonight she had seemed unsure, reluctant, and she had admitted the Dragon to be a danger to her. Could it be that she herself had been bewitched by a power stronger than her own?

At this thought Georyn's terror nearly overwhelmed him; for if any evil had befallen the Enchantress, what possible hope could there be either for himself or for his quest? Worse, the idea of harm being done to her was unbearable. Then all at once his eye fell upon the Stone, which he now saw had been bound to his belt by means of a leather thong thrust through its hole. And the Stone comforted him, for the Lady had not been unsure when she had given it into his hands.

Had she not warned him that he would be placed in a

terrifying situation that he could not hope to understand? And had she not clearly implied that the Stone would guard him from harm? It would avail little to give in to despair; he had been sent hither to learn, and learn he must if he was to benefit from that magic. Yet he knew not what powers the Stone would give him, save that it would in some manner ensure the potency of the charm that had failed Terwyn.

Looking up then, Georyn beheld a large sphere of some cold, shining substance, and it hovered above him; but as he watched, it began to fall slowly. Before long, surely, it would crush him. Perceiving that there was but one defense, he mentally formed the words of the charm and commanded the sphere to stop.

And indeed, it did stop. Yet he found that his mind must not wander, lest the sphere descend once more; and at this Georyn's heart was again filled with dread. Never during the encounters with the dark wizard had he been able to keep control of an object for more than a few minutes. Still, perhaps the Stone would give him this strength; he could but trust that it would be so, for he had no other recourse.

Then suddenly there arose a fearsome sound, a sound that grew in intensity until it became a deafening roar like nothing ever heard upon the earth. Georyn quailed; he was pierced by sound, it was unendurable. And how could the charm help him against an intangible thing? In panic, he let his mastery of the spell falter, and to his horror the sphere came plunging down upon him. It did not crush him after all. Rather, the surface of it burned with a cold fire the very touch of which was agony.

He had not thought that such would be allowed to happen. Out of his pain came awareness that mere possession of the Stone would not protect him; the Lady had

told him truly that its powers would be hard won. Seeing
naught else that could offer any hope, Georyn in desperation invoked the charm again—and thereupon the pain
was gone, even as the sphere rose to the top of the little
chamber. So too, instantly, was the sound. Joyfully then
did he realize that he could fight all that assailed him simply by controlling the sphere.

But holding the thing motionless near the ceiling did
not prove to be enough. All too soon the ear-shattering
sound swept over him once more, and with it another sort
of pain, the source of which he could not pinpoint; it was
not severe, but he guessed that it would become so if he
took no action. And the sphere could be raised no higher!

Georyn could not believe that the Enchantress had
intended him to suffer. He was sure, therefore, that she
had provided a means of deliverance, and had meant him
to find the way to use it. He was totally helpless physically;
his mental control over the sphere was his sole weapon—
so what course was open to him other than to deliberately
lower that sphere? Resolutely he tried it, and at once both
the sound and the pain receded, only to return as soon as
he allowed the sphere's motion to cease.

And with that, Georyn understood what was demanded
of him. He was required to keep the sphere moving.
Though this was a task of far greater difficulty than that of
causing it to remain poised in one spot, he found himself
equal to it. Knowing that it would not have been so, had
he not been faced with an intolerable alternative, he perceived that there was much wisdom in the Lady's way of
teaching. In truth, there was naught to be feared in this
business of being bewitched. But he was shaken with
weariness now, and since the ordeal showed no signs of
terminating, he was doubtless to be presented with yet
another lesson.

It was not long in coming, for in the ceiling of the cell there suddenly appeared a huge window looking out upon the enchanted realm. And the scenes the window revealed were fascinating indeed, although they shifted continually in a most disquieting fashion, a fashion that seemed in no way natural. Georyn could not take his eyes from them; whether they were fair or frightening, he was inescapably absorbed. But alas, in turning his thought thither, he lost control of the sphere and was clutched by pain once more. Easily enough could he stop it by giving his attention to the charm, but time after time he was drawn irresistibly back to the wondrous view that was unfolding before him.

Georyn felt as if he were being torn in two. For it was not in him to close his mind to such marvels as he was now being shown; yet neither could he resign himself to pain. Surely, for this too there must be an answer. At length he found it. Struggling to maintain the steady motion of the sphere despite his inability to ignore the enchanted window, he made a discovery: no need was there to devote his whole thought to the spell in order to control it. The new, magical function of his mind could be pushed aside and yet continued, even as the movement of his legs would require but little attention were he walking. It was not so hard, once he had grasped the idea. Gradually he gained confidence; the Stone was giving him resources beyond all expectation. No longer did the sphere slip from his command, and there was no more pain.

Then for a time Georyn beheld wonders the like of which he had never seen even in dreams. Some were terrifying—a hideous, snarling beast, a series of fiery bursts accompanied by thunder—but he soon realized that he would come to no harm from them; they were merely another manifestation of the spell under which he had been placed. And others were not dreadful, but only strange: there was a tremendous cluster of sparkling towers, for instance, that made him long to rise and step forward onto the silver-paved roadway that led to it; for he could see people there, vast crowds of people clothed in colors more brilliant and varied than the silks of a king. The sound he heard, too, was more pleasing than threatening; although it was unlike anything of which he had ever dreamt, it reminded him of music.

Suddenly, without warning, the window disappeared and there was silence. The Enchantress stood before him; reaching up for the sphere, she took it into her hands. It did not burn her, but neither could she hold it; it continued to rise, gently, while she stared at it in puzzlement. Then with quick understanding she turned to Georyn. "Let it go!" she said, laughing. "You are *too* good at this, now!"

Georyn released the sphere, and the Lady removed it from the chamber. In a few moments she came back to him; her hand rested on his arm, and he felt a sharp sting, after which tingling heat coursed through him, rapidly fading. "Stretch your limbs," she told him. "They will move again."

Finding that this was true, Georyn sat up. "The Stone has powers past belief," he said slowly. "I—I was only beginning to tap them."

She smiled. "You see what I meant. Its strength grows as you learn. Can you forgive me for subjecting you to this, Georyn?"

"There is nothing to forgive. It was not terrible after the beginning. The last of it, indeed, was in itself worth what had gone before; I would not have been sorry to see it continue."

The Enchantress sighed, saying, "I know, and I hope that that will not prove to be the worst of the whole affair. I do not want you to be hurt."

To Georyn, her meaning was all too clear. The helplessness, the brief touches of pain, were now over with and he had taken no harm from them. But the memory of that magical window was something else again; having been given a glimpse, he now wanted more than a glimpse, and he suspected that he was not going to get it. "Lady, where are we?" he said wonderingly. "What is this place?"

"I am not permitted to tell you, nor may you know how you leave it." In her other hand, she held a steaming cup, which she now extended to him. "Drink this, now. Do not be afraid; it will only make you sleep."

Georyn sipped the drink; it was hot and had a pungent flavor that was not unpleasant. "Guarded by such enchantment," he told her, "I do not think that I shall be afraid of anything! But the Stone has indeed its perils, and they are not as I imagined them."

"Ah, Georyn, you do not know them all; nor, I fear, do I," sighed the Lady. She sat beside him, cupping her hand around the Stone, and for a moment spoke less to him than to herself. "Is it by *this* that a mighty Dragon shall be overcome? I dare not guess where it will lead us! A stone's so very small a thing to change the fate of a world."

The Fire

The sun was high when Georyn awoke. He was lying upon his own pallet in the shelter that he shared with the Starwatcher; at first, he wondered whether he had only dreamt that he had been bewitched and taken to the dungeon of an enchanted castle. But when he saw the Stone still bound to his belt, he knew that it had been no dream. It had been real, as the power of the Stone was real; and although parts of it had been nightmarish, he felt all the better for what he had undergone. In truth, he felt far more eager to set forth upon the quest than on the previous evening, for surely the worst of Dragons could be no more terrifying than this past night's experience.

The Starwatcher was nowhere to be seen. But when Georyn went to the river for water, he found the Enchantress there before him. She sat upon a mossy log watching the clear stream swirl over the rocks, and when he went to her she rose and held out both her hands. He did not take them, for it was not fit that he should entertain the thought that had come suddenly into his mind.

That she should bestow an Enchanted Stone upon him was miracle enough; who was he to dare the hope that, in parting, she might honor him with her kiss?

"Lady," he said, from a desperate need to fill their silence, "did I indeed travel to the enchanted realm while I was bewitched?"

"No, Georyn, you did not," she answered. "It was an illusion."

"It was a wondrous one, then; for I have lost all fear even of being turned to stone!"

"That may be true, for the spell was so designed. But there is a difference that you must not forget! Last night your danger too was illusion, but with the Dragon, it will not be. The Stone can give you power, but it cannot make you invulnerable."

He smiled at her, and touched her hand. "Only your faith in me can do that," he told her.

Suddenly shy, the Enchantress turned away. "Georyn," she said hesitantly, "perhaps it is best that you should set out upon the journey today after all. Do you feel ready for it?"

"I feel entirely so, but must I not wait to consult the Starwatcher?"

"I—I think that that will not be necessary. You already have his blessing and all the aid he can give you. And now there is little time to waste."

Georyn said, "That is so, for I do not wish to prolong your peril for a single instant. And yet—" He paused, for it seemed to him that the ordeal now ahead of him would demand far more courage than the confrontation of the Dragon. To go, and not to see her again! To turn and walk away, knowing that in the moment of his victory, if victory he won, she would pass into the forever-unreachable realm beyond the stars! He could not find any words that were adequate to be his last to her.

And then Georyn saw in the Lady's eyes that he did not need words; she not only understood his feeling, but shared it. This farewell was no more to her liking than to his, yet to postpone it further was beyond her power.

She answered his unspoken thought. "That is *not* beyond my power, Georyn, for I have decided to come with you. But we must not tarry, for the Starwatcher will soon return, and he will not be pleased at my choice, I fear."

Firmly Georyn replied, "I shall not take you into further peril."

"My peril will be no greater than it is here!" she exclaimed, and he knew this for the first falsehood she had ever told him. "I cannot help you in the final trial, but I shall hide in the woods and watch it; and afterwards, we will meet again before—before I go from this world. I cannot bear that it should be otherwise!"

"Lady," Georyn declared resolutely, "I must go to the Dragon alone, as you yourself have told me is a necessary condition for the breaking of the evil spell that guards the monster."

"It is necessary only that I not be seen," the Enchantress said determinedly. "Do not set yourself against my will, Georyn. I have not given you *that* much power!"

"So be it, then," Georyn said. "But my heart forebodes that this will lead us to an ill fortune. That you should be with me on this journey is a greater joy than I could ever have wished for, but if any harm should come to you the defeat of a hundred dragons would be no victory."

It was absolutely crazy, of course, for me ever to set off for the Imperials' camp with Georyn. Not that Father had ordered me *not* to go; he'd just naturally assumed that there was no need to, any more than there was a need to order me not to go there with Evrek. But I knew well enough that he wouldn't allow me to take such a risk if I consulted him. And I had no real idea as to what good might be done by it; I simply felt that I couldn't bear to send Georyn into a danger that I didn't share, not after what had happened to Terwyn. At least I told myself that. Actually, I suppose, when it came right down to it I just couldn't bring myself to say good-bye.

Father had gone to the village that morning, since we were out of supplies again, and Evrek was away keeping tabs on the invaders. The plan was for Georyn to rest up after his night's ordeal; his departure wasn't to take place until the following dawn. But I knew that if I was to go along, we must leave before Father got back. I did not think he would stop me once I had taken the decision into my own hands. After all, I'd ignored his desire to protect me on two previous occasions, and he had not been angry.

Nor had I been sorry. My experience in the village had not taught me caution; it had been painful, but that kind of pain—the kind that comes from facing up to life—isn't a harmful thing. No harm had ever come from my rash acts. I could not believe that this one would turn out differently.

The site of the Imperial colony lay on the other side of the "enchanted" forest. Since Georyn and I had started fairly late in the morning, we had no hope of getting there before nightfall; we planned to build a campfire and take turns tending it, for we traveled light, without blankets or even packs. (I had sense enough, at least, not to take any offworld artifacts with me other than the clothes I was wearing, for which I had no substitute; I even resisted the temptation to carry along extra food in the form of concentrates.) However, just as it was getting dark enough for us to be choosing a place to stop, we spotted the glare of a large bonfire off in the distance, glimmering through the trees.

It never occurred to me to be leery of that bonfire. As we approached we could see that there were quite a few men clustered around it; that these men might be unfriendly to us never even entered my mind. Georyn was wiser; he insisted that we should size up the situation before making ourselves known. There was one of the typical Andrecian stone huts nearby, abandoned by folk who, although bolder than most concerning the forest, had fled in fear from the invaders; we watched from the cover of its shadow. The mere fact of men being in the Enchanted Forest at night was suspicious, but I didn't take that in until Georyn mentioned it. I didn't realize that anything was amiss until we saw the girl.

The girl was young, younger than I certainly; she sat leaning against a tree on the far side of the fire, away from its warmth. She was clad in a shapeless garment of dark, rough-looking cloth, none too clean, and her long blond hair hung limply across one side of her face. At first we wondered what one lone girl could be doing in such a place. The men did not seem to be paying any attention to her; they gave her a wide berth, in fact. Then, as we circled in closer, we saw that she was a captive; her hands and feet were bound, and in her eyes was an expression I had never seen on anyone before: not terror, but a look of having gone beyond terror to the apathetic resignation of despair.

Aghast, I asked Georyn what was going on. He didn't know, at least he said he didn't. I think now that he must have had a fairly good idea. He understood the Andrecian mind in a way that I never shall; and moreover he knew that no villagers would camp in the Enchanted Forest, this close to the place of the dreaded "dragon," merely for pleasure. Perhaps, if I had never gone to the village with him, he would have told me of his suspicion; he would have assumed that it lay within my power to deal with this situation as with all others. But to Georyn, the probable fate of this girl must have been a very horrifying thing. He now knew my reaction to horrifying things and did not want to cause me any sadness. It was very ironic, because I would have taken a more optimistic view of this particular truth than he.

As it was, although I had no inkling of the actual intent of these Younglings, it was plain enough that they were up to no good. And I'm afraid that I didn't have a very realistic idea of my powers as an enchantress! So far the only Andrecians I had met had respected me and welcomed my aid; I was under the impression that any villager would offer me, if not the adoration that Georyn did, then at least the deference that his brothers had accorded me. Cruel as they might be toward each other, their malice surely couldn't extend to *me*. I actually thought that I could walk into that camp to demand that the girl be freed, and be obeyed.

Georyn tried to stop me. "Are you sure that it's right that you should be seen?" he asked, clearly indicating beneath the respectful tone that he was not.

"But Georyn, those men are likely to do something awful to that poor girl! I've got to stop them!"

"I don't think," he said slowly, "that it's been laid upon you to right all the wrongs of the world; for haven't you told me that you are here only to help defeat the Dragon? And isn't it possible that if we try this thing and fail, our quest may thereby be jeopardized?"

He had hit the nail on the head, of course, just as he

usually did. A Federation field agent should not need a Youngling to interpret her responsibility for her; but if she does, and is lucky enough to have one who's capable of it, she ought at least to listen to him. Unfortunately I didn't listen, for my decision was already made.

It's one thing to understand Service policy concerning large-scale actions, and something else to apply your understanding to small and seemingly trivial actions. I knew perfectly well that intervention in the affairs of the natives was forbidden. But I honestly didn't think that the rescue of one mistreated girl could fall in that category! Father had explained why we couldn't eliminate hunger from Andrecia, but he hadn't scolded me for giving food to the starving children in the cottage. How would this be any different? It couldn't possibly involve Imperials, so the outcome of our mission could hardly be affected.

Sometimes you just have to learn the hard way, I guess. I hope I was motivated more by genuine pity than by the desire to exercise my power. In any case, throwing off the Andrecian cloak that covered my offworld clothing, I entered that firelit circle, Georyn followed, an act that required more courage than I appreciated at the time. Then, as it dawned on me that the stares that greeted us were undeniably hostile, that the men did not immediately fall back in awe at my presence, I began to see how foolhardy I had been. This wasn't merely a matter of policy. I'd risked Georyn's safety, and my own.

Though I was supposedly protected from violence by the Shield, to tell the truth I was not exactly confident of my ability to safeguard myself. I hadn't ever really used the Shield, at least not against anything other than what children usually run into. Not against any serious threat.

I had mentioned this to Father not long after we had arrived on Andrecia, and he had been very reassuring. "I wouldn't worry about it if I were you, Elana," he'd told me. "I know you haven't been trained to bring the Shield under voluntary control, but I'm positive that if you ever really need it, you'll have it."

"Couldn't you teach me?" I had suggested.

"I don't think it would be wise for me to try. I haven't the facilities to do it safely; that type of training can't be made too tame, you know. If it is, you simply fail and lose your confidence. The Shield's the same as psychokinesis and all the other things; you can't just practice, you've got to be faced with a real challenge."

Father had gone on, "There's only one real danger you have to watch out for, and that's panic. If you ever land in a situation where you have to rely on the Shield, you're going to be pretty frightened; but just remember that fear will do you more good than harm, so long as you don't let it throw you. There's a difference, though, between the useful kind of fear and panic. If you panic, you won't be able to exert any psychic control at all." He added thoughtfully, "The Shield for you, at this point, is rather like psychokinesis for Georyn. You've an inborn capability, but it's not under your conscious command."

"Father, could Georyn ever achieve the Shield himself?"

"No. Younglings haven't such power, not even in latent form; they simply haven't evolved far enough. If we could have given him *that,* the job would have been made a lot simpler."

So here we were. I was protected on a very problematical basis, and Georyn was not protected at all. However, I had got us into this, and I would now have to see it through. I waved my arm toward the unhappy captive and said with all the determination I could muster, "You must release this girl, at once!"

The general tenor of the reply was, "And who are *you* to say so?" I couldn't understand all the words, and though the thought behind them was forceful I could not read it readily, as I could Georyn's. There was some rapid talk, very little of which I caught, during which I began to get very scared indeed; in spite of the nearness of the roaring fire I felt chilly. Then finally Georyn, at my insistence, told me what he now knew for certain: the girl was the victim not of these men's brutality but of a calculated scheme involving the whole village. She was intended as a sacrifice to propitiate the "dragon."

And the plan would not be given up because of any objections from a strange being who appeared out of the forest. Not that the men doubted my supernatural origin; they were all too well convinced of that. But there was a side to being an enchantress that up until this point I had not seen.

High into the dark leaped the bonfire, and upon the faces of those gathered around it a red glow was cast. Georyn stood beside the Enchantress, his hand upon her arm, as she made answer to the men's enmity. Her eyes flashed proudly and her voice was clear and cold, demanding: "Do you dare to defy me, you who have less knowledge of this Dragon than babes at their mother's knee?"

There were angry mutterings, followed by an ominous silence. When at length it was broken the villagers spoke not to the Lady, but to each other. "She has cast a spell upon us!" declared someone. "She speaks in the tongue of demons, yet we understand as though it were human speech."

"*I* do not understand," answered one surly fellow. "But

she is a witch, without doubt; one has only to look at her to see that!"

"A dealer in fell magic," agreed another, and fear was in his eyes, fear masked by hatred. "What else should we expect if we are fools enough to come into the Enchanted Forest, to remain, even, past nightfall? Are we now simply to stand here and let her bewitch us all?"

"Not unless we are witless," a third man growled. "There are ways of dealing with a sorceress, whether she come out of the Enchanted Forest or no."

The greatest danger in the Enchanted Forest at the moment, Georyn thought, might well be from the fearfulness and mistrust of men rather than from any magical force. Grievous misgivings had he had about the wisdom of confronting these people; without questioning the power of the Enchantress, he had deemed there to be many things in the real world for which she was ill prepared. An understanding of enchantments was one thing, knowledge of the ways of men something else! Ever since the day she had gone with him to the village, he had known that the Lady had but little of the latter, and he now saw that his concern for her safety had been well founded. The tone of these men's comments was not at all to his liking.

Their best hope, it seemed, lay in boldness; so Georyn took a step forward and said firmly, "Not all who practice magic are to be feared. This Lady is a wise and powerful enchantress, whose notice you are unworthy to receive; pay her the honor that is her due."

The biggest of the men, who was evidently their leader, stared thoughtfully at Georyn. "She may indeed be a powerful enchantress," he conceded. "But does she serve good or evil? That is another matter, and one that must be looked into."

"She is entirely good!" cried Georyn. "There can be no question!"

"No question? Ah, but stranger, how do we know that she has not bewitched *you*? If she has, you would surely defend her."

"I defend her because I know her for what she is," Georyn insisted. He turned to the Enchantress; she stood frozen now in silent dignity, but he could tell that underneath her calm demeanor she was both angry and bewildered.

"There is a way to find out!" shouted an excited voice. "Let her be put to the test! If she is innocent, no harm will be done by it; and if she is not it will be no worse than she deserves." There were cries of approval and the men moved in closer, surrounding Georyn and the Lady.

"What foolery is this?" Georyn demanded, but inwardly he quailed, for he already knew.

"No evil witch," the leader said darkly, "can face the ordeal of fire and emerge unscathed."

"No!" Georyn declared. "I will not have it so!"

"Have you so little confidence, then?" the man inquired, with a slow smile.

Georyn did not reply. It would not be wise, at this point, to mention that he had far more confidence in the goodness of the Enchantress than in the validity of the test. He put his hand upon his sword, but there were angry shouts, and his arms were seized on either side. His protests could avail nothing; the Lady was beyond his aid.

She too had been seized, but she remained unshaken; she spoke softly to Georyn while the villagers watched with growing suspicion. "Georyn, tell me what is happening!" she urged. "What have I done, that they should treat me so?"

Then did Georyn reveal the grim truth to the

Enchantress, for he realized that she had not taken full meaning from speech not directed toward her; and to his dismay he sensed that she was appalled. Yet her expression did not change. "I am not afraid, Georyn," she said quietly. "I will submit to this test, if the men demand it."

"Will your powers protect you, Lady?"

"Yes, I shall be shielded," she replied calmly, but she was very pale. "Do not fear for me; I will come to no harm."

"Can you know that certainly, before you are tried?" Georyn asked. He was troubled, for he guessed that she had not faced this particular sort of challenge previously, and were not enchantments at times capricious?

"Whether I can or not," she told him, "there appears to be no choice in the matter; and should I fail in courage, my Shield would then surely fail also."

That the Enchantress should have a need for courage was a totally new thought to Georyn; he had supposed her above that sort of thing. But if enchanted folk were subject to fear and pain even as men were, she should not risk this ordeal. "If there is any question, Lady," he said, "I will take the thing upon myself. If one of us must depend blindly upon this Shield, it had best be me; for have I not already committed myself to the protection of the Stone?"

The Lady managed a weak smile. "That you should make such an offer touches me as has naught else in all my life. But you could not do it, Georyn, even if the men would permit you, which of course they would never do, for it would not suit their purpose."

"Build up the fire!" shouted a harsh voice. "Bring the witch; let her look upon it and tremble!" Logs were piled on, and a tower of hot sparks rose upward into the blackness of the Forest. The Enchantress was dragged around to the opposite side of the circle so that she was facing

Georyn across the barrier of the fire. The leader of the villagers thrust a long stick into the blaze and drew it out again, a flaming brand; he approached the Lady and brandished it before her. She shrank from it, her eyes dark with apprehension. Georyn could see that she was indeed trembling; he strained for freedom, but his captors held him fast.

Then in desperation he raised his voice, saying: "Look you, if this enchantress passes your test, which I am sure she can, you will only have made her angry; and the wrath of one so powerful as she is best avoided. Why should you risk that, when there is an easier way? For I have in truth been bewitched by her, even as you said, and therefore you can determine by testing *me* whether her enchantments be good or ill."

"There is sense in what he says," muttered someone.

"There is indeed," agreed the leader. "And besides, it is in my mind that this witch would be better suited to our main purpose than yon hapless maid; yet if she is guilty and dies under the test, she will be useless to us; whereas the fate of the man is of little account."

Shouts of assent greeted these words, whereupon Georyn was pushed roughly forward toward the fire; his hands were bound securely behind his back. He was very much afraid, but had he not been afraid before, during the tests to which the Lady herself had subjected him? Surely, if he was indeed destined to challenge the Dragon, which she had assured him that he was, the Stone would protect him now. "And in any case," he thought, "for it to fail me, if things should come to that, would be better than for *her* Shield to fail; they might then at least grant her an easier death."

Burning brands were now taken up by several of the other men; Georyn considered using the magic charm to rip them from his tormentors' hands; but this at best would be but a temporary respite, and if he was indeed to draw the attention of these people from the Enchantress it was more to the purpose that he should offer no resistance. He drew a deep breath, hoping that he would be able to meet the coming trial without flinching.

But even as the villagers advanced upon Georyn, the Enchantress caught their intent, which was by this time all too clear, and the studied calm of her face changed to a look of stark terror. "No!" she cried out. "It is beyond the power of the Stone!" And with that she shook off her startled captors and strode quickly forward to the very edge of the bonfire, which was now blazing furiously from a fresh load of logs. The men murmured in astonishment, for none dared to stand so close as she.

The hot red light blazed on her silvery garments, and upon her breast the Emblem shone, its myriad facets reflecting the brilliance. Heedless of the scorching heat, she knelt. Georyn, across the circle from her, could not actually hear the words her lips formed, but in his mind they sounded as clearly as if she had been speaking to him alone amid the stillness of the wood. *Georyn!* she said to him. *Whatever now betides, remember the Stone! Though it cannot give you the Shield, it is powerful; and its power is independent of mine. If I fail, you still must carry through the quest!*

There was an uncertain pause; the men clustered around, silently. Though they were still hostile, there was no more jeering. The Enchantress looked up toward the stars for a moment. Then, slowly, she stretched her hands out in front of her, plunging them into the heart of the blaze.

And there was a gasp of awe, for behold! there did indeed seem to be an invisible Shield around the arms of the Enchantress. She held her hands steady, and though flames leapt about them, they were not burned. She smiled triumphantly, holding the eyes of each man in turn, and her face bore no trace of pain.

Then was Georyn seized by wonder and a great joy; and he stared at the shining Emblem, struck anew by its power and by the valiant spirit of the Lady whom it guarded. None but he knew how very brave she had been. To the others, she was a witch, born without feelings; but he knew that enchantress though she was, she had a human heart, a heart that had known real fear. And he deemed that she had won the protection of the Emblem, even as he had been required to earn that of the Stone, by her willingness to trust in it. There is ever a cost to magic so mighty, he thought, for enchanted folk no less than for men; but surely now we are well armed against the most horrendous of Dragons!

But not so soon was the ordeal ended, and the bravery both of the Enchantress and of Georyn himself was presently to be sorely tried. For the leader of the villagers strode up to the Lady and pulled her back from the fire, by his roughness breaking the aura of respect that had for a time surrounded her; and as she stumbled to her feet her unscathed arms were grasped and twisted from behind. "Fools!" cried the man, "are you frightened merely because fire cannot hurt her? She can still be made captive."

"What are you saying!" exclaimed Georyn. "She passed your test; she is innocent!"

"Such innocence I want no part of, nor do you, if you are wise."

"But she may help to save you from the Dragon!" Georyn protested, using the argument that he felt would have the most weight.

"She may indeed. The Dragon is angry and has taken

many of our best men; we intend to offer it a maiden from our village so that it may be appeased and leave us alone hereafter. But why should we give up one of our own women when fortune has placed this witch in our hands? We will now send her to be the Dragon's victim and see how well her powers can protect her *there*."

Georyn grew cold; had she not told him that for her to confront the Dragon would be disastrous not only to herself but to the entire quest? He turned to her, reluctantly telling her the gist of this new threat, for she must perforce be warned of it if there was to be any chance of escape. To his horror her eyes grew large with dismay; far greater fright was in them than when she had knelt before the flames.

The big man held up his torch, illuminating the now-white face of the Enchantress. "Look at her!" he called out. "Dragon's fire is a hotter flame than our poor blaze; and that, she fears!"

"If you do this thing," Georyn said despairingly, "who knows what evil you may bring upon yourselves? The Dragon may *not* be appeased; it may become more powerful than ever, and then where will you be?" But he perceived that such logic would be of no avail, for to the men, torn between their dread of the Dragon and of the Enchantress's magic, the vulnerability they now saw in her had been only too welcome.

"At dawn," their leader was now declaring, "this witch shall be taken to the place of the demons. For now she shall be bound and kept in yonder stone hut, and you with her, stranger, so that whether you are bewitched or not you cannot help her to escape. In truth, I think that we shall give you to the Dragon also."

Thereupon both Georyn and the Enchantress were forced to enter the hut, which was dark and cold, having neither windows nor fire; and their hands and feet were tightly bound with cords. And the Lady was rudely stripped of her shining raiment and given a coarse shift of dark cloth in its place. But the men, rough though they were, dared not touch the Emblem; and, when the door creaked shut behind them, a ray of firelight shining through a wide crack illumined it faintly, the one glimmer of light in that dark place.

Dulard had seemed only too happy to assign Jarel to the supply ship that was to leave in two days' time. Probably, Jarel reflected, Dulard felt that since his, Jarel's, sympathies were so openly with the natives, he was too disruptive an influence on the colony's morale. For Dulard, of course, such an attitude could lead to nothing but trouble. All Dulard had said though was, "All right, someone's got to go in any case, to look after the natives. The regular crew's got enough on their hands."

"Natives?" Jarel had inquired. He could not see why there would be any natives aboard the ship.

"Specimens for the Research Center. As soon as those head shrinkers hear of a new species they start pestering headquarters about it."

Jarel had with great effort concealed the sick feeling that hit him. He was familiar with the Center for Research on Humanoid Species; it was a very old and very respected institution with the highest of scientific reputations. The science of psychology had no doubt been immeasurably advanced by its work. Certainly little would be known of the primitive species of the galaxy without it. All the same, he found the idea rather unappetizing. To him, the natives were not mere "specimens" but people, and he did not like to see people kept in captivity.

"The only problem," Dulard remarked, "is that they want a female. If Kevan had captured the one he blasted a while back——"

At last, Jarel had thought bitterly, someone had come up with a legitimate reason to regret one of Kevan's impulsive killings. Perhaps, though, the poor woman was lucky to have been killed. The Research Center didn't mistreat its specimens, but still. . . . He was glad that no native girls had ventured into camp, for he didn't think it likely that a scouting party would be sent out to find one. Dulard was not the man to put the request of some distant scientists ahead of his construction schedules.

"Anyway," Dulard had gone on, "we'll send three or four of the males. Pick out the ones in the best physical shape and give them the standard inoculations, or whatever you medics usually do. I don't want them contaminating the ship any more than we can help; just having them aboard will tie it up in quarantine long enough as it is."

It was a matter of opinion, Jarel had decided, as to who was most likely to contaminate whom. But he had said nothing, thinking that to indulge in any sarcastic remarks just because tomorrow was his last day under Dulard's command would be a fool thing to do. If he was to have any career in medicine at all, he must leave the Corps with a good record.

Now, crossing the clearing under the cold black sky, Jarel was more depressed than ever. He wished that he could resign on the spot, without waiting for his tour of duty to be up, without having anything to do with this latest piece of dirty work. Yet there was no escaping it; the natives would be taken aboard the ship with or without his help. The Research Center would undoubtedly want him to start the preliminary medical workup en route, and as a physician he could scarcely refuse.

Tomorrow night would be his last on this planet, his last on any virgin world, he reflected. It could have been such a thrill, being here, if it had turned out to be anything like what he'd expected. Was he really so green? he wondered. Was Kevan right when he called him a starry-eyed idealist?

It was too bad he'd never gotten a chance to do any exploring; he still didn't know much about what lay beyond the forest. What were they doing out there on a night like this, those simple, innocent village folk? Probably sitting by their firesides, little knowing that some of their kind had fallen victim to a cold-blooded bunch of strangers who intended to use them for their own dubious ends. How could they ever imagine the way that "civilized" men were likely to behave toward anybody who happened to be both different and weak?

Jarel was not proud of his heritage at that moment. He wished, even, that he had been born a native of this world himself. It would be nice to belong to a people with a cleaner slate than the Empire's.

No hours so dark had Georyn hitherto known. Hard indeed was it to be an unarmed and helpless prisoner, yet harder still did it seem that the Lady should share this doom. He sensed the apprehension in her mind, and he perceived that in some strange way, mighty as was the enchantment that guarded her, she now had need of *his* strength. It was a situation that he had never thought to meet; until this night, all his hope had been founded upon his confidence in her wisdom and power.

At length, he worked his way across the dirt floor of the hut to where the Enchantress sat, but try as he would he could not loosen his hands to reach hers. "It was not fit that they should touch you!" he exclaimed angrily. "They will pay for it, if I am ever free again."

"Do not be sorry that they have clothed me thus, Georyn," she said in a sad, quiet voice. "It is better so, if I must face the Dragon. Even the Emblem must be hidden, if I can find a way to do it; and if I cannot, our position will be still worse than it is now." She struggled with the cords that bound her hands, but it was useless.

"Why is that?" Georyn asked, and great was his consternation, for he had considered the Emblem her sole protection.

She sighed. "I must tell you the truth. Though my magic is powerful, there is a restraint upon it, a restraint that I am bound to obey. The condition under which I wield the Emblem is this: if it or its works are ever revealed to the servants of the Dragon, a great evil will be the result, for the Emblem can aid our cause only so long as they remain unaware of its existence."

"Would it then become powerless, if it were seen?" he asked despairingly.

"For this venture, yes," the Enchantress replied. "But worse than that, it would change, and bring disaster upon the world. Whatsoever good might have been wrought by my coming here would turn to evil; no longer would there be any chance for the Dragon to be killed at all, by anyone! And even if it were *not* seen, should my identity become known, I would lose my power to help you."

As she spoke thus an appalling thought came to Georyn, and he cried in horror: "Can you not then save yourself, as you did from the fire?"

"That specifically is forbidden me," she said gently. "But we must not lose courage, Georyn. The breaking of the spell that guards the Dragon will surely require that we be tried in many ways, not all of which I am permitted to foresee, and mayhap our capture is but one of them."

Then did Georyn recall the other condition of which the Enchantress had told him, that in the end he must lose that which he deemed most necessary to the triumph of good in order for the Dragon's spell to be unmade; and despair weighted his heart. For naught could be more necessary to good than the Lady's safety, and was she not facing deadly peril? Gladly would he die to defend her, if that could be of any help; but how could he fight this strange evil enchantment that he could not even understand? Bad enough had it been that he must meet the Dragon without any real plan of attack, but if she too was now bewildered and afraid, their plight was grievous indeed. It appeared that instead of going to the Dragon as challengers, they would in truth be taken there by force, no doubt to be fed to the beast! And if that were to be the end of it, it would almost have been better to have died by fire.

The Lady answered, as she so often did, his unexpressed thought. "Is *that* your fear? Oh, Georyn—I promise you that no matter what happens to us, we will not be eaten! We may, perchance, die in some other fashion; yet we are not defenseless. Remember that the Stone too has power, and it is not bound by the condition that holds the Emblem. There is more magic in the world than even I know of."

"The Starwatcher! Can he help us?"

"Perhaps. If he can, he will; but he too is under restraint, for he too wears the Emblem."

Surprised, Georyn exclaimed, "I have never seen it!"

"It is hidden, but he is far more the master of its powers than I."

Often of late, Georyn had wondered as to the nature

of the connection between the Starwatcher and the Enchantress, for it was a thing never mentioned in his presence. The Starwatcher did not wear the garb of the enchanted realm, and his hair was white, whereas the Enchantress was from her appearance a young girl; but who can judge the age of a woman who possesses magical powers? These two might be more to each other than he would care to think.

Again, the Lady replied to words that had not been spoken aloud. "I see that no secrets can be kept from you! The Starwatcher is my father, Georyn. I am only a student of the art of enchantment; I must pass through much before I am fitted to wield the full powers of the Emblem."

She sounded very young, not at all commanding; and from that Georyn got the boldness to ask a thing that he had hitherto kept hidden in the depths of his mind. "Lady, if we succeed in this venture, is it *sure* that you must return to the realm whence you came? Might not your father be persuaded to—to give you in marriage to a mortal, if that mortal could prove himself worthy of such an honor?"

She dropped her eyes, and Georyn could see even in the dim light that there were tears in them. "No," she said sorrowfully, "that he would never do. For I am bound by a vow to serve the Emblem, and may wed with no one but another who is so bound."

"I will take any vow he asks of me!" Georyn declared, hope rising within him.

"Georyn, Georyn, the stars are not for you! The ways of enchanted folk are not your ways; you could not bear the Emblem, not if you were to slay all the dragons that exist! Valor is not enough."

"Yet if I learn to wield the Stone?"

"Give it back to me now, if that is in your thought!" cried the Enchantress. "I would not have you do it through a false hope, not though we all die, not though the whole world is lost to the Dragon."

But Georyn said, "No, Lady, I will not presume to that which must remain beyond my reach. But if I may not wield the Stone to win you, still will I do it to save you, if that is how it must be."

At first, I was too stunned by the narrowness of our escape from the fire to give much thought to the difficulty of our present plight. For, by the power of his belief in the Stone, Georyn had already saved me; he really had saved me! If he had not acted as he did, I might easily be dead.

For I had gone to the fire in my own time, of my own free will, and I'm not at all sure that I'd have had the courage for that if Georyn had not forced me to it. Not even though I knew, theoretically, that it would be a wise thing to do. To use the Shield you've got to have absolute trust in it; you've got to be *sure*. If you commit yourself to its protection voluntarily, well, in that moment you are sure. Whereas if you wait, if you allow yourself to become a helpless victim, then you're all too likely to find yourself besieged by doubt at the very time doubt can be fatal.

With me, it had been touch and go for a while; I had been really afraid, with a terror that made the sort of fright to which Father had exposed me seem very mild indeed. Georyn had known—and though he hadn't understood enough of the truth to know how he was helping me, he had unerringly done the one thing that could jolt me out of it. And yet the Stone was proving truly perilous for him; we'd given him too much faith in it. What would surely have happened if I hadn't been in a position to counteract his rash offer was just too awful to contemplate.

My strength was now at a low ebb; sustained use of the Shield takes a lot out of you. Then too, I was horror-stricken not only by what lay ahead of us but by what I'd very likely done to the chances for our mission's success. For although the Imperials probably wouldn't kill me, they would see me at close range; they would know I was not of the same race as the Andrecians they had previously encountered. They'd have no cause, perhaps, to suspect that I was not a native, so long as I was very, very careful not to reveal any understanding of their ways. Yet if I failed to hide the Emblem . . .

If I couldn't get my hands free to drop it beneath the high neckline of the shift in which I was now clothed, the whole thing was as good as blown. The Emblem is made of a substance that is not found on Andrecia. It is not found anywhere, as a matter of fact; it can be manufactured only by a very advanced technology.

One thing was in my favor: the loss of my own clothes. It hadn't been easy to stand still for that; but exhausted and dazed though I was, I had known it was the only thing to do. Now, providing the Emblem wasn't seen, there seemed very little danger of an actual disclosure resulting from my capture. The peril was in the colonists' suspicions being aroused, so that they would not accept Georyn as a typical native. My being found in company with him could easily mean that anything he might do in the way of psychokinesis would be in vain, since our entire scheme depended on their making the assumption that all the natives were alike.

Beside that problem, the question of my personal fate wasn't very significant. Yet I must admit that it *seemed* significant, as I shivered through that miserable night of captivity. All in all, that night was even more of an education than my first night alone, let me tell you! Georyn, eventually, slept; but Georyn had both a clear conscience and an unshakable belief in the efficacy of magic. I had neither. I sat through until dawn, propped against the cold stone wall; scarcely moving, scarcely noticing even that I was hungry and thirsty, that the rough garment chafed my skin, that my arms ached from the tight cords. And when morning came the only thing I was sure of was that I would never, never again jump into anything without thinking through its implications.

The Sacrifice

Shortly after sunrise, Georyn and I were dragged from the hut by the villagers and forced to set out with them toward the invaders' camp. Our feet were untied, since we were required to walk, but our hands remained bound behind us. While our captors did not actually inflict any harm on us, I think their restraint arose more from a desire to deliver the dragon's victims in good condition than from any inclination toward mercy. Georyn's face was set in a hard mask of anger at their remarks, which were loud and, presumably, crude; it's just as well that I did not really know much of the Andrecian language. If you are going to be an agent, you must be prepared to take things as they come. Still I'll confess to having wondered, for a while, whether the saving of Youngling worlds was not a somewhat thankless task.

It wasn't a pleasant journey. Food being too scarce to waste on anybody who was slated to become a meal for the dragon, we were given nothing to eat. Georyn was more or less inured to hunger, but it was a new experience for me; I felt dizzy and faint. I was also unused to going barefoot, and my feet soon blistered. To top it all off, the sun was hotter than it had been before on Andrecia. Spring was giving way to summer. The part of the forest through which our path now lay was less dense than the area nearer the river, and there was little shade.

Georyn and I did not talk much; we were too dejected. Yet Georyn did not seem to have lost any of his faith in the Stone, and that bothered me. He would have gone to the fire, unshielded—he almost had. And now he was approaching what was in his eyes an even worse danger, confident that he would be guarded against all evil. It would be nice to feel that you were protected by an enchantment that couldn't let you down. Still, what right had I to have started such a hoax? How could we ever have thought that we could save Andrecia by such means? Perhaps I'd never really thought so; perhaps that was why I'd insisted on coming, so that I could comfort Georyn in his inevitable defeat, if he survived it. Oughtn't I to enlighten him now, not only about the Stone, but about my actual status in the scheme of things? I was not, after all, worthy of the reverence he paid me; it had been my own stupidity that had gotten us into these straits. Now that we were in them, now that the chances of pulling off the fantastic, harebrained scheme in which we'd made Georyn an unwitting pawn were practically nil, didn't he have a right to as much of the truth as he could absorb?

Certainly he ought to be straightened out about the dragon! My one poor attempt to warn him that he'd have to give up what would seem like the only true victory had probably only confused him; if he remembered the "condition" at all, he was undoubtedly expecting to find a way to fulfill it and destroy the beast. Well, I wasn't going to let this go on any longer.

"Georyn," I began determinedly, "there's something I've got to explain—"

But at that moment I was interrupted by a sudden, unexpected telepathic contact: the heart-warming touch of a familiar mind. Evrek! It was Evrek, somewhere nearby! *Oh, Elana, what are they doing to you? How did you get into this?*

When I told him, he reacted with even greater horror than I had expected. *To the Imperials? But that means . . .* His thought cut off, abruptly; he had masked it.

Disclosure, Evrek? No! I'll pose as a native. They'll know I'm different, but they won't be able to tell I'm not primitive. Will they?

Not at first. But Elana, it's worse than you've been told!

Will they kill me, then?

There was a long pause. Then he answered, *No, I don't think they'll kill you. There's another thing they may try. Look, you mustn't panic; I'll rescue you somehow! But there are too many men guarding you now.*

I know. Oh, Evrek . . . I poured out the whole turmoil of my mind, even including my decision to tell Georyn the truth.

Elana, you can't! he protested. *You'll ruin everything!*

If I don't, Georyn may try some other crazy stunt—throw himself in front of the "dragon" or something—and die for it! The plan will never work, now!

There's still some hope! If he has as much faith as you say . . .

Faith in what? In a stone? Or in me, in my magic powers?

In what you represent, if you hold to it. Surely it's worth the risk!

You say that because you don't care what becomes of him. I do care, and I know he can't count on mere faith to pull him through.

How can you expect him to, if you've lost yours?

*I don't expect it; that's just why I'm going to level with him.
Have you forgotten that you're sworn?*

*Of course not! If I honestly believed there was any real chance
left, I wouldn't interfere with it.* Was I rationalizing, I wonder? Suddenly I remembered my most pressing problem.
Evrek? What shall I do about the Emblem?

Get rid of it! Take it off!

My hands are bound.

With your mind, then.

I don't know why I hadn't thought of that. To lift the
chain over my head by psychokinesis was tricky, but surely
possible; I guess I'd been blocked by the idea that I could
never just toss the Emblem away somewhere. Yet the
Imperials must not see it, and now Evrek could pick it up
later. Why hadn't I given it back to him before this? I had
no right to it anymore, not to *his!* You don't wear a man's
pendant—or his pin, or his ring, or anything else of his—
unless he has your whole heart.

But I could not, of course, do the thing under the eyes
of Georyn and all the men. There would have to be a
diversion. Georyn would have to provide it; there was no
other way. *You know where I am, Evrek? You'll find it?*

*I'll find it. And I'll get help to you, later. Don't worry, dar-
ling!*

Tears sprang to my eyes. Darling? Not anymore, really.
Poor Evrek, how unfair to him, how useless. Yet I just
couldn't help the way I felt. What must he think of my
having rushed off with Georyn this way? I wondered, suddenly, whether Father could have told him the truth.
Surely not. Evrek was good at hiding his feelings, but
hardly *that* good; his recent stiffness, I thought, arose simply from the fact that he'd been ordered not to let his concern for me interfere with the job we both must do.
Besides, though Father almost certainly knew, he had not

tried to come between me and Georyn, and had in fact been making a seemingly deliberate effort to keep Evrek away from us.

The heat of the afternoon now seemed worse than ever, but the sun was no longer shining and in the distance thunder rumbled. Apparently we were in for a storm. "Georyn," I said quietly, "I've got to get the men to stop watching me for a moment. Can you attract their attention somehow?"

"Yes, if you want me to," he replied. Georyn always came through gallantly; in this case, he responded with a foredoomed escape attempt. It accomplished its purpose; I managed to get the Emblem off, and into a clump of ferns beside the path. But the cost was high, for in the scuffle Georyn was knocked senseless. I rushed to him, sick with fear, but I was shoved roughly aside. At that moment the first flash of lightning illumined the woods around us.

A couple of men picked up the now unconscious Georyn, and we went on. Miserably I stumbled along, setting my teeth against the pain of my badly blistered feet. I'm not any better off than a Youngling when it comes to handling pain, not yet having been taught the more esoteric psychic defenses. I wondered, despairingly, how much further we had to go. And then I knew—for, between the rolls of thunder, I heard a more ominous sound: the unmistakable noise of heavy construction machinery, not too far off.

My captors halted abruptly, their faces livid with terror. One of them, however, ventured cautiously into the dense thicket ahead. In a few moments he reappeared, beckoning, and the others pushed me forward. A suitable spot for the sacrifice had evidently been found.

They gripped my arms, and I took deep, steady

breaths, trying to slow the racing of my heart. It wouldn't
do any good, I knew, to struggle; I had best behave as
regally as was possible under the circumstances. I didn't
feel regal. What, I thought frantically, could there possibly
be about the Imperials that was "worse than I had been
told?" What had Evrek meant, *there's another thing they may
try?*

Near the center of the small open space into which we
emerged was a tall, rough-barked tree. To this— despite
the lightning that was now coming alarmingly close—I
was securely bound. The men weren't gentle; the ropes
bit into my legs and shoulders until I drew in my breath
sharply at the pain. My hands were still tied behind me in
an awkward, cramped position. Georyn, who had not
regained consciousness, was dumped unceremoniously at
my feet.

No rain had yet fallen, though the sky kept getting
blacker. The heat was really oppressive, perhaps that was
why my skin was wet and the sweat was trickling down
my face. The villagers stayed just out of sight, watching
me; they undoubtedly expected the dragon to claim me at
any moment. They were, I was sure, quite interested in
my reaction to the monster's roars, which now rivaled the
thunder in volume. We were very close to the colonists'
clearing, and I knew that guards would be patroling its
borders.

I must be calm, I told myself, and take what comes. Yet
suppose Georyn was seriously hurt? Suppose he died,
with me tied there, helpless? Of course, they might kill us
both when they found us.

Another blue flash lit up the trees, a flash that reflected
on the glaringly alien material of pressure suits and helmets. Imperials . . . four of them!

Our Andrecian captors fled; they had delivered us to

the dragon's globe-headed servants, and as for the spectacle of our demise, well, was not discretion the better part of valor? Two of the invaders lifted Georyn while the other two approached me, their weapons raised. It was the utter, hopeless end. I did not have time to be afraid, I simply turned my whole thought to the sad necessity for *not* using my Shield.

I succeeded. My first reaction was astonishment at being alive to know that I had succeeded; then I realized that the weapons were not lethal ones, but merely stunners. Father had prepared Georyn for the experience of being stunned; he had not prepared me. And it *is* frightening! It's not painful, though you somehow feel as if there's pain out there, just beyond the edge, waiting to pounce. What's bad, though, is the helplessness, the feeling of having no control over your body whatsoever. That can be just awful if you fight it. And not fighting it's easier said than done! It goes against all your natural impulses, and you have to learn the trick to it.

I had not yet learned the trick when I was untied from the tree and carried into the invaders' camp; I was so wrapped up in my sensations that I didn't even get a good look at the "dragon." Georyn, of course, did not see it either, since he was still unconscious. All in all, our entry to the field of battle was not very heroic.

When the girl was brought in, Jarel was outraged, not only because it looked as though he would have to deliver a woman to the Research Center after all—which for some reason bothered him even more than taking the men—but because of the circumstances of her capture. He had not expected cruelty on the part of the natives themselves, somehow; it was very disillusioning. What could they have against this unfortunate creature that would make them deliberately turn her over to beings whom they must surely believe to be some sort of demons?

But this was the smallest part of the mystery. For the girl was of a different race, obviously unrelated to the other natives; an enigma, any way you looked at it. Why hadn't they known that there was more than one race occupying this part of the planet? Where were all the rest of them? Were they slaves, perhaps? This girl's ragged garment, plus the fact that she had been a prisoner of the others, might indicate that; yet her hands were smooth, and there wasn't a mark on her other than those made by the ropes with which she had been bound. And where would the natives have obtained such slaves? She didn't appear to fit the description of any race that had been spotted elsewhere on this planet, though Dulard hadn't made much of a survey.

Moreover, this girl didn't have the attitude of a slave, Jarel realized as he shooed away the cluster of people that had gathered to gape at her. She had an air of assurance that made him feel not only that she deserved to be treated with respect, but that she expected it. She was frightened, yes; but underneath the fright he saw a glimmer of something else: a kind of poise that he wouldn't have expected to find in a young girl, not in any girl, let alone in an uncivilized one. Even the stunning didn't seem to have dented her spirit. He hoped that she would be able to hang onto some remnant of it during the prolonged ordeal to which she would undoubtedly be subjected.

After a quick examination of the other new captive, the unconscious man, Jarel cut the tight cords from the girl's arms; they had bruised her wrists badly and even chafed away some skin. Her blistered feet were also in need of medical attention; and he could see that she was suffering from thirst as well as from hunger. He was anxious to get her inside where he could do something about these things, but Dulard showed up just then and Jarel resigned himself to a delay. Though Dulard might not enjoy gloating over the girl in the way someone like Kevan would, he was likely to be totally indifferent to her feelings if he had something more important on his mind.

The girl's uniqueness aroused mixed feelings in Dulard. He was disturbed because a doubt had now been raised as to the adequacy of his information about the natives; he hated to divert men from construction to survey work, but it couldn't be avoided now. Who knew how many more surprises might be lurking out there? But at the same time he was pleased by the obvious scientific value of the find. The scientists at the Research Center would be overjoyed to be presented with not one, but two new species. He stared moodily at the girl and said, "They'll be glad to get *you,* all right! They may be so wrapped up in finding out what makes you tick that they'll get off my back for a while. On the other hand, they may want me to get busy and find some more like you, and that will be a devil of a nuisance. These guys never stick their noses out of that lab of theirs, yet they think the Corps has nothing better to do than scout around collecting more aborigines to ship to them. . . . "

Dulard rambled on; Jarel didn't pay much attention, for he was watching the girl's face. Briefly, her eyes registered an incredulous horror that was different from anything she'd previously shown; he wondered what had triggered it. Within moments she became impassive, almost as if by conscious effort. It surely was merciful that she couldn't understand anything Dulard was saying.

He smiled at her, hoping to counteract Dulard's all-too-evident coldness. "You look as if you've got courage. That will come in handy, I'm sure, when you find out what you've had the honor to be chosen for. The Research Center people ought to be happy about it, anyway; I should think it would make a specimen more durable. I don't suppose they're always so lucky. But then, the things they'll do to you are painless, so why should any fortitude be required?"

This last was said with a meaningful glance at Dulard, on whom the irony was not entirely lost. "I wish you'd quit anthropomorphizing these savages," he told Jarel bluntly. "They don't mind being studied the way a man would. Nobody's going to do anything cruel to them. I should think a medical man like you would be wild to get started."

Jarel didn't reply; argument, he knew, wouldn't buy anything. It was quite true that no bodily harm would be inflicted on these specimens. They were much too valuable for that. It was their minds that were to be analyzed. The drugs that would be used in the process were in no way dangerous and would simply serve to open those minds to investigation. It was incomprehensible to most people that to deprive a savage of conscious choice concerning what he revealed might be unkind.

The electrical storm that had been threatening had not passed directly overhead, but a heavy shower of rain began, putting an end to the discussion. With relief Jarel took the girl into the barracks. He managed to find a small empty cubicle in which to put her, for he was unwilling to throw her in with the male prisoners, though it would never have occurred to either Dulard or Kevan that a thing like that could make any difference to a savage. He also refused to leave her even partially stunned. The building was well enough guarded at the moment so that she couldn't escape, certainly. She couldn't even if he were to help her. If he had thought there was a chance, he would have been very much tempted to give it a try.

He brought her food and water, then went off to tend to the man, who was now regaining consciousness. But he couldn't get her out of his mind. There was an indefinable quality about her, a quality that just didn't seem to fit in with his impression of the other captives. It was more than the racial difference, and more, surely, than the fact that she was the first native woman he'd seen. She was just— well, *special*. He wondered, suddenly, how old she was. Her face was young and lovely, yet her eyes seemed laden with the weight of years. A witch, he laughed to himself. A wise old witch, the seeress of her tribe, who had discovered the secret of eternal youth? He might not know all there was to know about the natives, at that.

It was too bad she wasn't really a witch, a witch who could escape by magic. What had this girl ever done, Jarel thought angrily, that she should end her days thousands of light-years away from home, family, even from the familiar sights and sounds of her world? That she should lose not only her freedom, but the right to the inviolability of her personal thoughts and memories? She was very likely experiencing another sort of anguish, too, he realized, as were all these victims, that of separation from their mates. He remembered the way she had looked at this man, who although not of her own race had apparently shared her mistreatment at the hands of the villagers. Maybe she loved him.

Well, there was one thing he could do, perhaps, to make things easier for her. He had not yet selected the men to be sent. It would be a difficult choice on whatever basis it was made, but if he were to pick this man, for whom the girl obviously had some feeling, they might be able to comfort each other. Besides, if she did not arrive with a mate, the Center might very well decide to choose one for her, so perhaps this would help to make the best of a bad business. Jarel hoped that if he was wrong, she would understand that he had meant well and would forgive him.

I wish I could say that I was calm and fearless in the hands of the Imperials—intrepid, the way it seems as if an agent ought to be. But I wasn't. I'd known beforehand, of course, that I was in for an ordeal. But I hadn't anticipated just how much of an ordeal. I had not been in possession of all the facts.

The Imperials are not bad people. They're not villains; they're just—well, they're Younglings, that's all. You can't expect Younglings to know how to act; you can't condemn them for the way they look at things any more than you can blame a baby for having learned to creep instead of to walk. I told myself that, but it's hard to be objective when they're about to do something awful to you, and you've no way to stop them short of causing a disclosure.

I must admit that I was pretty shaken up when I found out about the plans the Imperials had for me. I had assumed that I might be killed as Ilura and Terwyn had been. But not this other business—it would have made any agent's blood run cold. And it hit me by surprise. I'd had no conception of the sort of thing I might find myself faced with. Georyn came closer to the mark than I did in his expectations; he correctly surmised that his captors' aim would be to get information from him, and was wrong only in his ideas about how they would go at it. For I later found that Georyn had been fully convinced that he was to be subjected to torture. The Andrecian picture of imprisonment is not a bright one, and he had no reason to suppose that the methods of the dragon's henchmen would be any less fiendish than those of the King.

The Imperials, of course, do not do things like that; they are, according to their own lights, humanitarians. They do not torture the natives they capture; they study them scientifically. And they have a research center on their home world for that purpose.

This center is notorious; anyone who has studied their civilization at all knows of it. It's a sort of zoo, to put it bluntly. The "animals," being valuable, are well-treated; the only experimentation done on them is of a psychological nature. The Imperials believe that this is the way to learn about the primitive peoples of the universe. They are very serious about it. They do not think of it as being cruel.

I now know that Father was aware even before we landed on Andrecia that if we were captured alive by Imperials we would be earmarked for their research center. He did not inform me because he didn't plan to let me go anywhere near the invaders' camp; and he felt that the less I knew about the risks he and Evrek were taking, the better off I'd be. Evrek himself, of course, knew all about this center and what it would mean to be sent there before he ever volunteered for the mission. Unfortunately, I had never heard of the place until my guards discussed it at length in front of me, addressing themselves directly to me in such a manner that I was able to pick up their thoughts. It was not the ideal way to find out.

Have you ever imagined what it would feel like to spend the rest of your life as an inmate of a zoo run by Younglings whose civilization was nowhere near to the level of yours—and to have to pretend, *always,* that you could not communicate with them? To know that you could never again show any evidence of having any mental life at all, lest they discover you for what you really were? It is not an inviting prospect. Although Evrek had promised to rescue me, I had no real hope that either he or Father would be able to do so. They were sworn; they could not risk disclosure to save me, no matter how much they might want to. So I didn't doubt that I was going to have to accept my fate, and to report that I was panic-stricken is putting it mildly, to say the least.

I was almost hysterical for a while, I'm afraid. I was alone, for they had me in a small room inside one of their unsealed barracks, separated from the other prisoners. You can snap out of it when you *have* to, though. Soon one of the guards came in, one of the few colonists who wore no helmet, being apparently immune to Andrecian bacteria. With great effort I arranged my features into some semblance of innocent fright; an authentic native would not have known what was going on.

This particular guard was evidently a doctor, for he proceeded to treat the raw rope burns on my wrists as well as my blistered feet. As he did so he talked to me, not unkindly, trying very hard to get me to respond; naturally he had no suspicion that I could understand him. He was a young man and his face showed more decency and compassion than I would have expected, somehow, though of course there was no reason to think that Imperials would not be good men as individuals.

"You needn't be afraid of me," he told me repeatedly. "I'm on *your* side. My name is Jarel. Jarel. Can you say that?" He pointed to himself and, if I had not been so overwrought, I would have been hard put to it not to burst out laughing. "I won't hurt you. Poor girl, I'm sorry for you. Why can't they leave well enough alone? It's bad enough confining the natives to reservations, as they'll be doing soon enough; do they have to drag you away from your own world, lock you up to be exhibited like some peculiar insect? Pardon me, I'm bitter, I guess. I'll let you in on a secret: as soon as I get home I'm going to resign. I'm going back with the ship tomorrow, and I'm glad of it. I only wish you and your friend weren't coming, or any natives for that matter."

It was all I could do not to show my shock. Tomorrow? My friend? Who could that be but Georyn, who was captured with me? Georyn to be taken, too? He must have regained consciousness, then. That was some comfort; but perhaps he'd be better off if he hadn't.

The doctor was not insensitive; he noted my concern and made a surprisingly accurate guess as to its cause, considering that he thought his words meaningless to me. "He's all right," he assured me. "Do you want to see him? I think I can fix it, though it'll be only for a minute or two. I know you've got no idea what I'm saying, but I'll fix it anyway." Purposefully, he left the room.

I must pull myself together, I thought, if I am to see Georyn. I must behave like an enchantress. No, not that; I must tell him the truth, the way I started to. The plan was definitely in ruins now; if the colonists' ship, their only means of quick retreat, was to leave tomorrow and if Georyn was to be kept in isolation until liftoff, there would be no opportunity for him to impress them before it was too late. Or for him to be led into any rash moves by his trust in the Stone, either. Still, we were in for some horrible experiences; wasn't it best that he face them realistically?

And yet, perhaps I was thinking less of him than of myself. If I told Georyn the facts, there would be no more mystery between us, no sham, no deception. But would there really be more of truth? He might take me off the pedestal and love me simply as a girl; he might kiss me, even, if we were ever allowed any privacy. Yet wouldn't I be taking from him the one thing that was in my power to give? Under the present circumstances it might be cruel to disillusion him. Absurd as it seemed, perhaps his belief in my nonexistent magic powers was the only solace he now had. . . .

I decided to keep quiet; maybe I was as obligated to that as to the role I must play for the Imperials. Yet what does an enchantress say, when she has no more magic to offer?

That he should be cast into prison without ever having set eyes upon the Dragon was a grievous blow to Georyn. Well did he know that he was in the power of the monster's dread henchmen, for it could not be doubted that the surroundings in which he found himself were manifestations of some evil enchantment. Moreover, he could hear a fearsome clamor from without that could be naught but the roaring of the beast. Yet he was apparently to face a time of waiting before the final confrontation, and the thought of what might easily occur during that time chilled him to the marrow.

Since he had so far been neither fed to the Dragon nor killed in any other fashion, it was evident that his captors were planning some torment for him; and Georyn had seen and heard too much of such things not to be very frightened indeed. His greatest fear, however, was not so much of pain itself as of what he might be forced to say under its influence. Torment usually had some purpose, and it was reasonable to suppose that it would be so in this case also. Only too well could he guess what that purpose would be, for had not the Lady impressed upon him that he must under no circumstances reveal that she was an enchantress, warning him that the servants of the Dragon would do their best to learn her identity? If the quest was doomed, as seemed likely, it was probable that the world would end in dragon's fire very soon now; and it did not matter very much what happened to *him*. But the Lady had implied that for her to be discovered would bring an evil fate upon herself as well as upon the world, and to prevent this he must now find strength to endure whatever was about to befall him. He hoped that the Stone would offer some measure of protection.

When the guard, who had not the form of a demon but rather a face resembling that of an ordinary man, came to him and beckoned, Georyn did not resist. He knew that it would not do any good, and was it not better to walk than to be carried? So he followed resolutely, expecting to enter some fell dungeon. The place to which he was taken was not a dungeon, however; rather, it was a small room where, to his joy, the Enchantress awaited him. So far, at least, she was unharmed. She still wore the ragged shift in which her original captors had clothed her; her dark hair was lustrous no longer, but bedraggled; weary and pale was her countenance. Yet to Georyn she was no less beautiful than on the day he had first beheld her. To see her thus at the mercy of the Dragon's slaves was a thing past bearing.

"You do not wear the Emblem!" he exclaimed. "They—they have not taken it?"

"No," she said, "they have not touched it, nor seen it either; it is hidden." Her voice was low and sounded almost as if she had been weeping.

"Lady," said Georyn urgently, "tell me what is now before me, that I may prepare myself for it."

She hesitated. "It is not a cheering prospect, I fear."

"As you know, I am loath to walk in the dark. Tell me

at least whether an attempt will be made to learn anything from me."

"Very well, Georyn," she said slowly. "I will be honest with you; we are in great trouble, and we face a fate that will be hard to bear. You have guessed truly that they seek information from us."

"From *us*, Lady?" he asked, appalled. "From you also?"

"Yes, but I shall not give it to them."

"Nor shall I," Georyn assured her. "I will die under the torment before I reveal any of your secrets."

She blanched. "Still am I struck with horror at the ways of your world. It will not be as you think; they will inflict no pain upon us. Nevertheless, we will need all our courage; for we are to be taken far away to a prison from which there is no escape."

"Shall we then spend the rest of our lives in prison?" cried Georyn. This was far worse than a quick death in battle with the Dragon!

"It appears so. I tell you this, Georyn, because I believe you have a right to the truth; but you must not despair, for in the end some power beyond my seeing may save us."

He clasped her hands between his. "I shall not despair," he told her, "so long as I have the Stone. But the quest, Lady? Have we yet hope of killing the Dragon, or must evil indeed overcome the earth?"

The Enchantress bent her head. "I must confess to you, Georyn," she said sadly, "that there is now very little hope."

As she spoke thus, the guard returned to take Georyn away, and wretched was the time that followed; but not yet was the hour of complete hopelessness come. For in his heart, Georyn did not believe that the power of the Enchantress could be defeated. It was possible that *he* should fail, die, or be cast into perpetual imprisonment, but not that the Lady should. Yet she now seemed to consider it so. How could this be, when her wisdom encompassed so vast a realm, past all knowledge of men?

At the beginning, Georyn had assumed that the Enchantress's magic was infallible: that she knew all truth, and could control much of it. He had by now perceived that this was not so; the Lady herself was liable to perplexity and also to danger. Had she not told him that even she could have no specific foreknowledge of all that must come to pass ere the Dragon could be challenged? And in the matter of the final condition that was so puzzling, the requirement that he must give up that which he deemed most necessary to the triumph of good, she had been unable to offer any guidance. *When it has been fulfilled, you will know*, she had said. It had not been fulfilled yet; and was that not, perchance, the reason for their present desperate case?

The thought of the paradoxical condition had long disturbed him; he knew not how he could meet such a requirement. Still, he was aware that he was not meant to know. It is ever the way with forces that are arrayed against evil, that they run deeper than a man's understanding; had he not heard tales aplenty of wicked spells broken through the fulfillment of conditions that on the surface seemed quite impossible? There was yet a chance, surely, that the opportunity to fulfill this one would come to him in some unforeseeable fashion.

But as he pondered this, Georyn knew a dire foreboding, and the implications of it smote his heart. For one thing above all else did he deem essential to good, and that was the Lady's well-being; and he could see no logic to her captivity if it were not to serve some mysterious end. He had thought himself willing to make whatever sacrifice was demanded as the price of the Dragon's defeat, but not until now had he guessed how cruel a choice he might face. With dark forces indeed was he dealing, should the breaking of the spell involve any hurt to the Enchantress! Thus at last did Georyn fear that he was to meet a trial in which he could do naught but yield; and for this anguish, even the Stone held little comfort.

I lay in the dark, wondering whether this was my last night on Andrecia. Where would I be this time tomorrow? Would they let me be with Georyn? Would I ever see Evrek again, or Father? Would I ever see anyone again with whom I could communicate? My guard, the doctor named Jarel, wanted to communicate—he tried so hard, it was doubly difficult not to respond. For I could see that Jarel was not an unkind man or even an unthinking one; however immature the attitudes of his people might be, he was sympathetic, and sympathy's much harder to stand out against than cruelty. Was it even possible to hold out forever, for days and weeks and years? *Oh, Father,* I thought desperately, *what do you do when the challenge you're given is just too much for you?*

Elana?

Father? We hadn't ever communicated over any distance; I hadn't been sure it was possible, even under the stress of the emotion I now felt.

What's happening to you, Elana?

I told him; almost before I could form the thought I sensed his response, swift and strong and heartening, though grim. *I suspected that. Evrek and I are nearby; we're going to do everything we can. But I'm not going to pull punches. You're in a pretty serious fix.*

One reason you can trust Father so implicitly is that you know that if there's something really bad to be faced, he'll give it to you straight, no matter what it costs him personally. He'll be brutally honest, and then he'll offer you the only help there is to offer, his belief in your ability to bear up under it. It was so in this case. He didn't ease into it; he simply presented the facts that I had to know.

The Imperials have a research center, their own way of studying primitive people psychologically. . . .

I know. I understand their talk. I'm not sure if I'm brave enough, but I'll try to be. I'll fool them.

Elana, you don't understand! You can't fool them. Imperial psychologists aren't that backward. They have drugs, facilities; they can get all they want from your subconscious mind. There would be a very extensive disclosure indeed; all that you know of the Federation would soon become the property of Imperial science. Their own race would be harmed—but more than that, there are things they'd misuse, things that could help them invade not only this world, but others.

It'll be worse than if I sat right down and explained the plan to them, I thought wretchedly. Andrecia will be theirs for sure; and on top of that, once they're warned, the Service will never be able to save any planet from them by this kind of a ruse. And what if—what if their development is thrown out of kilter? What if their whole future's jeopardized, because of *me*?

There was a pause. Then finally Father continued, *An agent doesn't let himself be put in that position, Elana.*

But I don't see how I can prevent . . . I didn't complete the thought, for all at once I did see. No, an agent does *not* allow such a disclosure to take place, not when the stakes are as high as all that.

I think I really must have known before he brought it up; I just didn't know that I knew it. If you commit yourself totally to a principle, eventually you have to think it through to its fullest logical conclusion, and I'd done a lot of speculating after the incident of the fire. Ever since the day I'd seen Father communicate with Ilura in the moment before her death, I'd been aware that deliberate sacrifice of an agent's life is not, in the Service, a subject beyond the pale of frank discussion. The Oath makes fearful demands of a Senior Agent; he is bound, in circumstances such as these, to introduce that subject.

Is that an order? I queried, half-hoping he'd ease the agony of the decision by saying yes.

No! I don't give such orders!

And that clinched it. Because it wasn't just that I was his daughter; he would, I realized, have replied the same to anyone—and that was another reason why the Service was so careful about selecting people in the first place. This was a matter not of an externally imposed duty, but of the Oath. *Above all other considerations.* How could there be any question? When you dedicate your life to that, you do it without reservations.

I knew I could find some means. It is easiest if you are equipped beforehand with a small red capsule, as I later found that Father and Evrek had been all along. (Both of them having known more about Imperials than they had seen fit to mention to me.) But there are other ways, and my captors were not watching for that; it was not a move that they would expect from the natives, and they didn't suspect that I had any inkling of their plans for me.

So I assured Father, *You needn't worry about me. I won't board their ship.* I wondered, though, if I'd really have what it takes; whereas the prospect of life as an Imperial captive was an appalling one, I did not want to escape in that manner.

Elana! Don't be afraid! Underneath, things aren't as terrible as we make them. Besides, it may not be necessary. We've still got some time; we may be able to find a way out. I'm not giving up hope yet, and you mustn't either!

I won't. Not till the very last minute!

After a short interval he contacted me again. *Look, I'm going to do something that may help a little. I don't know if it'll work over this distance, but we'll give it a try. Just relax for a while, if you can.*

Relax? Well, that was a rather unrealistic suggestion, I thought. I lay back on the bunk believing that very likely I would never close my eyes again; but pretty soon I began to feel better, somehow. Maybe it is less painful once the decision's made, I reflected. And yet, I didn't see how I could possibly feel reassured and safeguarded at such a time. Then I realized that he was transmitting to me in the other way, the way that gives you not words, but deep knowledge. In this case it was a sort of faith in the underlying rightness of things that I would never have found in my own mind. He was giving me his conviction that no matter what happened, it *would* turn out all right. And with that feeling, I fell easily into a dreamless sleep.

When I awoke it was still dark beyond the window, but inside the room there was a light; the young doctor, Jarel, was holding it over me. He smiled sympathetically. "Don't be frightened," he said to me. "I wish you weren't so scared of me. I'm not going to hurt you. I wish I could get you to believe that."

I avoided his eyes, trying to look as if I didn't understand without overdoing it. After all, even the average Andrecian would pick up some reassurance from his tone and his expression. How ironic it is, I thought. He really means it! He really means me no harm! Yet surely he must know that for anyone, even a person much more primitive than an Andrecian, the life of a zoo specimen would be intolerable.

No, not exactly intolerable. I knew better, now. There is nothing that teaches you the value of life for its own sake faster than the prospect of having to give it up.

Jarel went on talking to me as he had before, conversationally, as a man does to a dog he is fond of. He didn't dream, of course, that I could understand him; and he spoke mainly to reassure himself, I think, for it was evident that he did not enjoy this job. "I'm sorry to wake you up this early, but we're leaving in a few hours. I've got to get you ready. Look, I'll have to stun you again; you won't like it, but it can't be helped."

He raised the stunner. Resolutely I made the mental adjustment to drop my Shield (I hoped it would work; it had before). Inwardly I was in a dreadful turmoil. A few hours . . . so little time. What if I couldn't find any means to do what must be done? What if I was stunned until I was taken aboard their ship? Could I possibly *use* the Shield and then fake paralysis? No, I could never pull it off, not well enough to convince a doctor.

Suddenly Jarel burst out, "I don't care what they say, you're *human*. You're entitled to human dignity, if you can figure out what to do! Here, put these on; I'll turn my back for a minute." He presented me with still another set of clothing, and I realized that his own instructions had been to immobilize me and dress me forcibly. I debated briefly as to whether I was duty-bound to pretend not to understand, but decided that enough was enough; I changed quickly, hoping that he would keep his back turned long enough to be oblivious of my practiced way with buttons. It was a relief, anyway, to get out of that awful Andrecian garment and into a clean white tunic.

After I was dressed, he did stun me; the paralysis wasn't total, just enough to keep me helpless, and I was still able to move slightly and to speak. (I tried not to take it too calmly, since a native would be understandably upset.) I wondered if they had done the same to Georyn, and was again thankful that we had prepared him, for it's hard to bear when you don't know what is going to happen. In this case, various things were done to ensure that none of the alien bacteria of which the Imperials were so afraid would get onto their ship; Jarel gave me shots and the like, besides treating me with some sort of ray that I suppose was designed to have an antiseptic effect. He'd be surprised, I thought, if he knew how well protected I already was! The Federation's methods would make his seem no better than those of a primitive medicine man.

Everything that I had was taken from me; it was lucky, certainly, that I hadn't tried to rely on hiding the Emblem beneath my clothes. But as I realized this, I realized something else: the Stone! If they had done this to Georyn, they had taken the Stone.

I don't know why this struck me as the final, unendurable climax to all our troubles. Beside some of the other things, it was a mere trifle, for the Stone did not really have any power, after all. I must be going over the edge, I thought; I must be starting to believe that it was magic! And yet, Georyn believed. I had made him believe, and I had decided to let him go on believing. It was clearer than ever that without the Stone, he would be much worse off than before he had ever had it. He would think that he had fallen into the power of evil, as indeed he had.

For the first time the enormity of what was about to happen to Georyn really came through to me. Before, our captivity had been a shared misfortune, a thing that, if we were brave enough, we could face up to. But I had not known as much then. Georyn would have to face the ordeal alone, and he would not go as an unthinking victim, as some Andrecians might. Drugs? Facilities? Georyn's clear, penetrating mind torn open to the clinical probing of Imperial science? *Are we then to spend the rest of our lives in prison?* he had asked me, and he had not been able to hide the horror that prospect aroused in him. Georyn would die! Sooner or later, no matter how "humanely" they treated him, he would die; but before he died he would suffer terribly.

And it was my fault. If I had not come with Georyn, the thing would have gone according to plan; he would very probably have either succeeded or died quickly, as Terwyn had. For that matter, if I had not taken on the role of an enchantress in the first place, he might never have come anywhere near the Imperials at all.

Jarel stood by the window; he was still talking, more to himself than to me. "I know you don't understand what's happening to you. Maybe it's just as well you don't. Sure, they'll give you plenty of food and the best medical care there is, and your quarters will be comfortable enough. It's a top grade laboratory, nothing but the best for the glory of Imperial science. All the same, it's a pretty rotten business as far as I'm concerned. I saw some films of the experiments they do in that place while I was in medical school. Strictly psychological stuff, you understand. They aren't going to dissect you or anything, not physically. We're above that sort of thing, didn't you know? That would be inhuman! The biologists are always lobbying for it, saying they've got as much right to reap the benefits of interstellar exploration as the psychologists have, but they'll never get the bill through; it would be a backward step, I'd say. But of course belief in the inevitable progress of civilization has gone out of fashion, and who am I to express any faith in the destiny of man after what I've seen done on this world? Sometimes I wonder whether what we've got ought to be labeled 'civilization' at all."

Turning, he came over to me and patted my hand gently. "Poor little native girl. You don't know anything at all about such things. And who's to say that we're really ahead of you? Maybe we'd be better off if we'd never lost our innocence. It's a long, long road from your culture to ours, and it's even money, perhaps, that it ought never to be traveled. Is there anything it leads to that's worth the cost? If so, it's something we haven't found yet. Why, you almost look as if you could guess what I'm saying!"

I was staring at him, having been startled out of my determination to keep my eyes expressionless. He really doesn't know, I thought. How sad, that he doesn't know if the road goes anywhere!

"If in some strange way you can guess," Jarel went on, "if there's a kind of knowing beyond anything we humans understand, the way a sick animal knows, sometimes, if you're about to put him out of his misery—well, I want to tell you one thing: I'm sorry. If it were in my power to free you, I would do so; and what's more, if it were in my power to hand this planet back to your people I would do that, too. I'd give anything to be able to fix it so that our glorious Empire would simply pull out and leave the place as we found it."

He meant it. I knew beyond the faintest doubt that he meant it very sincerely. And all of a sudden I got a wild, preposterous idea. The power to free me? No, Jarel didn't have that; I was a unique specimen, one that he could scarcely persuade them to give up. But to free Georyn, to free him and give back the Stone—that might be a different story. The choice between the captives must have been more or less arbitrary. What would happen if he knew that Georyn had special powers? If Jarel knew, and no one else? If he really did want his people to leave, wouldn't he cooperate?

In order to understand, though, Jarel would have to know the whole plan. If the point of the plan was revealed to him, he'd see why he mustn't tell, the immediate reason, anyway. And if he didn't tell anyone, neither the Andrecians nor his own people could be harmed by the disclosure.

But it would mean breaking the Oath—deliberately.

I would be giving up the one thing I had to cling to, the only sort of comfort I had left. And I'd have to die knowing that if I'd misjudged, if Jarel proved unworthy of the trust, my death would be in vain. Well, not really in vain, because of course I wouldn't give Jarel anywhere near as much information as the Imperial psychologists could get from me, but still not wholly effectual.

It was an awful chance to take. Yet wasn't it the *only* chance, the only hope of salvaging anything at all out of the whole business? After all, Andrecia would certainly be lost to the invaders if Georyn wasn't released—whereas if I acted, there was a bare possibility, perhaps, that it might not be. Once free, Georyn would try the thing.

If Jarel kept quiet, I would be the only one who'd be hurt. It would be a strange paradox, though, if good could be brought about by making a deliberate disclosure! This decision was harder than the other one. Agonizing though that had been, I'd at least known what I ought to do; I'd been committed beforehand. Now I had no such help, and I knew well enough that I was being swayed by love.

Jarel gazed down at me with a sort of desperate longing for some sign that I had recognized his compassion toward me. And I gave it to him. I looked straight into his eyes and said, "Do you *really* want to give this world back to the natives, Jarel? If you do, you're going to get a chance to prove it."

The Dragon

J arel stood looking down at the girl, wondering for the hundredth time what it was about her that seemed so special. There was something behind those unfathomable dark eyes, something that he couldn't quite pinpoint. Not just intelligence; the tall blond man who was captured at the same time was intelligent, too, even more so, on the surface. But with this girl, he couldn't help feeling that there was more beneath the surface than there appeared to be. It was almost as if— well, as if those eyes were deliberately veiled!

The psychologists at the Research Center would, of course, crack her open very quickly; if there was anything to be found, they would find it in short order. And undoubtedly some guy who had never set foot on an alien planet would get publication credits out of it that would establish him as the authority on this primitive species. Logic told Jarel that he ought to be looking forward to that. He was curious, wasn't he? Curious enough to have been haunted by the thought of this girl ever since she was brought in?

But he was not looking forward to it. The thought of her mental privacy being stripped away seemed indecent, somehow, just as it had suddenly seemed indecent not to give her the physical privacy he would accord an ordinary patient. Besides, wasn't it possible that if she were approached with genuine kindness, as you'd approach a kid, perhaps, the girl might prove to be educable? If he had a little more time, he might be able to teach her to speak a few words of Basic. Or he might even learn her language; presumably she had one, though he hadn't been able to get her to open her mouth so far.

If only he could make her trust him. He focused on her eyes, willing them to signal some trace of comprehension—and, to his amazement, they did. In one brief instant of transition the veil was removed and those eyes came alive, alive with power and assurance and a very evident understanding not only of his wish but of many other things. At the same time the girl spoke to him in a soft, steady voice; it seemed almost as if she was saying, "Would you really like to give this world back to the natives, Jarel? Are you willing to prove it?" But of course, she couldn't actually have said that! The words she used were of a strange language, just so much gibberish as far as he was concerned.

"Say, you *can* talk!" he exclaimed excitedly. "I sure wish I could understand you!"

"But you can, just as I can understand you. Can't you?" For a moment she wavered, as if she were no longer quite sure.

Jarel blinked. He was losing his grip! Too much senseless worry over these natives. He'd started to imagine things. Or maybe it was only wishful thinking.

"We haven't any time to waste, Jarel. Must I draw pictures? I could diagram your Empire's chief solar systems, point out your colonies, and all that; but the natives don't need such proof. They hear me speak and they answer, that's all there is to it."

He stared at her, overwhelmed. If he were imagining a conversation with the girl, she would not have said *that*. "Telepathy?" he asked incredulously. "We're reading each other's minds?"

"Not exactly 'reading.' I only get what you direct toward me; you have control over it. And of course, you only get what I choose to tell you. Keep on talking out loud; that's easiest."

"Who are you? You're not a native at all!"

"No. Who I am and how I got here needn't concern you. My name is Elana." The syllables of the name itself came from her spoken words.

Jarel sat down on the edge of the cot on which she was lying. She was still immobilized, of course, but it didn't seem to bother her; he had the feeling that the fright she'd shown before had been no less a mask than the lack of comprehension. "If you can do this, Elana," he said slowly, "why did you keep quiet so long? You were faking, weren't you? You understood all along?"

"I understood."

Suddenly realizing what that meant, he let out a horrified gasp. "All of it? About the Research Center, too?"

"That especially!"

"But that's awful! You're on *our* level!"

"Not exactly," she said calmly.

"You're above our level? More advanced?"

"Quite a bit above, Jarel. My civilization, I mean, not me personally. I tell you this because you must know, to understand what I'm going to ask of you."

Jarel shook his head sadly. "I can guess what you're going to ask. And I can't do it. Oh, I'd be happy to set you free, but I just couldn't get away with it. You'd never get out of camp."

"I know that. You'd have let me go before now if you could have."

"Yes, I think I would. You have me figured pretty well, haven't you? But look, it won't be so bad, now. When I tell them what you are, they'll treat you differently. They'll roll out the red carpet for you, back home."

She broke in quickly, "That's just what you mustn't do, Jarel! You've got to promise right now that you won't tell anyone that I'm other than what I seem—or you will not hear one more word from me! I'll go back to faking, and I'll stick to it. I can, you know."

He looked at her with astonishment. "But why? What are you hiding?" Frankly, he came out with the only possibility that occurred to him. "Are your people hostile to the Empire? You're not a spy or anything, are you? Because if you are, you'll never get away with it, not at the Research Center."

She laughed. "I'm not a spy, and my people are not hostile to yours, I swear they're not! Oh, that's funny! If only you knew!"

Her amusement was genuine, Jarel realized. In any case, it was impossible to imagine this girl as an agent of some alien power. She was too young, too innocent. Her involvement in this must surely be accidental, though what sort of accident could have stranded her on this planet, he couldn't begin to guess. "But look," he protested, "you can't fake at the Research Center! You don't know—"

"Yes, I do," she said seriously. "I have a way of dealing with that problem, Jarel. So long as you don't tell, the secret will be safe."

Well, no doubt anyone who had command of telepathy had other abilities beyond anything he could ever imagine. Still, the Center's methods were very efficient; and physiologically, she was humanoid. "It'll be pretty rough, you know, for anybody with a mind like yours," he said with concern.

"Let's not talk about it."

"Okay," Jarel agreed reluctantly. "You've got nerve, I'll say that. More than I'd have. I don't see why you've got to keep up the pose, though. I don't even see why you were posing to begin with."

The girl said urgently, "Jarel, did you mean what you said about wanting to make the Empire give up this world?"

"Yes, I did." It was disloyal, traitorous even, Jarel thought. He could be court-martialed if Dulard knew, yet he did mean it.

"Well, my people want that, too. We don't want the planet for ourselves. I've been told you might think that we do, but you're just going to have to trust my word that we will let the natives have it, if we can get your colonists to leave."

"Get us to leave? *You?* How?"

"By playing a little trick on you. Nothing that will hurt anyone, I promise you."

Jarel frowned. "But look, if you're more advanced than we are, you must have superior weapons, so why don't you just——"

"Lay down an ultimatum? Use force? Is that your definition of advancement, Jarel?"

"Not mine, but . . . you're really beyond that? Is *any* civilization beyond it?"

"Yes! We have other ways. But they're not foolproof, sometimes they fall through. And this one is about to, unless you help."

Aside from his desire to see the natives come out on

top, Jarel was not at all adverse to the idea of a trick being played on Dulard. It was a rather intriguing notion, in fact. And besides, he would never be able to live with himself if he were unwilling to stand behind what he'd been saying all this time. He drew a deep breath. "I'm probably out of my mind, but I'll help, so long as I don't have to get my shipmates killed in the process."

"You don't. They won't be harmed. Now listen, would you be able to release one of the captives? Not me, but the man who was caught at the same time I was?"

To set him free temporarily? Yes, Jarel thought. It would be easy enough to cook up a story about having discovered a physical defect that made the man unfit for the Research Center—a bad heart, or something—to explain having to replace him; to Dulard, one native was like another, except for this girl. But what good would it do? He would only be recaptured or perhaps killed. "This man's not one of *your* kind," he said, puzzled.

"No. He's a real native."

Then they *were* people, Jarel thought triumphantly. To a race that was far, far ahead of the Empire, even, the natives were people. For he couldn't have been mistaken about the way she looked at him.

"But he's the key to our plan," the girl went on. "Jarel, have you ever heard of psychokinesis?"

"Psychokinesis—PK? Like the experiments they do with dice?" Jarel nodded numbly.

"It's more than just influencing dice. Would you like to see a demonstration?"

"Now I *am* out of my mind."

She didn't answer, but the stunner that he had laid on the table rose, drifted across the room, and hovered in the air above the paralyzed girl. Jarel didn't say anything; he was speechless.

"Does it frighten you, Jarel?"

"Yes, I guess it does, a little. Not the way it would most people, though. It's funny—we were actually talking about ESP the other day; I was saying that some races might have developed paranormal abilities instead of technology. Except I didn't mean it, really. The other guys laughed, and Dulard said that if those natives ever started doing anything of that nature, he'd pull out so fast—" Breaking off with a sudden gasp of excitement, Jarel exclaimed, "Oh . . . I think I see!"

"I'm glad you do; it saves a lot of explanations."

"But you can't fool Dulard, Elana! He's no anthropologist, but he's sharp enough to be suspicious if you try anything like that, when you're obviously of a different race than the others."

The girl said, "Do you suppose we didn't think of that? That's why we trained the native to do it, the man I want you to free."

"You mean they do have such abilities?"

"Not normally. It's an advanced thing, Jarel. But it can be awakened, sometimes. You see why no one must know about me; if they guessed I'd arranged it, it wouldn't work any better than if I did it myself. There are other reasons, too, reasons that have to do with protecting your people; but those are pretty complicated."

She's right, Jarel thought. If she were to let her abilities be discovered, Dulard would smell a rat for sure. But that means she's sacrificing herself for the natives, the same natives that turned her over to us. And she talks about the other reasons being for our benefit, which is even worse, considering what we're doing to her.

"I won't give you away," he promised soberly. "And I'll get your key man released, somehow. This man—you taught him? Elana, the implications of that . . . "

"It's not as easy as it may seem, to teach, I mean. I probably couldn't teach you."

"Because we're not good enough?" he asked unhappily. "We haven't the capacity for anything beyond gadgetry?"

"No, whatever gave you an idea like that? You've progressed far above these people, haven't you? But you see, I wouldn't be able to give you a Stone."

"A stone?" Jarel suddenly remembered something, something that had seemed strange to him when he'd prepared the native who was now to be freed. There had indeed been a stone, and when he had taken it he had noticed inexplicable anguish on the man's face. It had surprised him, not only because it was such an odd thing in itself but because the man had reacted so stoically to everything else that had been done to him. He had displayed no fear at all, although he had been alert rather than apathetic. And the stone itself was extraordinary; Jarel had kept it, thinking that it might make a good paperweight.

He pulled it out of his pocket, while the girl stared as if the thing were a priceless jewel. Mystified, Jarel protested, "What does a stone have to do with psychokinesis? It's just ordinary river rock; it can't possibly have any special properties."

"None that you would understand, Jarel. But to the man you took it from, it's magic. With it he has power; without it, he does not."

"You mean he's superstitious about it?"

"I guess you could say so. I don't think that's exactly the way to express it, though."

Jarel fingered the smooth surface of the stone. There was so much, so very much, that he did not understand. But if he was to free the man, he must do it now. He would be sticking his neck out, certainly. Yet he was willing to play along with this fantastic girl to that extent; in fact he'd known right from the beginning that he was going to do whatever she asked. He only wished that it could be something that would save her. Helplessly he asked, "Isn't there anything I can do—for you, I mean?"

She hesitated, and for the first time since she had revealed herself she averted her eyes. Finally she said, "Well, there is one thing."

"What?"

"Don't leave me stunned. Don't let them carry me aboard that ship; I've got to walk under my own power."

He smiled. "That's a small request. You won't be able to escape unless you can fly like a bird, but if by some miracle you could, I'd be glad of it!"

"Thanks," she whispered. "It's—important, Jarel." He administered the neutralizer; she sat up. "Jarel? I'll tell you one thing more, since I've gone this far. The road you spoke of—it is worth traveling! There's something beyond what you know, something hundreds of years in your Empire's future, that justifies 'faith in human destiny' as you put it. Only you aren't permitted to see, that is your people aren't, because the seeing would interfere with the traveling. Do you get what I mean?"

"Not at all," he said slowly. "Only if you say so, I'm just crazy enough to take your word for it. Can't you explain it a little more?"

"I'd better not."

"But we'll find your people's worlds, surely, maybe soon—"

"No, you won't."

"Why are you so sure?" Jarel demanded.

"Because we don't want you to find them."

"Elana, you can't just leave it there! Am I to hear, to know, that there's a civilization existing somewhere, a civilization that has *answers*, and then never find it? That's no easier than the other way. It's harder, even. Don't I deserve better than that?"

"It isn't supposed to be easy. It isn't a matter of deserving, either. Someone, a very wise man, once told me that to make things easier for the most deserving would be the surest way to mess up the whole business. Well, I may already have messed it up; if you break your word and tell, I surely have."

"I don't understand!"

"I don't expect you to. I don't either, very well. Not yet. I'm not really educated yet, you see. But I guess it's that if your people don't find the answers for themselves, they won't find them at all. Or else if they do, those answers won't be what they ought to be."

Jarel said softly, "And this future, it's really worth all of what leads up to it? Our history isn't very pretty, Elana. You don't know! Your people probably don't have all the black marks against them that mine do— "

"I do know. It's the same for all worlds."

All worlds . . . she's so casual, he thought. How many worlds have her people seen? Apparently *they* haven't found star roving an empty dream. "Worth all the sorry mistakes that've been made in the name of progress?" he persisted. "Worth men dying for?"

"Oh, yes," she told him. "Certainly worth dying for." And then, with surprising intensity, she added, "It had better be."

It must be a fine future at that, Jarel reflected, if she's any sample of it! Idealism may even come back in style. He smiled at her. "I'm going to wake up in my own bunk pretty soon and find that I've been dreaming all this. Don't worry, I won't tell anybody. They'd lock me up if I admitted that a girl I met on a primitive planet, a girl barely out of her teens, had been giving me the inside dope on human destiny—and that I *believed* her! And you're going to be the docile, uncomprehending captive again, aren't you? Your eyes are going to be dull and blank, just as they were before. What proof will I ever have for myself that you even pretend to know anything about what's back of things, about what's in the future or what's worth dying for?"

She returned the smile, though hers was a rather grim smile, he thought. "Oh, you'll have proof," she assured him, "very soon."

B lack indeed was the dread and the despair into which Georyn was now plunged. In the dead of night he had been turned to stone, had been jabbed with sharp needles, and had undergone other fell ministrations that were unquestionably concerned with the casting of spells upon him. Yet because many of these terrors had not been unlike those toward which the Lady's own spell had hardened him, he had borne up valiantly. Once the Stone had been taken from him, however, he had fully believed himself to be beyond hope of deliverance. Worse, the cause for which he had been brought to this pass was now totally and irredeemably lost. Georyn was well aware that although the Enchantress might have been right in her promise that he would not be subjected to physical pain, his captors would have plenty of other ways of making him suffer; she had, after all, warned that his imprisonment would be unending. And not the least of his torments would be the knowledge that she too was at their mercy, and that should the Dragon indeed consume the world, she might perish utterly.

Why he felt called upon to meet his fate bravely, Georyn could not have said, for what purpose would be served now that all hope was quenched? Yet somehow not to do so seemed a betrayal, a betrayal of something that he could never willfully abandon. It seemed near to being sorry that he had chosen to pursue the quest, and he was not sorry. He had failed, but that which to him was represented by the Enchantress still existed; there was yet the Emblem, hidden though it was, and some good would therefore surely abide. So as the long night wore away he endured, and mastered his failing spirits; and he told himself that he could withstand any trial the Dragon's slaves might devise for him, save only one.

But at first light of dawn that one seemed all too likely to confront him, for he was taken again into the presence of the Enchantress; and at once he perceived that she faced some new and overpowering jeopardy. Pale and drawn was she now, and her eyes were distant; Georyn felt that in her mind, perhaps, she lived again in the enchanted realm, that fair realm from which she had exiled herself for the sake of this ill-starred venture. She was clad in a simple tunic of white, the collar of which lay open, and her neck was bare of any chain. He dared not think that she might have been deprived of the Emblem, even as he of the Stone. Yet her terror was now painfully evident: she shivered, and when she greeted him her voice trembled. He resisted the desire to question her, for the guard stood by; but he had little doubt as to the purpose for which he had been brought here. And indeed, his suspicion was soon confirmed, for behold! that guard held forth the Stone, temptingly, and as he did so he smiled an ominous smile.

Georyn gazed at it with longing, yet stayed his hand. He was aware that his mere imprisonment or death would not satisfy the Dragon's minions; they could have killed him long ago had that been their sole interest. Rather, the free surrender of his will was wanted, and that it should be sought through threat to the Lady had long been his most harrowing fear. He saw now the full measure of the submission that they would attempt to force. *Much evil could be wrought by its misuse,* the Enchantress had warned when first she bestowed the Stone upon him. And had she not said that those who served the Dragon were but men bewitched? This one was now smiling upon him as if to say that such thralldom was not really so bad; and that if he would but consent, he could win the fellow's friendship! Well convinced was Georyn that the Stone would be given back on no terms save as the instrument of his enslavement, and that he would refuse not at his own peril alone, but at the Lady's also.

"You hesitate, Georyn," she said softly. "There is nothing to fear; take the Stone."

He turned to her, perplexed. She would not counsel him to yield, even to save herself; of that he was certain. "It is not to be thought that this henchman of the Dragon, whether he be demon or merely bewitched, offers me power out of love for good," he demurred.

"Is it not?" the Enchantress answered. "Perhaps you can scarce believe so. But no matter, for the Stone is regained, and you are free now." Seeing that he made no move toward it, she took it into her own hand; and by that token he knew that the thing itself was unsullied.

"Free? To what end am I free, with the fell creature's eye upon us both?" Georyn protested. "There are terms, Lady, and I cannot accept until you name them."

"They are beyond your understanding. Go now, Georyn! You are to be released; go while you have the chance."

"I shall not leave you in their hands."

"You must, or all the quest is vain. There is very little time."

The quest? Had hope been born anew, then, that the defeat of the Dragon could be accomplished? Perhaps he could yet turn the Stone to good if he took it with that purpose! But more terrible would be the penalty if he defied them thus; looking upon the Enchantress, Georyn was sure that she had resigned herself to some dire fate of which she was desperately afraid. For he knew her mind; and although her eyes were resolute, he sensed much that lay behind them; and his heart forebode that her confidence was feigned. Thus was he convinced that the prophesied doom was indeed upon him, whereby he must give up either that which he most valued or the quest itself.

"Lady," he said slowly, "you have always spoken truth to me, save only in the matter of your own peril, which you have oft kept hidden. I must have the whole truth now: is your life forfeit if I continue this venture?"

A look of surprise crossed her face, and he saw from her wavering gaze that he had struck close to the mark. But she evaded it, saying, "We deal with graver matters than my life or yours, Georyn; we influence the futures of worlds."

"You have not answered my question. Is it not true that if I challenge the Dragon now, either with or without the Stone, its servants will kill you to punish my defiance?"

Steadily the Enchantress replied, "To my certain knowledge, they will not kill me whether you succeed or fail, nor will they do me any other injury."

Georyn could not believe that the Lady would tell him so direct a lie, yet it was obvious that she was concealing something. "You will be unharmed, though you remain hostage?" he persisted.

"That is not for you to choose. If you forsake the quest and go at once from this place, you may save yourself bitter sorrow; but you will not help me by it, and much that has been will go for naught. Oh, Georyn, do not lose courage now!"

Then Georyn bethought himself that should he in this evil hour fail to attempt the thing, he would betray the Lady's goal as well as his own; if for her an ill fate was indeed appointed, she would suffer it to no purpose. There was thus but one course he could take. Yet how could the Dragon be vanquished when the final condition had not been met and the dark spell was still in force? If his worst fear was unfounded, and no action of his could seal the Lady's doom, then the mysterious sacrifice was yet to be made; that it should be remitted was clearly impossible. The ways of enchantments were not so capricious as that!

He stretched forth his hand, and once again the Enchantress placed the Stone therein; but as she did so her fingers shook, and her eyes brimmed with tears. He was going now to a sure defeat, Georyn realized. He had not even any sword. All was in ruin, for the condition could never be fulfilled; yet if for a while the Stone would give him the power to oppose evil, then it was better to die thus than to submit.

"I know little of magic, Lady," he said haltingly. "I am but a woodcutter's son, and there is much that is not given to men to understand; but of this I am sure: there is more to things than we imagine. Beyond the stars are worlds without number, perhaps, and had I never sought to look beyond my own I should be the poorer for it. Is it not so with you also, that your spells have meaning whether the Dragon be killed or no? And mayhap there are other forces for good, which we do not see."

With a wan smile, she replied: "The wisdom that you set out to find has been yours from the beginning. It is as you say, or so the Starwatcher has told me."

"Then surely the Emblem will guard you, though you be forbidden to use it openly; I cannot believe otherwise!"

"You must not expect that," she said in a low voice. "Believe rather that should I not be guarded, and should aught befall me that is a grief to you, there will be no cause for your trust in enchantments to falter. For I no longer have the Emblem, and its power will be no less for my misfortune."

He stared at her, aghast. Small wonder she stood now in fear of darkness to come; the Emblem was in truth not hidden, but gone! "You have not given it to them?" he demanded.

"No, Georyn, I have not. You know, surely, that I would never do so; rather, it has passed beyond chance of their seeing," she told him.

Then ere he could question her further, the guard came forward, speaking strange words to the Lady; and she answered in her own tongue, the tongue of the enchanted realm. With growing dismay Georyn perceived that no more was she feigning the manner of a simple village maid, and he cried out, exclaiming, "He knows you for what you are!"

"Yes," she admitted slowly, "he, but no other. I have told him the truth; it was necessary, and it has not harmed our cause."

"It was he who gave back the Stone," Georyn whispered. "Lady, was that the price? Did you bargain *thus* for the Stone's return?"

She did not answer. She had no need to answer; he knew. If neither the Lady nor the servants of the Dragon had the Emblem, then it was doubtless unmade, vanished into the very air after the manner of enchanted things. Had she not told him that should her enemies ever learn that she was an enchantress, she would cease to wield any magic? "You have lost it, lost it by revealing yourself," he said sorrowfully. "You have bought back the Stone at the cost of your own power!"

"That was not quite the way it happened," said the Lady, but she did not meet his eyes. "Let us speak no more of it, Georyn! It is nothing that need worry you." But Georyn was sore distressed. She had given up her power for his sake, when he was so soon to die in any case. It seemed likely to break his heart.

And then suddenly a light burst forth upon him, and wonder took him, and a great resolve. This was the thing that had been foretold! The sacrifice had been not his to make, but hers. Naught had been specified as to *who* must break the spell that guarded the Dragon; it had been said only that the one who did so must give up whatever that person deemed most necessary to the triumph of good and must face an apparently grievous failure. To the Enchantress, what could be more necessary to good than the talisman from which all her magic sprang, and what failure more grievous than recognition by the servant of evil from whom she had vowed to hide her identity? Yet she had revealed herself and thereby lost the Emblem, and even so had the final condition been fulfilled.

Thus it came to pass that hope unlooked for surged through Georyn, and the Stone in his hand pulsed with a mighty strength; and he went forth in expectation not of defeat, but of victory. For he knew that the evil spell was now indeed broken after all, and the time for the slaying of the Dragon was come.

As soon as Georyn had been released, Jarel came back to escort me to the ship. After the hours of agonizing suspense it was a relief, I guess, to have the time run out. But I was scared all the same. Scared and a little rebellious. If something's hard but necessary, well, you may have to do it, but you don't have to like it.

Up until that moment I hadn't been able to find any way to accomplish the thing demanded of me. The room was absolutely bare of possibilities, no sharp objects, nothing. I hadn't contacted Father again; in fact when he'd tried to communicate, I'd withheld response, once I was sure it was not a rescue attempt. I couldn't have borne an exchange of thoughts with him, now that I'd broken the Oath. And besides, it would have been too hard on *him*. Some things you have to take on alone.

Jarel smiled at me. "Your protégé's free, for the moment," he said quietly. "As far as the Research Center's concerned, he's off the hook. I told them his heart wouldn't stand the liftoff. I'd have said the same about yours, but on that, they'd check me; we'd blow the whole deal."

"Will he have any chance, do you think, to—"

"I just don't know, Elana. Right now everybody's wrapped up in getting that ship off, which is the only reason I got away with letting him go when it was assumed that I'd thrown him back with the other prisoners. But if he sticks around camp, he'll be recaptured. And this isn't going to work unless it's timed just right; he's got to make it pretty dramatic. I hope he's aware of that."

I fought down rising nausea. How could Georyn possibly be aware? I was fooling myself if I thought that I'd made the disclosure from a real hope of saving Andrecia by it. And even if by some miracle he did succeed, I would never know it.

"He seemed reluctant to take back the Stone," Jarel remarked. "Is he afraid of the thing?"

"No! It's sort of mixed up, Jarel. You wouldn't be flattered by Georyn's view of things, I'm afraid. He believed that you had tampered with the Stone, that you had sold out to the powers of evil and were trying to force him to do likewise."

"He may be right," Jarel said unhappily. "About my selling out, I mean. I talk a lot about what's wrong with the Empire. Yet I stand by and watch, while——"

"You haven't a choice! And if you weren't standing by, how could you help when there's a chance to? Oh, Jarel, you're as naive as he is in some ways, I think; you've just got a different framework for it." I broke off; I was not in any mood for a philosophic discussion! But I've thought about it since. Poor Jarel, his dragons were less concrete than Georyn's but no less menacing; and he wasn't nearly so confident that they could be successfully fought. Of all the stages Youngling peoples have to go through, I do believe the age of disenchantment must be the hardest. To see so much, by methods you think are scientific, that you've no faith in there being anything you *don't* see—it must be awful.

"Look, we've got to go aboard now," Jarel was saying. "I've delayed as long as I can; they'll be coming after us in a minute. I'm sorry, Elana. I know it's going to be rough for you."

He doesn't know the half of it, I thought grimly. And when he finds out, he'll feel worse than ever; he'll blame himself.

I knew what I was going to try. I'd watched out the window, desperate for an idea, and I'd gotten one; needless to say I was not enthusiastic about it, but it was the best that could be managed. Carrying it out might be a problem, though. To drop the Shield was possible for me; I'd proved that with the stunners. But to drop it in this case—well, I just hoped that my nerve would hold.

Jarel took my arm. "I'll come to see you often during the trip," he promised. "And later, at the Center, too. I'll tell them I've got a scientific interest in you. Don't worry, I won't let anyone catch on."

I didn't dare to answer, I was so afraid I'd give him a hint of the truth. He'd feel bound to stop me, of course, if he knew what I was planning. And underneath I knew I wanted him to. We went outdoors into the dazzling sunlight of the clearing. Ahead, between us and the ship, was the "dragon." It *did* look rather as if it were alive; I had noticed that from the window. And certainly the racket it made would have done credit to the most ferocious of beasts! The colonists had finished burning off vegetation for the time being and were now using the machine to dig a foundation for their first permanent building; it was scooping up tremendous gulps of dirt and rock, crunching them to rubble, and heaping that rubble in what had once been a grassy valley, but which was now almost level with the grade of the clearing. I watched for a few moments, then averted my eyes.

It's funny what you recall when you look back on a thing. I remember how brightly the sun shone, and how the light streaming through the leafy wall beyond the blackened rim of the clearing reminded me of the way it had been in that other place, the place by the river where Georyn and I had spent those few happy days. I remember how I thought of my first moment on Andrecia, of the way I'd looked out at the shimmering green meadow from the door of our landing craft and seen visions of thrilling, glorious adventure. Thrilling? Glorious? That was a laugh. Maybe when a character in a book or a film gives his life for some noble cause, it seems that way. But if you've been through it, you know that when you are about to die you don't feel glorious, you just feel sick. You are not looking for glory; you are looking for a way out—or, if you're past that, you are just numb, and are not looking for anything at all.

I raised my hand, unconsciously, to where the Emblem had once hung, and of course it was not there. What was more, I no longer even had what it stood for. Georyn, not for the first time, had seen clearer than I: *You have lost it by revealing yourself,* he had said to me. *You have bought back the Stone at the cost of your own power!* Yet when you lose a thing, that doesn't mean you stop believing in it. I'm not doing this because of the Oath at all! I realized. I've already broken that. I am already forsworn. So why am I doing it? I guess just because underneath the ritual there's a goal, and the goal's worth backing all the way.

I looked up, and across the clearing I saw Georyn. My heart lifted for a moment. He was free! Free to walk off into the forest. If only I could go with him. If only I was really the Andrecian girl the Imperials thought me! If I ran to Georyn, would they vaporize me? That would be the easiest way. But they would not; they would only stun me again, and I'd have lost my chance.

And of course Georyn did not walk off into the forest. Instead, heroically, he approached the "dragon." He still had hope, I realized, of "killing" it! I should have clarified that, at least. Again, I wondered what he'd made of my paradoxical warning; it was unlike him to ignore what I said, and he might very well have put a disconcertingly literal interpretation on it. He might even believe that the magic wouldn't work unless he made some sort of sacrifice!

For once in my life I was not acting impulsively; I had thought the situation through very, very thoroughly, until I was dizzy with thinking. Yet its implications weren't evident. Sometimes I marvel at the way things work out, beyond all logic. It's something the Federation doesn't know any more about than the Younglings do.

It all happened quickly and yet, looking back, I see it in slow motion; time stretches when you believe that you haven't any to spare. I was pretty shaky, and for a moment I was afraid I wouldn't be strong enough to go through with the thing. Then suddenly Jarel's hand tightened on mine. I held my breath. Several Imperials had now confronted Georyn and stunned him, but one of their weapons was moving slowly through the air toward his motionless hand! He was *doing* it, the mission might succeed after all! If only I'd explained that "final condition" better so that in the end, when the monster didn't die, he would remember and be comforted.

Every invader in the clearing froze, eyes held by the unbelievable thing that was taking place. Only the machine worked on; whoever was running it apparently had not seen. I realized that since most of the men were helmeted they could speak to each other only via their radios; I would not hear even the tone of the reaction. *Tell me what they're saying!* I urged Jarel.

He stared at me, startled, but had the good sense to know that he could answer silently. *They're incredulous, frightened . . . but not frightened enough yet, I'm afraid. . . .* His thought broke off, to be replaced by a stronger one driven by anger. *Oh, no! That fool—not again, not now!*

An Imperial was coming up behind Georyn with weapon raised. I could see that it was not a stunner. *Oh, Jarel, do something!* I implored.

Jarel's face darkened. For a moment he seemed torn by indecision; then, without hesitating, he pulled out his own stunner and fired. Not at Georyn, but at the man who in the next instant would have dealt with this strange and unwelcome phenomenon by vaporizing the native responsible for it. And that man was abruptly immobilized, the lethal weapon falling harmlessly from his extended hand.

Several other men started toward us, their momentary awe of Georyn forgotten in the shock of seeing one of their number attacked by a shipmate. *This* was something they could cope with, and they were no doubt telling themselves that while they were coping, the other problem would go away. Jarel dropped my arm; there was barely time for him to turn the neutralizer on Georyn, freeing him from paralysis, before he himself was stunned.

There was no hope then, not for the mission, not even for Georyn's escape. They were not sufficiently impressed; they would simply capture him again. The single demonstration was not enough. We'd always known, of course, that it depended on luck, on an opportunity to do something really spectacular.

But I had no time to worry about that, for what I myself had to do, I must do while the men were preoccupied, before anyone took it into his head to stun me. I ran forward, toward the "dragon" whose victim I was literally to be, and though I was sorry about a great many things, I was sorriest of all, I think, that Georyn was going to have to watch. He wouldn't understand, I knew; in the face of his own failure, he would see me die, and he would think it an act of ultimate despair.

When Georyn at last beheld the Dragon, the sight was more fearful than anything of which he had ever dreamt. The monster's bescaled body reflected the sun's rays, dazzling his eyes, so that little could be made of its form; yet all too clearly did he see that the creature was of gigantic size. Even its mouth was large enough to swallow a man in one gulp. And that mouth was filled with jagged teeth, teeth that could bite into solid rock; for apparently, when no choicer morsels were available, this was what the beast fed upon.

It was feeding now, swinging its long neck from side to side, then swooping that neck down into a vast pit that it had eaten into the very earth itself. After each mouthful, it spit out a great mass of crushed rock, which it no doubt found indigestible; and that rubble had inundated a sizable valley. All the while it ate, its roaring continued, a dreadful sound at which even the ground trembled. This was a monster of awesome strength; to draw near to it would indeed require courage!

Georyn took a deep breath and strode steadfastly forward. He had no idea of how he could slay this evil thing. By all logic, such a feat was impossible. No longer was he troubled by his lack of a sword, for he perceived that no sword could penetrate the hard silvery scales with which the beast was covered. Nor was it likely that a man could get within sword's length of the creature. At the moment, the Dragon was not breathing out fire; but all around the ground was charred, and the trees also, evidence enough that when it wanted to do so, it could.

Yet firmly did Georyn believe that victory was within his grasp, for had not all the conditions been brought to fulfillment? Thus surely some means must exist whereby the monster could be conquered. And even as he approached the beast, Georyn deemed that he knew the answer.

He was meant to face impossible odds. How could one expect them to be otherwise if one was to save the world not through battle but through magic? From the first, he had been tested for one thing only: not his prowess in the art of killing, but simply his ability to endure terror; and ever had that magic aided him according to the measure of his fear. If through defiance of fear alone could the Stone be wielded, then clearly, to call forth such power as would overcome this creature, he would need to be terrified indeed. He saw now what was demanded: he must deliberately court terror; he must walk forward to meet the Dragon without any knowledge of the way to victory, in full expectation of death. If the Stone could save him, it would; and if it could not, then no other strategy would be of any avail.

But in order to reach the Dragon, he must first frighten away its awful servants. There were dozens of them in sight, and most were monstrous, bloated creatures with glistening skin and shiny faceless heads that had an evil look. Georyn wondered, with a shudder, whether they had been born so or whether this was the result of their bewitchment. Would he himself have been so transformed had he remained subject to their sorcery? Far better, in truth, would it be to die in battle.

Fortunately, as to his present course he had been given direction: he must take their mysterious magic wands from them by means of the charm that the Enchantress had taught him. In a steady voice all but drowned by the Dragon's roars, he began to recite, fixing his will upon the nearest one; and behold! the thing came easily to his hand! He stared at it in wonderment. It was made of a material like to silver, but surprisingly heavy, and odd-shaped knobs protruded from its sides. Unquestionably, this strange object possessed the dread power to turn men to stone—provided, of course, that he who held it knew the proper magic words. Georyn did not know them, nor had he any wish to; such knowledge, surely, would lead less to wisdom than to the dark sorcery he had rejected.

He dropped the wand at his feet and prepared to

obtain another, striving desperately to quell his rising panic. The grotesque bewitched ones had not given way at his challenge, but were instead closing in around him. As they brought forth more wands and pointed them, Georyn's heart quaked. They would turn him to stone! To be sure, he knew from experience that the charm would continue to work while he was immobile, but it was nevertheless an appalling prospect. If struck by the spell, he would have no choice as to his tactics in regard to the Dragon. He would have to wait for the monster to advance upon him, as it undoubtedly would do as soon as it noticed his helplessness.

Clutching the Stone, he once again committed himself to its protection and turned his mind firmly to the employment of the charm. And alas, his fears were borne out. His limbs froze—whereupon the Dragon swung around, gnashing its teeth, and made a lunge toward the spot from which he was now powerless to move.

Georyn began to be horribly afraid, a circumstance in which he supposed he should rejoice; but he could *not* rejoice. A chill shook him, and he knew naught but a bitter, sick misery. He did not really expect that he would live to enjoy the Stone's triumph, and it was torment to stand as he now must stand, in ignorance as to the manner of the approaching end. The downfall of this raging monster could scarce be imagined; was not its hide impenetrable? Perhaps despite the Lady's assurances, the beast would devour him, Stone and all, and would be struck dead from within.

Giving an ominous snort, the Dragon halted its charge; still there could be, it seemed, no possible deliverance. Yet suddenly, at the blackest moment of Georyn's terror, a thing past hope occurred: as he wrenched the fell wand from a second enemy's grasp, there came an unlooked-for release from the spell that had bound him.

He was frozen to stone no longer. Once more he had command of his body, although he was weak and trembling from fright. With resolution born anew, he started forward, but even as he did so, he caught sight of the Enchantress.

Now indeed it was well that he had been taught to use his magical powers without giving them his full attention, else he would surely have lost control. For a heart-stirring thing was taking place! The Lady had broken away from her guards and was running across the clearing, the white of her gown flashing in the sunlight. A thrill of hope pierced him. If she could but reach the forest while all eyes were on him, she might yet escape.

Then, to his horror, Georyn saw that the Enchantress ran not toward the forest, but toward the Dragon! Unarmed, unshielded by any magic, she was challenging the monster herself, to what purpose he could not guess, for she had told him from the beginning that she had not the power to do so. Even with the Emblem she had not; and now, without it, she could not possibly save herself from harm. And indeed, he realized in anguish, it could only be that she had no intent to save herself. In some mysterious fashion she was seeking to appease the evil creature after all.

The Dragon let forth a frightful roar, raised its head, and again prepared to spew out a tremendous mouthful of rock. Its fury did not abate, but rather grew more fearsome than ever. Without pause, the Lady advanced boldly into the region strewn with its gravelly vomit, only to stumble and fall to her knees directly beneath the jaws of the beast. She glanced up briefly, then with a cry of uncontrollable terror she buried her face in her arms. There was no doubt as to the outcome: within the next moment, when those jaws opened, she would be crushed.

Thereupon Georyn was struck with a fear greater than any that had hitherto been aroused in him, beside which his own fear of the Dragon was as nothing. In his wrath and desperation he did not wait to think the thing through; instantly, rather, he acted as he had been readied to act by the days of testing and preparation. All the strength of his will to oppose evil and of his love for the Enchantress was channeled to one end: he ran toward her, raising his fist containing the Stone in the direction of the Dragon's threatening jaws, and threw the whole force of his mind into an invocation of the charm.

And lo! a great marvel came to pass, for the Dragon's jaws gaped open and the rock indeed spewed forth, only to be arrested in midair! The Enchantress knelt stock-still beneath a hovering cloud of rock, once again gazing upward; and it seemed that even she was assailed by astonishment and by an overpowering awe.

A hush lay upon the clearing, broken by naught save the triumphant song of a solitary bird. Georyn walked forward. No one stopped him; those who were bewitched stood back, giving him a clear path. With the hazy fragment of his mind free for such trifles, he sensed that the Dragon had made no move to harm him; in truth the monster was now silent, motionless with outstretched neck as if it had itself been turned to stone.

Then, although the stillness remained undisturbed, he became aware of the Lady's exultant voice: *Oh, Georyn, Georyn! The power of the Stone is greater than I knew!*

And his heart responded, *Great was the need, Lady, for that you should perish as this Dragon's victim was not to be borne!*

He took her hand and led her back from the place; then slowly, gently he allowed the mass of rock to settle onto the ground. Still no sound was uttered by the

Dragon nor by any of its slaves, who stood dumbfounded in the presence of so puissant an enchantment. A giddiness came upon Georyn; he opened his fist and stared at the Stone in wonder, aware that he had tapped a power that surpassed any he had previously used as sun surpasses firelight.

The mind of the Enchantress was now far away, listening as was her wont to the eerie voices of the enchanted realm. Suddenly with radiant countenance she turned back to him, crying with a glad voice: "Now truly have you vanquished these foes, and we have come beyond hope into a brighter morning than you know. For the spell that you have cast is stronger than their will. Their trust is in the might of dragons; they know naught of such magic, and are bewitched as is the way of men by fear of what they do not understand."

Then a great rapture welled up in Georyn, and his heart seemed like to burst with the fullness of it. "I had not thought," he said dazedly, "that even in victory my life would be spared."

"Nor I mine," she whispered. "It is strange, that through my peril should have come so wondrous a success."

"Less strange by far than if your peril served no end," declared Georyn. And as he pondered this, the design that had been hidden became plain, and the long-sought reason for her captivity was laid bare. For he deemed that if the Stone's powers had increased a hundredfold, it was because in the final extremity he had released them less through terror than through love.

The Ending

A t first, Jarel could not believe that it had happened. Even though he'd been forewarned, he could not believe *this*! That a small object like a stunner should be lifted by the force of mind alone was one thing—an incredible thing, a thing in itself upsetting to a bunch of confirmed disbelievers like Dulard and Kevan. But a great mass of rock—a total defiance of every natural law known to science . . .

An advanced thing, she'd called it. An advanced thing that could be "awakened" in a man who was not in himself different, not superhuman? By what means? By belief in a stone? What are we missing, he thought, we of the Empire who are so all-fired proud of our technological prowess? We who study men as if their minds were no more than perishable computer circuits, who analyze their behavior and their brains in Research Centers as if they were simply a superior strain of white rats? How could we have blocked out a whole area of knowledge in the name of the very science that should have revealed it to us? Scientists? Why, to *her* people we must seem no better than primitive tribesmen hiding from a thunder-storm!

But in this case it was a good thing that Imperial science was backward, Jarel thought dazedly. If it wasn't, Dulard would not have been so overcome as to give the order for retreat.

It had not been only Dulard, of course. Some of the colonists had witnessed the thing, and they had been the first to demand that the ship be held until they could get aboard. They had come here prepared to deal with all sorts of hardships and hazards—but not with this. Not with a threat that was immeasurable because its very existence invalidated every measuring stick by which they had been trained to judge. What good is superior technology against something that breaks all of technology's rules?

It's a lot more comfortable to live in a world where the rules still apply.

So this would become an "off-limits" planet, like the ones with virulent bacteria that couldn't be tamed, and the ones with inhabitants who were in the habit of playing around with radioactive poisons. These natives had now been shown to be equally dangerous. "To think we stunned them," someone said. "Kept them locked up, and all—"

"Personally," another man remarked, "I think those 'helpless' captives were running the whole show all along. They didn't need to worry about trifles like stunner effects with what *they've* got."

"What'll they do to get back at us? They wouldn't have shown their hand unless they were ready to act!"

"They're probably gathering out there now. They'll disarm us all, and then destroy the ship."

"I don't know about that," said Dulard. "But I sure as heck know that this is something we want nothing to do with."

Unreasoned fear, thought Jarel. How did Elana's people know that the colonists would be so afraid, just on the basis of one man's demonstration? A man who didn't even try to harm them? Of course, he had reason enough to want to. Perhaps the colonists were being deliberately trapped by their own consciences. Were all peoples thrown by what they didn't understand? It seemed such an unnecessary drag on progress. And then Jarel thought, no, it wasn't. It was a built-in safety factor. Dulard was right, but for the wrong reasons.

The forces of the mind dangerous? You bet they were! What would the Empire *do* with them if it had them? And imagine such powers "awakened" in a guy like Kevan! An advanced thing . . . a thing further down the road. If there *was* any sort of natural progression, and Elana said there was, why, it worked out very neatly to keep the matches away from the baby.

Within a few moments of the native's display of power, the decision to turn the other captives loose and to start work on the reloading of the ship had been made. Dulard was a realist. It was not that he was afraid personally. But he had not gotten to be a commander in the Imperial Exploration Corps by ignoring the dictates of prudence. He was charged with the responsibility for the long-term safety of the colony. If that colony was wiped out, it would be on his head; and he could see no justification for such a risk, not when they could start again somewhere else.

In the excitement, Jarel hadn't had time to consider his own position. He himself had been stunned in the instant following his stunning of Kevan, but had been released from paralysis shortly thereafter. Now for the first time he began to realize what he'd gotten himself into. There were men at his elbows; he was under arrest.

They were motioning him toward the ship. Quickly, he "spoke" to Elana, telling her of the success of her plan, for he suddenly took in the fact that without him, she would have no way to be sure that the ruse had worked. Her reply flashed into his mind, strong with the overtones of incredulous joy.

Not until then did it dawn on him what had actually happened when she dashed toward the rockchewer.

She had not known what form the thing would take. She hadn't expected the native to save her; she had expected to die. Yet she had not been in despair; she had done what she did not out of rebellion against a horrifying fate, but solely out of concern for the keeping of her secret. It had been premeditated, several things she had said now pointed to that. She had never had any defense against the Research Center's methods at all; when she had claimed "a way to deal with that problem," she had meant *this* way. This was why she had begged him not to leave her stunned, and when she had promised him proof of her belief that she knew what was worth dying for . . . well, this was the proof.

The secret was that important. Not just to this world, but to others; she'd said there were complicated reasons. . . . Before, Jarel knew, he might have told someday—not the circumstances, not enough for anyone to connect it with this planet, but just the fact that there was an advanced civilization, a civilization with answers, a reason for hope. A fact that would seem helpful for people to know. But Elana had said that it would not help. And what she had said, she had been ready to back

up. He knew now that he would never tell anyone a
single word.

I t was like nothing I'd ever imagined—the zenith of all
hope, the bright pinnacle of joy that you think can never
come to anyone outside of a storybook! One moment like
that makes all the rest worth going through: all the peril,
all the grief, and yes, even the nightmare of believing that
you are going to die. None of the bad part has any impor-
tance at all beside such a thing as happened to us on
Andrecia in the moment of our triumph.

I felt suspended, light, almost as if I too were floating
on air! When you're convinced that you'll soon be dead,
you are free in a way that you can never be at any other
time—free in the sense that *anything* can happen to you
and you will not mind, because you have already faced the
most frightening thing there is to face. So if what happens
is something good, something so good as suddenly knowing that you are going to live after all, why, that in itself is
pretty tremendous. But if on top of that you know that a
whole world, a whole race of people with a practically
unlimited future has been rescued too, rescued because
someone you love has achieved a success far beyond anyone's highest expectations, there just aren't words for it.

For I knew, even as I looked up at the hovering mass of
rock that magically did not fall, that Georyn had saved
more than my life; I knew that our mission had been fulfilled, that the invaders would leave without captives, and
that the freedom of the Andrecians was now assured, at
least as far as removal of this particular threat could assure
it. Don't ask me how I knew, because it really wasn't evident at that point. Not until Jarel told me, silently, what
his commander had said did I get any confirmation.

Father contacted me almost immediately, and the emotion that drove our thoughts was pure elation. He and Evrek, after an unsuccessful attempt to free me that I so far knew nothing of, had hidden in a dense clump of trees at the furthest edge of the clearing, and had seen everything. At first our exchange was wordless; we were just plain overwhelmed. Finally I began to think a little more coherently, coherently enough to take in the marvel of it. *Oh, Father—I never guessed, I never dreamed . . .*

You did a very brave thing, Elana. Sometimes the outcome of that can surpass all hope.

The outcome of belief in magic can certainly surpass all hope, I realized dazedly. I thought of how close I'd come to taking Georyn's away from him. Why, if nobody believed anything except what they understood, how limited we'd be!

The ecstasy didn't last, of course. Heights of feeling never do, and in this case I still had plenty of worries left to close in on me. For in a very little while I remembered the thing that the excitement had driven from my mind, the thing I must now find courage to confess. I had broken the Oath. You shouldn't complain, I guess, when your life has just been miraculously spared, yet the thought of my career as an agent being over before it started was a sobering one; I hadn't expected to be around to face the music. Not that I would have acted differently if I had, but dismissal from the Service wasn't going to be pleasant. And what if the repercussions *were* bad, not only for me but for Jarel's people? Or what if Jarel told, and the colonists changed their minds about leaving? Jarel had put himself in a tough spot by stunning the man who had been about to kill Georyn. In our one brief exchange before he was taken to the ship, under guard, he assured me that no matter what happened he would not explain his true reasons for doing it. Still, mightn't they put pressure on him?

Father, you don't know! I thought despairingly. *I made a disclosure, a deliberate disclosure! I told one of the Imperials . . .*

Don't worry about it now. We'll talk later.

At that moment Evrek's thought came through to me, strong, urgent. *Darling, you're all right! Oh, Elana, when I think . . .*

I'm all right, Evrek. Everything's all right now. But I shied from the contact, for with Evrek and myself it was not all right, nor would it be for some time. And since it was not his fault, I did not want to ever let him know.

And there was another thing that was not all right. There was the inevitable ending. I turned to Georyn, realizing that without some explanation he couldn't possibly appreciate the full scope of this fantastic victory. I hoped for his sake that we could get away before the man who was operating the "dragon" recovered and brought the thing to life again! So far, all the Imperials seemed to be stunned—figuratively, not literally—but there was no telling how long it would last.

They freed us quickly; not only Georyn and myself, but all the other Andrecian prisoners. They chased us out of camp, in fact! We were a threat to the very foundations of their logic, to their most deep-seated conceptions of their own power. If a man can by sheer mental force defy the laws of gravity and keep a huge mass of rock suspended in the air—suspended so that not even a pebble falls to earth in its natural fashion—what is he likely to do next? Deactivate all the blasters, perhaps? Reduce the ship and the barracks to dust? I think they thought if they ever got us inside their research center we would blow the place to smithereens and emerge unscathed. I only wish it were true! If it were, I would be glad to volunteer.

As Georyn and I started toward the forest Father's thought came again, insistently. *We'll wait for you at the fork in the path. Let's say in an hour. One hour from now.*

An hour? What's the delay for?

There was a slight hesitation, after which he replied, *When you come, you must come alone, Elana.*

He did it the best way, the kindest way. He knew that our courage was at its highest pitch, that the elation of our victory would carry us through; to have drawn it out until the next morning would have helped neither Georyn nor myself. It would have been an awful letdown. As it was, the despair, the joy, and the final sorrow were blended into one climactic memory that will never be surpassed by anything I may experience later.

And it was no shock to Georyn; he was half-expecting to see me dissolve into thin air at the moment of the dragon's death in any case. But to me, at the time, it seemed heartless. Suddenly even the parting itself seemed heartless, unnecessarily so. I tried to express what I felt lightly, not trusting myself to be forthright. *Isn't the dragon-slayer always given a reward? Doesn't the fairy godmother always whisk him off to some fabulous castle where his every wish is magically fulfilled?*

Father could see well enough what I was leading up to, and he said what had to be said. *Elana, surely you know that what you're suggesting would not be a reward for either of you.*

I suppose I did know, but I wasn't quite ready to admit it. *Wouldn't it?* I persisted.

Have you forgotten that all too often the spell's broken? The magic castle turns back into a miserable hovel and the prince's fine raiments revert to rags?

Bitterly I responded, *That may happen in any case! We've done something that can't be undone, made him into something different from what he was, made him want things that Andrecia can't give him. He will never fit here or be happy here. Aren't we responsible for him now?*

We are, yet there's no help we can give. To take a Youngling aboard a starship is highly illegal, Elana; but that's not why I'm

refusing to do it. I would break policy if I thought good could come of it, as I have in certain other things. But it wouldn't be good for anyone, least of all for Georyn. He would not be a hero, away from his own time and place.

He's right, I thought. Inside, I can't deny that. Georyn would be a misfit in our world too, but at the bottom instead of at the top, and I'd be the last one to wish that on him.

There's one more thing, Elana. You must take back the Stone.

No! That, I won't do!

It's for his own protection. He may misuse it; if he does, then someday it will fail him.

It was the last straw, somehow. I had been warned; I'd been told on the night I was sworn that this job can exact a rather terrible price. I was willing to pay it. I hadn't balked at any of the big, important things.

Yet if one sort of magic can come true, why not another? Why not the "happily ever after" sort? I knew, of course, that that just isn't the way things work. But it seemed one demand too many.

H and in hand, Georyn and the Enchantress went forth from the place of the Dragon, and they came to a glade within the wood, hidden from the path along which the other freed captives were hastening. And Georyn knew that the time he had so long dreaded was now come, when the Lady must depart into the enchanted realm; and if it were not for the harm to her, he thought, he would have preferred to dwell beside her in prison than to endure this parting.

Then as they sat upon the grass, the Enchantress faced him, saying: "The Dragon has in truth been defeated by your magic and will presently depart into the dark region whence it came; no more will it ravage this land. The world is now safe for your people; so must we not rejoice, however hard this hour may be for us?"

"I rejoice indeed for the world," he answered, "and for your escape. But I fear that not all the evil has yet been vanquished."

"One can never vanquish *all* the evil," she said. "That we should have prevailed against this much of it is a thing of wonder."

"That is not quite what I meant," Georyn replied, troubled. "Lady, why did you approach the Dragon as you did? It seemed almost that you sought death. Terrible indeed must have been the doom that awaited you, if the monster's jaws were to be preferred!" But he did not voice his deepest fear, that having given up her power she might not wish to live.

Quietly she answered, "That was not the way of it; I would not have done the thing out of unwillingness to suffer, Georyn. But there are some evils against which no amount of bravery can prevail. Even before I revealed myself, I learned that if I were taken to prison, I would be forced to disclose the secrets of the enchanted realm by fell sorcery—sorcery against which I would be powerless, with the Emblem or without it."

"I hope," said Georyn darkly, "that the folk of this world are worth what has been risked! There are times when that seems open to doubt."

"You jest, Georyn! You do not really have any question, do you? Such doubts rise not from wisdom but from the acceptance of half-truths."

"Good magic would have little meaning, were there no good in men," he conceded. "But now, your peril is ended, and you are truly free? I cannot part from you thus without knowing that you will be safe hereafter."

"I am free and safe. You need have no fear for me."

"But you do not smile, Lady," he said. "And for you all is not as it would be, had you never come here."

"No, Georyn, for I have lost the Emblem, as you know," she said sadly. "I am no longer fit to wear it, since a wrong was done when I revealed myself, as had been foretold."

He pressed her hand, and for a moment he knew naught but wrath at the ways of enchantments, that she should be so punished for a thing that, like all her acts, had stemmed only from her goodness. It did not seem fair! Fervently he declared, "I would give my life to restore your Emblem!"

She managed a thin smile after all. "Do not worry about me, Georyn. Twice you have saved me from far worse fates than that which I took upon myself when I saved you. There is more to my world than you have ever dreamed, and—"

Georyn broke in, saying: "I would not have you think that I would turn your sorrow to my own benefit, and yet—I must ask, Lady, for I will never love anyone as I love you. Is there no chance, now that you no longer wear the Emblem, that you could remain in *my* world?"

Gently she drew her hand away from his. "There is no chance. My vow still binds me, though no more shall I be trusted to serve in the same fashion; but even if that were not so, it is not possible for enchanted folk to remain long in the worlds of men. I will not deceive you: I love you—oh, how terribly I love you—but I could not live in your world for more than a little time. The stars have a hold on me; I would miss them, and I—I would be torn in two, Georyn."

"Do not speak of it," he begged her. "I know it. I have always known, and it was cruel of me even to ask."

"Cruel? After what I have done to *you,* Georyn?"

Slowly he replied, "If by that, you mean you have shown me that which I cannot have, I would choose such cruelty over any other woman's kindness, Lady. For it is better to *know* of what exists than not to know. I would rather be helpless than blind; and if in seeking wisdom as my reward I got more than I had need for, well, that is not your fault but mine, for being what I am."

"And if you were not what you are, Georyn," she said, "you could not have conquered the Dragon; so there is nothing for either of us to regret. We are both captives still, captives of our own worlds' boundaries, for enchantments are not unworldly things, but only ways of seeing what is already there."

Georyn drew forth the Stone and held it for a moment, wistfully, upon the palm of his hand. Then he extended it to the Enchantress, saying: "You must take it back, Lady. For now, without the Emblem, you need it more than I."

"Oh, Georyn, I cannot! It may be of use to you again, someday—" She looked at him with concern. "Without it, you will have no magic powers at all, will you?"

"You know that I will not. But perhaps it is better so; for without you to guide me, I would not really know what to do with them; and as you have often told me, such things misused are perilous."

She paused, then with reluctance admitted, "That is true, and I have indeed been directed to take back the Stone. I had thought to disobey and let you keep it, for I would not deprive you of what you have earned at such cost. But since you offer it freely, I will accept—although not for my own sake, for even without the Emblem I have the powers of my people, which are greater than you know." Taking the Stone, she added thoughtfully, "Perhaps, Georyn, the condition of which I once told you has come true after all, since you must give up this that you have deemed necessary to your triumph."

Puzzled, he said to her, "But Lady, that condition was fulfilled when you sacrificed the Emblem."

She stared at him as if such a thought had never before occurred to her. "Did you see it so?" she whispered.

"But surely. How else could I have gained the full power of the Stone? How could I have succeeded, if it had not been for that?"

To his amazement, she began to weep. He put his arms around her, and she clung to him just as a mortal maiden might have done. "Oh, Georyn," she sobbed, "the ways of enchantments are indeed strange! I understand them no better than you, I think."

And Georyn knew that in this moment he was the stronger, and it was for him to comfort her, presumptuous as that seemed. He held her to him and stroked her hair, and he said softly, "Do not grieve, Lady! For us to love, and weep for it, was but the price of the victory; I knew that in the beginning, and I cannot believe that you did not. Without this love I could have done nothing, and the Dragon would have overcome the world even as you said. And were that not so, still I would not choose to reject what has been for the sake of the sorrow to come."

Thereupon he kissed her, and for a time they did not speak; but in the end she rose and said, "The time allotted me is past; shall we fail in courage now, we who have faced the fire and the Dragon? Farewell, Georyn!" And with those words she turned from him and walked out of the sunlight into the gathering mist of the wood.

Jarel lay on the bunk in the small, bare cabin, waiting for liftoff. He knew that what was ahead of him would be no picnic, and that logically he should be miserable. But somehow he couldn't be. He felt almost exultant. They were pulling out. The barracks had been dismantled in short order, the equipment had been loaded onto the ship, and the rockchewer was being brought aboard. In a few more hours all that would be left of the Empire upon this world would be the black scar of the clearing.

Someday, the natives might build a city over that scar.

It had been worth it. Sure, his future prospects were at the moment pretty grim; but if the girl, Elana, could do what *she* had done for the sake of this thing, for the sake of the secret that must now be kept not only to protect the natives, but also, she'd said, to protect the Empire, he too could face what he must.

Thinking about it, Jarel began to understand a little. It could hurt, all right, for the existence of an advanced civilization to become common knowledge. For instance, he was going to have to practice medicine from now on knowing that everything he did was far, far behind what had been discovered elsewhere; if everybody engaged in medical research knew that, they might give up in despair. Yet if they kept on, without knowing, then someday they might discover something totally new and significant just from having followed a different path, something Elana's people had missed. Thousands of years from now, the natives of this world might do the same!

If that was how it worked, then it was worth whatever sacrifice anybody had to make. And he wasn't about to back down, now that it depended on him.

In the old days a man who turned a stunner on one of his own shipmates might have drawn a jail sentence. For Jarel, it wasn't going to be that simple. Perhaps if he could present a reasonable motive, his assault on Kevan might be considered a crime; but if he gave *no* motive, if he looked his commanding officer in the eye and disclaimed all knowledge of why he acted as he did, well, there would be no court-martial. Instead, there would be a medical inquiry.

Anyone who suddenly attacked an Imperial citizen without apparent provocation was considered unstable, Jarel realized, and modern medicine did not allow such instability to remain untreated for very long. As a doctor, he had a fair idea of what he was in for. It wasn't going to be fun.

They would be able to uncover his motives from his subconscious mind, naturally. (The methods that the marvels of Imperial science had made available for that purpose were not confined to use in research on primitive species.) But the secret would not be endangered by this, for in his case they would not believe what they found. At least they wouldn't believe that it had any substance in reality. Not so long as he steadfastly denied any conscious knowledge of it, they wouldn't, which, of course, was what he must do. They would not want to believe. And on the face of it, any man who had subconscious delusions of having communicated by mental telepathy with a young girl claiming to represent a superior civilization was a prime candidate for therapy. Resisting that therapy might prove to be quite a challenge. Jarel hoped that he would be equal to it.

The whole business was pretty ironic. Here he had been ready to resign from the Corps, and now that she had given him back the dream, now that he wanted desperately to stay in, he was facing discharge. Whether or not he managed to avert that, an episode of mental imbalance on his record wasn't going to help his career. And with his sentiments about certain aspects of Imperial policy being what they were, his loyalty might be questioned.

That too was ironic, because he had never been more sincerely loyal to the Empire than at this moment.

And he couldn't tell anyone the reason for this sudden loyalty, this new faith in the Empire's future! He couldn't ever reveal why he believed that Imperial civilization was less corrupt than it seemed. There's nothing *wrong* with us as a people, he thought. We are not decadent, not wicked, not on the wrong road! We are going somewhere after all. We are as far below *her* people as the natives are below us . . . but someday! Is there a federation of mankind, perhaps? Is Elana's civilization the outgrowth not of one people's maturity, but of many? Is it *true* that there's good in reaching for the stars?

If it is true, Jarel reflected, then we must work for it. A hard job? Of course, because there were evils to be avoided in the process, evils like the one almost committed on this planet; and if you were involved, you had to accept personal responsibility, not some vague share of a collective guilt that didn't really exist. Yet you had to be involved. Where would anything ever get if everybody who had any moral scruples dropped out?

Suppose he'd never joined the Corps. Or suppose, two days ago, he had been able to resign on the spot. Neither Elana nor the man she had trained would have been saved; there would have been no miraculous demonstration of the natives' potential; and the takeover of this world would be proceeding according to plan.

He would never resign now. He would stick it out and fight—and somehow, someday he would win back the Corps's respect. There would be some rough going. The secret would be difficult not only to keep, but to live with, for there was a frustrating side to being shown only a glimpse. In spite of that, he wasn't sorry for anything. He would hang onto the memory of what had happened

on this planet for the rest of his life; of that, Jarel was
very sure.

W̶e stayed on Andrecia one more night. I was near col-
lapse by the time we had set up our temporary camp;
the reaction was setting in. So, although it was still early
in the day, Father made me lie down and gave me a strong
sedative. The next thing I knew it was morning, and Evrek
had already started back to the hut by the river. Before
following him, we checked up on the Imperials to be sure
that they had pulled out all their equipment.

I sat on the scorched ground at the edge of the now-
deserted clearing and looked around at the grim skele-
tons of the trees. It was a forlorn, gray morning; the
rents in the cloud cover had closed in, hiding the sun.
From somewhere deep in the forest came the piercing
cry of that elusive Andrecian bird I'd never managed to
catch a glimpse of.

Father and I had not talked the day before; he had
sensed what I was going through and had left me alone to
do it, for which in some respects I was thankful. He'd
passed no comment on my confession beyond requiring a
detailed report of what Jarel and I had said to each other.
Evrek had not commented either; in fact he'd made a
point of avoiding me, on Father's orders, I was sure. Evrek
had taken a terrible risk for my sake, though I didn't know
it at first, and my coolness to him must have been hard to
accept.

He had tried a rescue. To my astonishment—for I
would have thought the danger too great to be justifi-
able—I learned that he had actually been in the Imperials'
camp, under my window even, sometime during the
night. He and Father, I gathered, had been communicat-

ing, though they hadn't wanted to raise my hopes, or to further arouse my fears. For Evrek had been fully prepared to die with me if he was caught; we would not have had to rely on makeshift measures. Miraculously, he was not caught. But he found, of course, that to free me was just plain impossible. He could not even toss anything to me through the window, for Jarel was with me. As he told me this part, Evrek seemed about to say something more; but Father broke in quickly. "Later, Evrek," he commanded. "This isn't the time."

Now, Father came over and sat down on the low outcropping of rock behind me. For a while neither of us said anything. Finally, following my gaze to the charred undergrowth, Father began, "It'll grow again, you know. The forest will push its way back. To erase the clearing will take longer, for they sterilized the ground. But in time, time as we reckon it, no one will be able to tell that they ever came."

I looked at him; then, silently, I began to cry. He put his hand on my shoulder, and I burst out, "Oh, Father, I broke the Oath! I broke it, and if Jarel ever tells what he knows all kinds of damage may be done! They may grab a dozen more worlds, and we won't be able to stop them! I'm not any good at this; I couldn't ever become an agent now, even if the Service would have me."

"You will not be released that easily, I'm afraid. You made an irrevocable commitment, to which you're still bound."

I dropped my head to my knees and sobbed. For a time Father let me cry. Then, gently, he drew me around to face him. "Look at me, Elana. Be very honest: are you sorry you chose as you did?"

There was only one thing I could say; I met his eyes and said it. "No. I would do the same thing again. And the mission *did* succeed on account of it. Yet I betrayed the Service."

Astonishingly, he smiled. "No, as a matter of fact you didn't. There'll be a formal inquiry, but you've no need to worry about the outcome."

"But I failed to stick by what I was sworn to!"

"Elana," Father said seriously, "the Oath demands more of us than blind obedience. Its literal words are a mere reflection, a poor attempt at expressing something that can't be fully expressed. They are anchors, not shackles. You didn't fail by violating them any more than Georyn succeeded by repeating the magic spell you gave him; the Emblem is no less an artificial device than the Stone."

"Do you mean to tell me that breaking my sworn word is *all right*?"

"No, I'm not saying that. What I'm saying is a much harder thing to grasp: sometimes, when in our best judgment it is justified, we must be willing to do what's *wrong* and take the consequences. We wouldn't be fit for this work if we didn't have human feelings! And in this case none of the consequences were bad. You needn't worry about the disclosure spreading. If Jarel tells later, without proof, he will not be believed."

I stared down at the ground. There was a strange-looking beetle that had somehow escaped the invaders' destruction of native life forms; I watched it try to climb the rough surface of the rock beside me. All of a sudden I caught a hint of Father's thought, something that he wanted to tell me, yet did not know quite how to bring up.

"You knew!" I exclaimed. "Somehow you knew in advance what I was about to do and how it might turn out!"

"Yes," he said quietly. "During that rescue attempt, Evrek overheard your opening words to Jarel and realized that you were going to reveal the plan. I guessed enough of what could come of that to gamble on it; otherwise I wouldn't have let it happen. You know, don't you, what a strict interpretation of the Oath demanded of me?"

I nodded, not daring to speak.

"So you see," Father went on, "that I'm in much the same position as you are, and Evrek is, too. He did not stop you by force, which he was equipped to do; nor did I order it. For that matter, for him to try the rescue in the first place involved a risk of disclosure that strictly speaking ought not to have been taken. All three of us are technically forsworn, and not one of us has any regrets."

Awed, I asked, "How could you possibly have known enough about Jarel to trust him?"

"I didn't. I trusted *you*."

I'd judged Jarel accurately, of course. And yet— "They arrested him," I said. "He was the only Imperial who disapproved of what was being done to the natives. Why should he be the one to pay for it?"

"Because he was the only one willing to," Father answered.

"Everyone we contact is hurt by it!" I said unhappily.

"Yes. But from what you've told me about him, I think Jarel's as likely as the rest of us to find the game worth the candle."

Slowly I said, "Evrek's been hurt, too. And yet he took that awful chance! I didn't deserve it. Oh, Father, the whole mess was my fault. I got caught because of a feeling for Georyn that I never meant to have, that I knew was foolish and wrong—"

"That's not the way to look at it, Elana."

"What other way is there?"

He hesitated. "Why do you think I failed to do anything when I first saw how it was with you and Georyn, if not because I believed that the love between you, hopeless though it was, might lead to good?"

"But then you—you used me, in just the same way as you used Georyn! I was only another pawn."

"In that sense, Elana, so are we all. We act in the light of the knowledge we have. Do you suppose *I* see the whole picture? Do you suppose anyone does?"

He stood up and held out his hand to me; I scrambled to my feet. As we walked back across the clearing, Father said softly, "A very wonderful thing happened here yesterday, a thing that in some societies would be counted as a miracle. Don't let your joy in it be spoiled by the circumstances; for neither you nor I can be sure that it would have happened as it did if they had been any different."

"A miracle," I said bitterly. "Yet it was all a sham, a fake, right from the beginning."

"No! It was *real*, Elana! As real as anything ever can be. The Youngling interpretations of it may be superficial and naive; but so is ours. Our presumption in thinking that we saved this world by our intervention is, underneath, as ridiculous as Georyn's in thinking that he did it by slaying a dragon. Or Jarel's in crediting it to his personal humanitarianism. Yet the fact is that the invaders are gone, and they would not be gone if any of us had been less faithful to our own beliefs."

"That's almost like saying that Youngling beliefs are true."

"Of course they're true. How else could they be worth living for or dying for? But there are different kinds of truth. And if our kind is more mature than theirs, it's so only because we know that."

In the pocket of the cloak I was wearing was the Stone that Georyn had returned to me. Slowly I drew it out and stared at it, weighing it from hand to hand. Father watched; his face had a faraway look. Then suddenly he turned to me. "Let me have that," he said gently.

I hesitated, not wanting to part with the thing; it had come to mean something. Wasn't I to be allowed even this much of Georyn? "I—I was planning to keep it," I wavered. "As a sort of souvenir."

He reached for it and, reluctantly, I opened my fingers. "Souvenir? The word's cheap," he said. He began to reknot the leather thong with which Georyn had bound the Stone to his belt. Passing it through the Stone's hole as a single strand, Father fashioned it into a pendant.

Smiling, he held it out. "Wear it, Elana. You returned Evrek's Emblem; wear this in its place until you get one of your own."

I bent my head, overcome by an inexplicable surge of happiness. Father raised the Stone, free-swinging, just as he had held the Emblem before the campfire on that first night. I sensed what he was waiting for: *Not casually! With ritual, Elana!* And so very softly I whispered the now-familiar phrases, as I had at my investiture, and then with the formal words, the words of the Presentation, Father placed the thong around my neck.

It is still there. And though when the trip's over and we are home again I will receive a proper pendant to replace it, I do not think that that will have any more significance.

Father took my arm. "Come on," he said. "We've got to get back to the hut. Evrek's waiting for us, and I've recalled the ship."

I didn't move. Georyn! I couldn't just go, without telling him that I had the Emblem back again! He was undoubtedly still somewhere close by. "Do we have to sneak away like this?" I said desperately. "Couldn't you bring the ship—"

"Here? So that Georyn could watch you fly away in

your enchanted chariot?" He shook his head, and then with forced lightness he went on, "No, I should say not! They will have legends enough without that."

Now in the days following the slaying of the Dragon, Georyn went in triumph to the King and received of him gold, fine raiment and armor, and a spirited mount. But of this wealth he gave much to his father and elder brothers, who had been among the freed captives, and much also to the poor folk of the village; and for himself he kept only such as he could carry on a long journey. For he no longer wished to live as a woodcutter nor yet at the court of the King; and since the world beyond the Enchanted Forest seemed not so perilous as it once had, he intended to see it, for perhaps in the seeing he might find another sort of wisdom.

But ere Georyn set forth, he went again to the abode of the Dragon; and the monster had disappeared, and so too had all its fearsome servants, who had no doubt by now regained their natural form. It was a dismal place, upon which the destruction that the Dragon had wrought lay heavy, and he was not sorry to ride away. Upon leaving, he avoided the glade where he and the Enchantress had parted. Rather, he rode back to the deserted hut by the river; and he searched for some token that had been the Lady's, but everything that had been made by magic was gone. By his own pallet, however, he found the carven cup she had given him on that sunlit day when she had taught him the charm: the cup from which they had drunk the magical draught, seeing for the first time into each other's hearts. And this he put carefully away in his saddlebag, knowing it for a greater treasure than any the King had placed there.

He knew that he would not see the Enchantress again. She had passed out of his world—where, and by what means, he could not ever hope to understand, but he knew that it was not like dying; somewhere, in that strange enchanted realm beyond the stars, she lived as she had lived here, and experienced all the joys and sorrows to which her human heart was heir. And no longer did he fear for her; for once, at the moment of her going, she had spoken to him. She had been nowhere nearby, yet suddenly he had heard her voice as clearly as if she stood beside him, and he had answered.

Georyn!

Lady! Can you then speak, from the enchanted world?

No, I am still in yours. I speak in the way of my people; I did not know you could hear!

Your voice is clear to me. Could we have spoken so, all along?

We did, in a sense. But from this distance it is a rarer thing. It requires a feeling, an urgency—of fear, perhaps. . . .

Or of love?

Or of love, Georyn.

Will we be able to do this again?

Never again, for I am leaving. In only a few moments, I am leaving! But I could not have gone without telling you that I again wield the forces of good magic!

Your full power, Lady?

My full power. I wear the Stone, and it has, for me, the might of the Emblem; and someday soon I shall regain the Emblem itself.

Was there then no evil after all?

There was evil, but it is overridden. I am safe from it, for a time, at least. I thought you would want to know.

It is the only happiness now possible to me, to know that all is well with you!

Do not say that, Georyn! I cannot bear that it should be so for you! What will you do, now?

I shall travel to the ends of the earth, Lady, for have you not told me that the world holds wonders past my knowing?

You are wise, as usual; it is the best way, for you will indeed see wonders. I too shall visit lands beyond my present imagining; and in time this grief will lessen, for both of us. Let us remember only the joyous part.

I shall remember it as the core of my life.

Then, as the Lady's voice faded, he glimpsed the world as she saw it, from above. *Oh, Georyn, I wish you could see . . . our meadow is a circle of pale gold, and the river a shining thread, and the Enchanted Forest is not dark at all, but only a patch of greenness . . . and of the village road, I see both ends, though there is another road beyond it which is hidden. Georyn, we are rising above the clouds now. . . .*

And after that, she was lost to him. Yet he was sure, as he would be sure for ever after, that the powers that were hers to tap would endure beyond time and space, for as long as the worlds of men or of enchanted folk should abide.

Epilogue

A ndrecia shines below us, blue-green but swathed in white. We have remained in the vicinity for some days, awaiting our new orders, for the ship's original mission was canceled when we were diverted here. But we are breaking out of orbit now, and soon there will be only the emptiness of interstellar space. The next planet we see will be the world of a different people, and it may be thousands of years before a starship touches Andrecia again.

Will it be their own starship—Georyn's people's? Will they go out to invade some distant solar system, even as an older Empire once invaded theirs? And will the Imperials in that future time, perhaps, be the ones to wield the powers of enchantment? Where will *we* be then, I wonder; I mean, our descendants—mine, and Evrek's? For of course I'll marry Evrek someday, that hasn't changed. Only I think it will be quite a while yet before that happens. I've a lot of training to catch up on, for one thing, before I go on any more world-saving expeditions. The next time I want to be better equipped.

If good came of what I did on Andrecia, I can't really claim any credit for it. It was not by my design that things worked out; if Georyn and Jarel had been less than they were, my rashness would have brought disaster on us all. What's more, I did not even believe in my own spells, and I came awfully close to ruining everything on that account. It's only now that I know the magic was *real*, and that Georyn did what he did through a genuine faith rather than a false one. If that were not true, then nothing would be, and no people's symbols would have any meaning at all. And that cannot be, for then we'd all still be living in caves on the planets where our ancestors evolved.

Georyn and I won't ever forget each other. I don't suppose I'll be forgotten on Andrecia for some time, as a matter of fact. The legend will be handed down from one generation to the next: how the dark-haired Lady of the Forest bestowed an enchanted Stone upon the woodcutter's son and helped him to slay the Dragon, and was never again seen by any mortal. In time, people will laugh at the story, and long before they build that first starship, they'll be saying that magic spells and enchanted stones are only foolish tales. And none of them will ever suspect that the Enchantress was only an ordinary girl who wasn't very good at her job and who didn't want to be endowed with any supernatural powers in the first place.

Sooner or later, Georyn will find himself some Andrecian girl. The appropriate thing, I guess, would be for him to marry the King's daughter; I don't know whether the local king has a daughter, but if he doesn't there are doubtless other fair ladies worthy of a slayer of dragons. I hope that Georyn will love her, and that that at least will bring him joy. For he will never, of course, be content with Andrecia; the door we opened is not one that he can ever close, and I doubt that he would choose to, even if it were possible. There are worse fates than to see beyond your grasp.

As for me, I am as bound to my heritage as he to his. I am not supposed to cry, and I won't, anymore. For Evrek has come to stand beside me at the viewport, and together we will watch Andrecia recede, until the time when we are swept into the black night of the stardrive; and in the morning there will be another world to think about.

Afterword to the 2001 Edition

For most of my years as a writer, I led a quite isolated life. I got reactions to my books from reviewers but rarely from readers; people seem to be shy about writing to an author when they must do so in care of a publisher. The Internet has changed that. The opening of my World Wide Web site put me in touch with my audience.

Nothing in my experience has affected me more deeply than my discovery—via the Internet—that a lot of people remember this story, have often reread it, and are eager to share it with new generations of young people. To the many who have sent me e-mail, I want to express my thanks. And to those who haven't yet found me on the Web, as well as to new readers, I want to extend an invitation to visit my site.

Among the things you'll see there are my Phoenix Award acceptance speech for *Enchantress from the Stars*, a page about my view of space colonization, and an essay containing some of my ideas about paranormal abilities. There is a FAQ (Frequently Asked Questions) page with answers to some of the questions readers have had about my books. There's also a place for you to ask your own questions and enter your own thoughts—I welcome your comments, and I promise to respond personally.

My e-mail address is sle@sylviaengdahl.com and my Web site is located at http://www.sylviaengdahl.com. I hope to meet you there!